CAST IN STONE

CAST IN STONE is the second novel in the Leo Waterman series. G. M. Ford lives in Seattle, and is also the author of the highly acclaimed Frank Corso series.

G. M. FORD

CAST IN STONE

PAN BOOKS

First published 1996 by Walker & Co.

First published in paperback 1997 by Avon Books
an imprint of HarperCollins Publishers Inc., New York, USA

First published in Great Britain 2007 by Pan Books
an imprint of Pan Macmillan Ltd
Pan Macmillan, 20 New Wharf Road, London N1 9RR
Basingstoke and Oxford
Associated companies throughout the world
www.panmacmillan.com

ISBN 978-0-330-42752-4

1 3 5 7 9 8 6 4 2

A CIP catalogue record for this book is available from
the British Library.

Typeset by SetSystems Ltd, Saffron Walden, Essex
Printed and bound in Great Britain by
Mackays of Chatham plc, Chatham, Kent

Visit **www.panmacmillan.com** to read more about all our books
and to buy them. You will also find features, author interviews and
news of any author events, and you can sign up for e-newsletters
so that you're always first to hear about our new releases.

To my friend and guide

Vincent Castiglione

a man to match the mountains and the sea

CAST IN STONE

1

THERE WERE TWO TONY MOLDONADOS. One was the lovable fat guy we all knew from the TV ads. The one who dressed up like the Wagnerian opera singer, horned helmet and all, and proclaimed to all the world that "Da deal ain't over till da fat lady sings." That Tony had a thirty-year marriage, grown children, a successful string of auto dealerships, and, as we all knew, would beat any deal in town.

The other Tony was an entirely different matter. I hadn't figured him out yet and wasn't sure I wanted to. Tony number two was, if nothing else, a man of consistent habits. Unfortunately, those habits were consistently disgusting, which was where I came into it.

Once a year, like clockwork, Tony number two went on a binge. He'd fake an out-of-town business trip, pack enough luggage for a safari, kiss the wife goodbye, and take a taxi to the airport. From the airport, he'd take another taxi across the street to the hotel strip on Pacific Highway South, find himself a roach motel, and begin the serious business of partaking of those prurient pleasures that cruel fate denied Tony number one. Tony number two was into young girls. For that matter, young anything. The younger the better. Rumor had it that he billed himself as Tony Coitus.

For the past four years, Tony was no sooner out the door than his wife was on the phone to me. I have no idea how Rose Moldonado got hip to Tony's meandering ways; it didn't much matter. My duty was to see that Tony was returned safely to the bosom of his family. I wasn't supposed to stop him; I was merely to see to it that he survived the experience.

I'd been holed up for the past six days in the Pacific Vista Motel, a pink, U-shaped, cinder-block emporium that specialized in adult movies and a quick turnover. I was on the same floor, directly across the U from Tony's room, with an excellent view of the seemingly endless stream of demented debutantes who stumbled in and out.

The first year I'd been part of this little charade, in a fit of misplaced responsibility, I'd taken the room next door to Tony's, but the sounds and smells that filtered through the cardboard walls had for weeks afterward polluted my dreams. Rose Moldonado paid promptly and well, but neither promptly nor well enough for my dreams. There were limits.

I'd since cut a deal with the management. To reduce the chances of both apprehension and infection, they kept the rooms on either side of Tony's vacant, made an honest effort to provide disease-free specimens, and gave me the proverbial room with a view. Not only was I paying them, but tumid Tony passed out hundred-dollar bills like candy. It was the mythical offer they just couldn't refuse.

I was well prepared this year. I had enough food for a rural village, a couple of good books, and a new pair of slippers that kept my feet from ever touching the matted green shag carpet, which seemed determined to stick to the soles of my shoes. This year, I'd even brought my own sheets. Those provided by the management invariably looked like a road map of northern Bosnia, embossed, I'd always assumed, with the same substance that gave the carpet its adhesive quality.

I was up early. Tony's last volunteer, a prematurely purple prepubescent type in road warrior garb, had left at about 3:00 A.M. In spite of the massed mercury vapor lights, I'd been unable to ascertain the gender of this particular specimen. I had the feeling that it didn't much matter to Tony. Tony, I presumed, would be sleeping in.

I rummaged in my cooler and selected an onion bagel, some cream cheese, and the last of the smoked salmon for breakfast. I washed it all down with some orange juice, cleaned up my mess, and headed for the shower, careful not to let any part of my body touch an exposed surface.

The shower head had only two adjustments. The

first provided an incredibly fine spray that was like trying to wash in fog. The other setting could have easily been used for crowd control. It had been set that way the first time I'd used the shower. I'd gotten in, turned the handle up, and immediately been hit right in the groin by a water cannon. It paralyzed me. If I hadn't been able to scoot down by the drain, I'd still be pinned to the back of the tub with a hole in my chest. Thank God I'd been wearing my new slippers.

After about ten minutes of being alternately misted and bludgeoned, I squooshed back into the room, got out some fresh clothes, and stood up on the bed to get dressed. While I was lacing up my Reeboks, I wondered what Tony dreamed about at night, deciding that I probably didn't want to know.

I was putting my slippers on the windowsill heat register to dry when I noticed that Tony was about to have his first visitor of the day. This was a bit of a disappointment. I'd figured he would be running out of gas by now. Obviously the man had unimagined reserves of strength. I wondered if maybe he'd been going to the health club in preparation for his yearly sojourn, which, in turn, led me to wondering exactly what would constitute a workout for a sport like Tony's. How many sets of what? I quickly wrote this off as something else I didn't want to know.

This morning's repast was pretty much standard fare, about five foot seven, skinny, long blond hair grown out brown at the roots, wearing jeans, a green flowered blouse, earrings the size of hubcaps, and red shoes with impossibly high heels.

She knocked and was instantly admitted. Obviously, Tony had been up and expecting her. All was as well as it was going to be until I managed to get out of this virus culture of a motel.

I settled into the tape-patched coral Naugahyde chair by the window and got out my book. Nobody but John McPhee could keep me reading about oranges for two hundred pages. I was immersed in citric splendor when a sudden movement in my peripheral vision jerked my attention from the Indian River Country of central Florida to the door of Tony's room.

I was greeted by a scene that presented limited possibilities; either Tony was broadening his area of interest to include large black men—a notion that, while unspeakable, was not beyond the realm of possibility—or we were about to have a serious problem. As I grabbed the jacket that held my 9mm from its hanger, I got my answer. The larger of the two, using the balcony rail for leverage, reared back, cocked his leg, and planted one of his 14EEEs right in the middle of the door.

I had just begun my sprint around the third-floor balcony when the door splintered and both men disappeared inside. I was ready for trouble. I wasn't ready, however, for the scene that greeted me as I burst through the door. The smaller of the two was madly snapping pictures while the door kicker was holding down the center of the room.

The room smelled like a stable and looked like a back room at Central Casting. Costumes of all types were scattered about the room. A pink leotard and tutu, size fifty-two stout. A sawed-off canoe paddle with a taped grip. A World War I leather helmet, complete with goggles. A yellow plastic miner's hat. A pair of white, woolly chaps, with matching vest. Swim fins. Swim fins? Jesus. Whatever his myriad failings, the man led a rich fantasy life. You had to give him that.

Tony was backed up against the far wall, wearing his famous Viking costume, sans the breeches, trying valiantly to cover his distended organ with his hands. This type of intrusion would have deflated me in a hurry, but not old Tony. I made it a point not to look at him.

The girl was lying facedown on the unmade bed, naked from waist to ankles, making no attempt to cover herself. Her frilly dress was up over her head. What looked like an accordion was bunched around her ankles. If it hadn't been for the shepherd's crook leaning against the wall, I probably would never have recognized her costume. Now I was certain I didn't want into Tony's dreams.

I lowered my shoulder and launched the picture taker toward the middle of the room. He rocketed forward, tripped himself up in Zorro's cape, which was lying on the floor, and fell heavily into the back of the door kicker. They both went down in a heap. The big one started to jump to his feet. The picture taker began to reach into his coat. Staring down the muzzle of the 9mm put an immediate stop to both actions. A picture's worth a thousand words.

"Who the fuck are you?" asked the larger of the two, being careful to keep his hands flat on the floor. The hands were covered with a lacework of faded tattoos. He wore a mismatched gray suit over a red-and-blue Hawaiian shirt. The pockmarks on his cheek and the out-of-style Afro made him look like one of the heavies on "The Mod Squad."

"Funny, that's just what I was going to ask you."

At this point Tony, still clutching his organ—which, unbelievably, was still holding its own—piped in. "They said they were the police." I tried not to look at him.

The dialogue seemed to revive the picture taker. He ran a hand over his newly processed hair and started to rise.

"I wouldn't," I said.

"You're interfering with official police business. If you—"

"And if you move that right hand of yours another inch, I'm going to put one of these right between your nappy little eyebrows."

This seemed to have the desired effect. He settled himself back on his haunches and looked to the heavy for help. These two sure as hell weren't the police, but if this went on much longer, we were going to meet the real article.

I pointed at Tony. "Get your ass in the bathroom and get dressed." He was still holding himself. "And slam that thing in the door while you're at it," I added. He began to move.

"Who the fuck are you?" the big one asked again.

"I guess you could say I'm sort of the good shepherd."

The little one was persistent if not persuasive. "This is official—"

"No," I corrected him, "*this* is how it is. You and your girlfriend here are going to gather up Bo Peep and her belongings and get the flock out of here. The police shit isn't going to float."

This was all the girl needed to hear. She slowly slid off the far side of the bed and began to collect her street clothes. Her efficiency was somewhat restricted by the full-length ruffled pantaloons around her ankles, but she was a real trouper.

The two men began to slowly rise in sections. Shorty wasn't willing to quit yet. As he smoothed his suit, he mustered his best conspiratorial tone. "Listen man, this is a real sweet deal here. Do you know who this guy is?"

Bo Peep was struggling out of the pantaloons. I stopped her.

"No, don't get dressed, sweetheart," I told her. "Just gather up your shit and get out."

She was a much quicker learner than the other two. She had the pantaloons up in a flash, right over the dress, and was doubletiming it for the door. I stopped her.

"Take that with you," I said, gesturing toward the shepherd's crook.

Thoroughly confused now, she picked up the crook and clutched it to her chest. Mouth-breathing, transfixed by the gun barrel, she gingerly began to edge her way past me toward the door. Once out, she turned left and hustled down the arm of the U the short way. The pantaloons had a drop seat, which was still open. Yessir, a real trouper.

I turned my full attention to my two remaining friends. "Get out," I said.

The break in the action had given the door kicker a chance to regroup. "Wadda you gonna do, shoot us? Huh, right here, motherfucker?"

I didn't want to give this guy a chance to get his courage all the way back up. He was just dumb enough to be dangerous.

"You got it, friend," I said. "Unless those are pictures of his family that your partner keeps reaching for in his pocket, I'd say I can waste the two of you and walk." It was time to end the snappy dialogue.

"Put your hands on your heads and walk out of here. Now. Leave the camera." Shorty started to object. Not just persistent, but cheap.

"You can steal another one later. I'm not telling you again."

I backed to the far corner between the window and the bed. They were walking.

"We'll find you, asshole," mumbled the big one.

"I'll live in constant fear," I promised.

I followed them out, folding my arms over my chest, hiding the gun under my arm, down the steps and over to a blue Ford Galaxie. They got in, backed out into the lot, and drove out onto Pacific Highway South. Someone, years before, had ripped the vinyl top off the car. The back third of the roof was a uniform rust. Somewhere in the past, a spring had broken. The hook of Bo Peep's crook protruded from the right rear window. The car had a thirty-degree list to starboard. They headed south on Pacific Highway, looking like some sort of depraved Christmas ornament.

Tony had staged a major recovery. He was still the color of old custard, but he had managed to get dressed. He was stuffing the last of his paraphernalia into his suitcases when I got back. A remnant of shocking-pink lace was mashed in the crack of the smaller brown suitcase. It was obvious from his expression that he wasn't at all sure that I was any improvement on the other two. I decided to let him go on worrying about it. I picked up the phone and called him a cab.

"Get out of here," I told him. He had a blue pinstriped business suit on, collar buttoned, tie in place—and yet, amazingly, there was still hair sticking out from under his collar. I'd almost forgotten what he'd looked like in half a Viking costume. I was beginning to feel sick.

"Just go home, partner. This is your lucky day."

He was confused, but smart enough to know a gift horse when he saw one. He picked up all four bags and started for the door. He didn't fit. He had to put them outside two at a time and then follow them out.

"How'd you know they weren't the police?" he asked, as he picked up the bags.

"Even the police dress better than that."

"Come on, seriously."

"The tattoos on the big one," I said. I let him carry his own bags down the stairs. I guessed he was in training. It didn't bother him a bit.

"Cops have tattoos too."

He wasn't going to let this go.

"Not those ballpointed pen specials, they don't, buddy."

The cab arrived. The driver opened the trunk and began to load the bags. Before getting in, Tony grinned at me sheepishly.

"I suppose I should explain what was going on in there."

I opened the cab door.

"If you do I'll shoot you right here in front of the driver," I said without a smile.

Tony took me at my word.

2

I STARTED TO PUT MY WET SLIPPERS INTO THE TRUNK, had an unexpected spasm of lucidity, and instead lobbed them into the conveniently located trash receptacle. Better safe than sorry. As I packed the Fiat with the rest of my gear, I inventoried the positives. My calendar was clear. Rose Moldonado's check would keep me going for some time. The king salmon run was just getting started on the peninsula. An extended fishing trip was in order. The ground fog was just starting to burn off. The weather, for fall, was truly gorgeous. I was depressed. Goddamn that Tony.

I coaxed the Fiat into life and headed back to my apartment. I don't have an office. Waterman Investigations, such as it is, is just me and the answering machine in my apartment. When I'd first started in the business, I'd gone for the whole nine yards, office, secretary, the works, but it didn't work out. Now it's just me and the machine. Most of the time, the machine and I get along quite well.

By the time I crested the interstate, the black glass

of the Colombia Tower wore the last of the ground fog like a bad toupee. I wheeled through the cars and construction and thought about a feature spread I'd seen in the *Times* a few months back. If the pictures could be believed, the women's lavatories in the Colombia Tower were both larger and considerably more elegant than my apartment. At the time, I had dismissed this incongruity as a rather dubious link to lasting fame. It occurred to me now that maybe this wasn't as out of line as I'd once imagined. After all, back around the turn of the century, when my dad was a boy, the entire downtown section of the city had been regraded for the express purpose of getting the newly fashionable flush toilets high enough above the rising tide to prevent them from becoming sewage fountains every time the tide came in. This was, historically speaking, the town that toilets built. Maybe this helped in some small way to explain Tony Moldonado.

I stowed the 9mm in my desk, the cooler in the closet, and its contents in the garbage. The suitcase could wait. What I needed now was a beer. I decided to splurge and opened a Chimay for myself. Chimay is an ale brewed in Belgium by Trappist monks. I found it a bit pricey for day-to-day swillage, but for special occasions it provided just the right festive touch. It also provided a reasonable explanation as to why Trappist monks were silent. If they consumed much of this stuff, they were probably unable rather than unwilling to speak.

I made my way to the living room. The light on my machine was blinking. This was something of a problem. If I listened to the messages before arranging a fishing trip, I was probably going to find somebody who wanted me to do something. If I left town without listening to the messages, I'd spend the whole damn trip wondering what in hell was on the tape and how in hell I could be so irresponsible. I already knew the answer to the last part.

On the surface, I was still a great believer that there was absolutely no sense in working if you already had money. I was, after all, going to come into a pretty fair inheritance when I turned forty-five. My old man, locally renowned as an impeccable judge of character, had seen something in me even when I was a child that had inspired him to reach from the grave to save me from myself. His efforts had not been in vain. Despite the best efforts of my ex-wife's team of lawyers, the draconian complexity of my trust fund had managed to thwart even Washington's hellish community-property laws. To Annette's everlasting chagrin, my prospects remained intact.

In spite of this, however, some compensatory function of impending middle age was beginning to worm its way into my consciousness. I was starting to have visions of spending my declining years with the Boys, down in the vicinity of Pioneer Square, debating the body and bouquet of fortified wine with the other denizens of the district.

Fortunately, I was spared this moral dilemma.

The phone tinkled. I swallowed half the schooner of Chimay, wiped off my upper lip, and picked it up.

"Leo, jew chit. I seen you come in. How you doin'?"

It was Hector Guiterrez, the superintendent of my building. Hector looked out for things around the apartment when I was gone. An expatriate Cuban whose attitude toward the regime had earned him several years in one of Castro's more colorful prisons, Hector harbored a deep, abiding distrust of all authority figures. As my job tended to bring me into constant conflict with a wide assortment of officialdom, Hector had unilaterally adopted me as a fellow conspirator. I'd never been totally clear as to whom we were conspiring against or to what ends, but it seemed to make Hector happy, which was good enough for me. Off the pig. It was us against the world.

"Glad to be home, Hector. Thanks for watering the plants."

"No problem, Leo. The people we got to steek togeder. Jew know what I mean?" I offered that I did.

"How'd eet go? Jew was gone a long time."

"You don't want to know," I said.

"Somebody been looooking for jew." He hesitated. "A wooooman." He breathed. I was supposed to guess now.

"Rebecca?" I ventured.

"A beeg woooman. Muy . . . muy . . ."

What followed was a series of rough glottal noises, the origin and timbre of which made me yearn for a hot shower. He sensed my impatience.

"She come back tree, four times. Finally I took a note from her. Tole her I geev it to jew when jew get back. Eets on toppa de fridge."

"Thanks again Hector. Anything else?"

"Jour lawyer, he called me looking for jew. Said jew gave heem my nomber for 'mergency. Two maybe tree days ago. And"—favoring his flair for the dramatic, he let it hang ominously—"a couple of dose bums of jours was around. The one wid da wood coat and the real dumb one. Jew got to keep dem away from here, Leo. The odder tenants dey go batshit eberytime dey see dose guys. De Harrisons, in 4C, dose fokkers, dey called the corporation and beetched. You tell 'em to stay away, okay, Leo?"

"I'll tell them again, Hector. Sorry about that."

Hector was referring to what I affectionately call "the Boys." When I need a couple pairs of extra ears or eyes, I hire the Boys. Rebecca occasionally groused that referring to a group of grown men, none of whom was under sixty, as the Boys was a slur, but I knew better. The Boys didn't mind. In one capacity or another, they'd all known my old man and, as such, had been counted among my many "uncles."

Twelve terms on the city council had ensured that my old man was among the city's most well-known characters. Three half-hearted runs at the mayor's office, particularly the one when, clad in a red tuxedo, he'd campaigned from atop a spewing beer wagon, had lifted his status to legend. Through it all, however, he'd never lost the common touch. He never forgot his old friends—that collection of drunks and reprobates he'd started out with down on the mud flats, those who sobered up every four years or so for just long enough to vote for him again. Wild Bill Waterman always kept a place in his heart and a little cash in his pocket for a guy who was down on his luck.

Among my most cherished memories are those of being awakened late at night by muffled conversation and laughter, of sneaking down the back stairs that led to the kitchen, my mother's threats humming in my ears, of finding ragged, red-faced men who smelled of dust and desperation sitting around our kitchen table, dripping water on the black-and-white tile floor, dipping snuff and sipping whiskey. Even then they'd been relegated to the back kitchen. Unlike my father, my mother took her social position quite seriously and had, in stages, eventually banned these so-called "uncles" from her house.

The Boys were the last remnants of another era, my last tie to my old man. When sober, they made excellent operatives. The old and poor are invisible. They can hang around forever without attracting attention. They operate inside their own little force fields, which direct the regular citizenry away from them like incompatible magnetic poles.

Of the originals, only George, Harold, and Ralph

were still around. Buddy Knox had gotten himself killed on what I'd foolishly presumed was a routine surveillance. I was resigned that guilt was a major reason why I always tried to keep the Boys busy, even when I didn't particularly need the help.

To everyone's amazement, Buddy had left the other three enough of an insurance settlement for them to put a down payment on the rooming house in which they'd all shared a single, large room. Combined, their meager pensions provided just enough cash to pay for booze and utilities. No problem. They took up the slack with a combination of money they made working for me, panhandling, and an artful collection of insurance scams.

Since Buddy's death, they'd used the house as a makeshift shelter for the homeless. Neither their neighbors on Franklin nor the authorities were amused. Faced with a withering volley of suits and injunctions, the Boys had turned to me. I, in turn, had passed them on to my attorney, Jed James, who, while way out of their financial league, was such a lover of underdogs and lost causes that he'd seemed a natural. His approach was to meet salvo with salvo. Thus far, he'd kept the powers that be at bay with a veritable hail of writs and show-cause orders. Privately, he'd confided to me that it was just a matter of time before the authorities had their way. Perhaps that explained why Jed had been looking so hard for me and why the Boys, in spite of instructions to the contrary, had been around.

"There's a new Chucho Valdez CD." Hector interrupted my thoughts. In addition to conspiracy,
Hector and I also shared a love of jazz, particularly
the Afro-Cuban variety. Burro notwithstanding,
without Hector and his embargo-defying relatives in
Miami, I wouldn't have know Chucho Valdez from
Juan Valdez.

"Make me a tape."

"Chewer. Jew tell dem bums. Okay, Leo?"

"Okay, Hector. Later."

The answering machine yielded several calls from
Jed, a heartwrenching potential employment opportunity that involved finding a lost dog—Muffy, I
believe it was—and the usual collection of telemar-
keting schemes that besmirch the airways these days.

I wandered over to the refrigerator and pulled
the note off the top. The pressure of my hand
plowed a furrow in the collected grease and grime. I
reckoned somebody needed to clean off the top of
the fridge. There was printing on one side of the
torn-in-half piece of blue paper. Scrawled on the
unprinted side, the message was brief.

Heck needs you. He's in Swedish. Room 222.
                                        Marge.

Henry "Heck" Sundstrom was a major supporting
player in the movie of my life. During my high
school years, I'd worked three winters on Heck's
commercial fishing boat, the *Lady Day*—a jet-black

Limit Seiner, fifty-eight feet with a nineteen-foot beam, built and rigged to spend six months a year seining the obsidian waters of the Bering Strait for salmon and black cod and six months being scraped, painted, and refitted in preparation for another season.

When the *Lady Day* hit the dock in early September every year, Rudy and Angel were on their way south before the diesel fumes had settled. They were fishermen. Refitting was beneath their dignity. That was a job for a kid. My old man, as usual, knew somebody who knew somebody who knew Heck. It was the hardest work I'd ever done and the best time I'd ever spent. I dreamed of the days ahead when I'd be able to prove myself worthy of going fishing. While my mother was dreaming of law school, I was dreaming of ling cod.

Heck was a third-generation Seattle fisherman. With an uncanny combination of luck, hard work, and business sense he'd parlayed the mortgage on his grandfather's hand-built wooden fifty-two footer into the *Lady Day*, a paid-for, half-million-dollar, state-of the-art vessel whose staunch steel sides and cozy tophouse gave a man the courage to once again risk the hard northern waters for profit.

He'd been unmarried then, seemingly a lifetime bachelor. A man's man, he answered to no one. He'd lived on board, playing host to an ever-changing assortment of waterfront characters who'd stop by for a drink or two, disappear for a month, and then suddenly return to find the party more or less where they'd left it.

In those days, the air displacement of his physical presence seemed to bob lesser men about. I'd stay aboard on Friday and Saturday nights when the perpetual party, after enough booze and testosterone, sometimes degenerated into round-robin arm-wrestling sessions. I'd watch in amazement as Heck, his massive arm steady as a rock, would casually make small talk with onlookers while larger opponents, their faces beet-red, streaked with sweat, their bodies shaking with the strain, failed to move him an inch. When the desire moved him, he'd put them down in a single swift movement without ever interrupting the patter.

He was everything I could imagine a man wanting to be. Unlike my old man, who was forever moving and shaking behind the scenes, Heck grappled directly with reality and won. He was my hero. In those days, we didn't have role models yet. He'd seemed untouchable, somehow destined to forever continue his yearly migration to the sea, to the party and back.

Destiny went into the dumpster the moment Marge sashayed onto Dock 2 that day in early October more than twenty-three years ago. She was about twenty-two or so, not too many years my senior, and ripe in a way usually limited to a tropical fruit. Her family was visiting old Mel, who ran Lubber, the greasy spoon at the marina. Over six feet, she was nearly as big as Heck and put together in a package of truly fearful symmetry. On other women, the simple blue frock was just a house dress for ironing or a quick trip to the market; on Marge it was neon. The image of her that day, thick auburn hair backlit by the late-afternoon sun, seemingly on fire, is still burned somewhere on my retinas.

As she ambled down the dock fully aware of her effect yet profoundly disinterested, jaws gaped; the daily tasks of rerigging and cleaning up, so essential to boat maintenance, stopped dead on every craft she passed. I gawked with the others, filled with an odd mixture of excitement and anxiety, as if one of my fevered adolescent dreams had finally arrived, only to find me withered and wanting. Martin Henry, who kept the *Mary B* in the slip next to Heck's, later confided to me that he'd been fixing a rope end while gawking at Marge that day and had nearly severed his thumb. Like me, he still carries the scar.

In all the years since that day, I've never seen it again. As a matter of fact, if it weren't for that single moment, I wouldn't believe it at all. I'd figure it was just the exaggerated way people remember their pasts so that their lives will seem to have more drama and less sadness. I'd have been wrong. It was love at first sight. From three boats away, Marge and Heck honed in on one another like a couple of hormonally guided missiles. At first, I thought it was me she was looking at and was instantly lifted. Luckily, before I could make an ass of myself, Heck eased me aside. To this day, I'm convinced that anyone stepping between them at the precise moment when their eyes met would surely have been killed by the combined power of their gazes. In that single moment, Heck knew that life as he had known it was over. I knew that he knew. Marge knew that we both knew.

Rudy, Angel, and I found that our services were no longer required. Within a week, Heck was without crew. It wasn't just us either. The party was just plain over. Boarders were summarily repelled. The *Lady Day* gave up her berth on Dock 2, a Sundstrom stronghold for nearly forty years, and moved down to Dock 7, the nominal line of demarcation between the commercial and the gentlemen fishermen, a more civilized environ where tourists could stroll the docks on weekends without fear of so much as smudging their togs, let alone taking a broom support in the melon.

Marge, in spite of her limited years, was a woman who knew what she wanted. Instead of trying to melt herself amiably into the maze of Heck's past life and acquaintances, she'd simply started his life over for him. She kept his old friends at a distance. On those occasions when Heck and I got together after they were married, I could sense her impatience with any story that had transpired before she'd walked into his life. She'd immediately redirect the conversation to the present, as if the thirty-odd years of his past had merely been a prolonged prelude to her arrival.

One by one, she'd phased us out. Surprisingly, Heck didn't seem to mind; obviously, she was all he needed. God, how I'd hated her back then.

Within five years she'd gotten him off the boat and into wholesale. Fleets of Sea Sundstrom vans now supplied local restaurants with the fresh fish for which they were so justly famous.

They had also had a son. Over the years, I'd seen the newly prominent Sundstroms in the paper once in a while. Maybe it was my imagination, but Heck always looked vaguely uncomfortable and strangely out of place. Marge, to my great annoyance, looked good even in newsprint. The kid, Nick I think it was, had turned out to be a pretty good halfback for Ballard High. Rumor had it that Heck shared his success with a number of worthy causes. I thought back to the last time I'd seen him.

I'd spied on him, across the packed room, at a fundraiser for the families of those lost at sea. This was six or seven years ago. Instinctively, I'd squirmed and shouldered my way through the crowd to his side. Without thinking, we'd embraced, the intervening years instantly evaporating. His face cracked with an idiotic grin, he grasped me by both shoulders and held me off the ground at arm's length as if I were a doll. Before either of us had time to speak, the sea of humanity suddenly parted and Marge, more stunning than ever, appeared at his side, smiling that smile. She had someone for Heck to meet. So nice to see me again. She took him by the elbow. Heck barely had time for a quick look over his shoulder as they melted into the melee. It was a moment of such encompassing awkwardness that it resurfaced, fresh and hot on my face, every time I thought about Heck Sundstrom, which was more often than I would have chosen.

I leaned back against the fridge. Scraping the sludge off the printed side of the note, I could just make out what it had once been. It was a final notice from Puget Power. They wanted their three hundred seventy-four dollars and twelve cents, and they wanted it by last Friday.

3

SWEDISH HOSPITAL SQUATS AT THE APEX OF PILL HILL, the blond cement of her estimable girth warding off all challengers for that most lofty section of lower Broadway that has, over the past decade, evolved into the medical epicenter of the city. Not surprisingly, the presence of five major hospitals in a couple of square miles has spawned multifarious schools of specialists and technologists who hover and dart about the neighborhood, always alert for bigger, better office space, eager to bill, ever ready to snap up any crumbs that might float from the mouths of the great beasts. Whether medical services have improved is a matter of great debate; that parking has gone to shit is without question.

Unable to find anything legal on either Minor or Colombia, I wound down the hill toward Boren, getting lucky, finding a space on the shady side of St. James Cathedral, half a block uphill from O'Dea High School.

Any vestige of morning fog had been swept aside

by the earthy breezes of Indian summer. The uphill walk, padded by the first red maple leaves of the season, was enough to raise beads of sweat on my forehead. I skirted piles of sand, rebar, and wire mesh, the remnants of the ongoing state of siege that the unending construction left in its wake. I found a side door.

I didn't see him at first. In the hard hospital bed, he looked small, inanimate, and out of place. Several tufts of blond hair, mostly gone grey at the center, had somehow wriggled free of the mummylike bandages covering most of his head. His left hand, reddened and clenched like an oak burl atop the covers, sprouted a plastic IV tube that was anchored in place by yet another maze of tape. He was alone. I walked to the foot of the bed and plucked his chart from the built-in receptacle.

I was lost in the scribbles when he stirred, tightening his body, seemingly attempting to sit up. I slid around to his left side and put a hand on his shoulder. The touch seemed to comfort him. He relaxed again, smoothing the deep lines of his forehead, sending the blood back around the system, again making visible the network of fine pink capillaries that hatched his nearly translucent skin.

"He sat up twice yesterday. They say it's just muscle contractions."

Marge stood half-in, half-out of the door, her right arm braced on the beige wall. She wore a thick forest-green turtleneck sweater, a shade darker than her eyes, blue jeans, and what looked to be python cowboy boots. Large gold hoop earrings diverted attention from the grey in her thick hair. She wasn't twenty anymore. No sir—to my eye, at least, she looked a whole lot better than that. Nature, with uncommon kindness, provides most of us with a rationalized scale of beauty, a balanced image in keeping with our stations of life. Unlike Tony Moldonado, most of us manage to surmount the aching for buxom airbrushed cheerleaders and find ourselves one day mercifully able to envision strength of character in a facial line or two and intellectual weight in the slight sag of a breast. By synchronizing that which is possible with that which is desired, nature both ensures the survival of the species and keeps the costs down.

I waved the chart. "I was . . . trying to . . ."

"He's stable. That's all they'll say."

"Stable means?"

"Stable means, he's got a severe skull fracture and two broken legs but is in no immediate danger of dying. Whether or not he's going to stay like this or for how long is anybody's guess."

Her heels clicked as she crossed the room, took the chart from my hands, and returned it to its place at the foot of the bed. No perfume; just soap, leather, and hair spray drifted in her wake.

"What happened?" I asked.

"He was hit by a truck."

"Where?"

She hesitated before answering. "On First Avenue."

"When did this happen?"

"Three days ago."

"Did they get the driver?"

"It wasn't his fault. He stopped. Heck walked right out from between cars. There was no way he could have stopped in time."

"What time of day was this?"

"Just after midnight."

I retrieved the chart and again pretended to study it. This called for some discretion. Most of the things a guy could get on First Avenue at midnight were not things you wanted to discuss with his wife.

"What was he doing in that neighborhood at that time of night?"

When I didn't get a response, I rephrased the question.

"Did he have a meeting or something?"

My question struck some kind of nerve. Marge heaved a sigh, pursed her full lips, and reached a hand out toward me. She pulled the chart from my hands and hugged it to her chest.

"This isn't going to work," she said quietly.

"This what?"

"This . . . you . . . none of this. I thought maybe . . . you being a detective and all. I'm sorry, Leo. You were just a wild idea I had—but this isn't going to work." She turned away toward the bed, fussing with the pillows, as if Heck knew the difference.

"I'd like to help."

"Thanks anyway, Leo," she said, continuing to prop and preen.

When I didn't move, she tried again.

"Sorry for wasting your time. I'll tell him you were by."

"He's even easier to control when he's in a coma, isn't he?"

I don't know where that came from. It crossed my lips before it ever crossed my mind. I must have had it stored in some dank internal warehouse where the collected injustices and indignities of adolescence bide their time until that day when *they'll* all be sorry. She turned slowly from the bed with that big smile.

"Leo," she said with a bit too much control, "get a grip. Better than that, get a life. It's twenty-three years later. What? Am I supposed to still feel bad about breaking up the Ballard Boys' Club?"

"Still?" I countered lamely.

"You're right."

She stepped in close, nodding her head. We were eye to eye. Her face makeup seemed to contain little specks of gold glitter.

"When you're right, you're right, Leo. You always were the brightest of the lot, so let's get this over with. I didn't feel guilty about it then, and I don't feel guilty about it now. There. I said it. The man was damn near thirty-five years old. I don't care about what you and the other Lost Boys wanted. It was time for Superman to get on with his life. You and the rest of those perpetual adolescents ought to try clicking your heels together and repeating 'I'll never grow up. I'll never grow up.' See if that works."

I surprised myself again. "You could have done it differently."

She pivoted and walked past me to the west wall. I figured she was going to show me the door. Wrong again.

"I was young," she said quietly. "I only knew what I wanted and what was in my way. In those days, I didn't think much further ahead than that. I was—what's the word?" She studied a diamond-encrusted knuckle. "Smitten, I guess. I'd never seen anything like him in my life. I mean, he wasn't my first or anything."

She turned to face me.

"I was an early bloomer. They'd been after me since I was twelve. First my uncle Jack, then anything else that could walk or crawl—but nothing like Heck."

"He was special," I agreed.

The moment seemed to grant me a reprieve.

"Heck and I hadn't talked much lately. He'd been sleeping on board."

"On board what?"

"The *Lady Day*."

"I didn't realize you still had her."

"Oh, well, we couldn't sell never-never-land, now could we?" The bitterness crept back into her voice.

"Hell, we borrowed money at absolutely criminal rates when we expanded the business, rather than sell the clubhouse. He wouldn't even use the damn thing as collateral. He and Nicky were gonna—" She hugged the chart tighter. "They've warned him. They've fined him. They've threatened to take away his berth."

"Who's warned him about what?"

"Sleeping on board. There's no living aboard anymore. The city put a stop to that years ago."

The *Lady Day* was built to fish. She had berths all right and a galley and the obligatory head, but nobody in their right mind was ever going to mistake her for a five-star hotel. Whatever demons had driven Heck from a warm spot next to Marge to the sparse shelter of the boat must have been serious indeed.

"I'd like to help," I offered again.

Marge wandered over and leaned on the steel restraining rails of the bed. She gazed absently at Heck as she spoke.

"You know, he always kept track of you, Leo. He's got that famous picture of you and the two . . . er . . . two working girls, in the fountain in front of the Four Seasons, framed on his office wall."

That particular incident not being the highlight of my career, I didn't know what to say.

"He's got an envelope in his desk with all these clippings about you and your cases. All the times you made the papers. I found it the other day when I was going through the desk trying to straighten things out. That's when I thought maybe . . . I don't know."

"I'd like to help." Third time's the charm, right? "I'd consider it a privilege to do anything for Heck that I can."

"What about working for me? Would that be a privilege?" she asked. "The way things are"—she put a hand on Heck's chest—"it looks like . . . temporarily at least, you'd be working for me, not for Heck."

She patted him gently.

"You and I will have to work it out as we go along," I said.

She turned and looked me in the eye for a long moment. Her gaze had the same unsettling effect on me that it had twenty-three years ago. This time, I was the one who turned away.

"Fair enough," she said.

I pulled my notebook from my back pocket and turned around. She was seated in the heavy blue chair next to the bed. I clicked my pen.

"Where to start?" she said to no one in particular.

Usually, by the time people come to me, they've told their story numerous times and have it down to a science. Detectives aren't anybody's choice for a first resort. Marge's manner suggested the opposite. I had the feeling that I was the first person who was going to hear whatever was to follow. As she spoke she looked at the unmoving Heck as if at any moment he would rise up and save her from this painful duty.

"Nicky had—" I thought she was going to balk again, but instead she plunged ahead. "Nicky was diagnosed with cancer about eighteen months ago. Bone cancer." She hesitated. "For a while, it looked like he was going to lose a leg. Then they said they had it under control. Then, he needed to go for those treatments again. Chemotherapy."

She waved the words away.

"They're a bunch of witch doctors. They can maybe slow it down but other than that they don't have a clue."

She sighed heavily and reached out to Heck again, stroking his cheek.

"Heck took it hard. Harder than Nicky. Heck—" She began to edit herself. "To make a long story short—"

"No need," I said. "It's probably best if I hear it all."

She nodded resignedly. "Heck took it hard. Nicky meant everything to him. He must have forced that poor kid into about a dozen second opinions. Nicky was like a pin cushion, but Heck just had to do something. Couldn't stand feeling helpless. He just had to do something to fix things. He always had to fix things." She paused.

"Anyway, when he got more or less the same diagnosis from everybody, Heck had this hare-brained idea. He and Nicky were going fishing together. Back into business. They were going to refit the *Lady Day* and hit the high seas together." She shook her head. "I don't know what he was thinking. Other than taking the Clipper up to Victoria, Heck hadn't been out on the water in ten years."

Another pause, as she reminisced.

"Well, we did have a little thirty-foot Sea Ray for a while there, but somehow it just seemed to make him sad." She flicked a gaze in my direction. "So we sold it."

"Heck and Nicky were going fishing," I prompted.

"Heck said it would take Nicky's mind off it all. That the sea air would do him wonders. None of it made any sense, but he wouldn't listen, and Nicky— well—he just idolized Heck. Whatever his dad said was gospel."

She was winding up now. "He gave Nicky the *Lady Day*. Signed it over to him. He gave Nicky his trust fund so they could refit the boat. They knew damn well they wouldn't get the money from me," she added defiantly.

Catching herself, she went on.

"The boat was sound. Heck always kept it up, but it needed new electronics. The navigational equipment and radar were out of date."

She shot a murderous glance at the inanimate Heck. Her hands closed into bejeweled fists. I recognized the signs. Her resolve was waning. Clients often reach a point where they'd rather live with the problem than have to finish telling the story to a stranger.

"And?" I said.

"And, they almost got it finished."

"Then?" A chill ran down my spine like a drop of icy rain. She transferred her glare to me.

"And then Miss Allison Stark came along."

This time I waited.

"Nicky met her at one of his therapy sessions. I don't know what she was doing there. He used to go to these meetings with other cancer patients. You know, support groups. Where they could share. Heck hated it. He kept saying that Nicky didn't have cancer like those other people. Not like lung cancer or liver cancer. He couldn't face it, just couldn't stand it."

She was losing her thread. I poked her back on track.

"Allison Stark?"

"Allison Stark Sundstrom," she snapped, angry I'd reeled her in.

"They're married?"

"They're dead," she said quickly, hitching her breath. "Or that's what everyone except Heck thought."

I could hear Heck's smooth breathing, the muted hum of machinery somewhere in the bowels of the building, a toilet flushing next door.

"Let's start back with Allison Stark," I suggested.

"She came over Nicky like . . ." Marge mused, "like . . ."

She read my mind. "Yeah . . . like I did over Heck. But"—she wagged a finger at me—"this was different."

"Different how?"

"There was something about that girl. It's hard to describe."

My eyebrows gave me away.

"I know that sounds strange, Leo, but it's true. From the minute I met her, something in me knew the girl wasn't real."

"You're gonna have to fill this in for me."

Suddenly we were in a movie that Marge had run before. The original definition of the word rehearsal strolled across my mind: To raise up or resummon the dead. Grief, anger, and guilt all give us pause for rehearsal.

"First, there's the basic situation." Her voice rising. "We've got this beautiful kid, twenty-two years old, God love him, who's undergoing chemotherapy, who may well never live to see twenty-three." She rubbed her temples, going on. "His hair is falling out in clumps. He's a splotchy light yellow color most of the time from all the chemicals. It takes him three days to get up and around after each treatment, and what happens?"

I shrugged.

"Out of the blue, it's like suddenly this little beautiful creature just can't live without him. And does anybody but me find that strange? No way. Makes complete sense to them. Those two were just like the rest of you. They just blandly assumed it was Nicky's charm. Men always assume it's their charm. It's what makes them so damn easy."

I ignored the jibe.

"What else?" I prodded.

"The age thing. I mean she looked great, perfect little petite figure and all, no cellulite, not a ripple, not so much as a vaccination mark, but there was no way she was the twenty-six she claimed to be. Women can sense things like that. Heck wouldn't listen to me, but as I'm sitting here, she was no twenty-six. You couldn't see the lines because of that tan, but she'd had the work done, I know it. I've seen it before in my friends. Everything was just a bit too tight. You could have bounced quarters off her cheeks."

"Anything else?"

"The stories. This goes along with the age thing. You wouldn't believe the stories. At first, I thought she was just eager to please—you know, trying to make an impression—but it never let up. To hear her talk she'd been everywhere and done everything—model, advertising exec, aerobics instructor, river guide, travel agent, butcher, baker, candlestick maker. Leo, I swear to you, you'd have to be eighty years old to have had all the experiences she claimed. Yet"—she waved a finger again—"not one verifiable detail. Not one thing you could check.

Only child. Parents killed in a plane crash. Raised by a rich aunt. Supposedly from Wisconsin. It went on and on."

"And nobody but you noticed?"

"She charmed the socks off both of them. They were pathetic. Nicky was so in love she could have had horns and he wouldn't have noticed."

"And Heck?"

"Heck was just so relieved to see Nicky happy again." She shook her head sadly, anticipating my next question. "I had to either shut up or become the enemy. I shut up. I figured, given a little time, they'd see through her. God knows she was transparent enough."

"What did—" I began. She interrupted me.

"If I'd had any idea they were getting married, I'd have kept at it. I'd have set new records for bitchery. I wouldn't have cared what either of them thought of me. I'd have kept at it until they paid attention."

"The marriage was a surprise, then?"

She clicked her tongue.

"They were supposedly just going to Vegas for the weekend."

"Came back married."

She nodded. "That bitch had it planned all the way. I told Heck the day they left that they'd come back married."

"How did you know?"

"I just knew."

"And then?"

"And then what in the hell was I going to do? My only son was married. What was I going to do? I had to at least seem supportive, didn't I?"

"So they came back married. What then?"

"The honeymoon. They began to plan the honeymoon. We offered to buy them a Hawaiian honeymoon, the Bahamas, the Caribbean, you name it, we offered it. Oh no. They already had their minds made up."

I could sense we were coming to the end now.

"They'd, or rather she had, decided to lease a yacht for a month. Fifty-some-odd feet—just restored—a beautiful thing. They were going to cruise down to Baja and back. It was her idea. She said that would save Nicky the embarrassment of the public beaches, what with his hair and all the splotches. Just the two of them, you know. She was always so very thoughtful."

"So?"

"So, they left on a Thursday morning, a month ago next Thursday. Heck and I went down to Magnolia and saw them off. Champagne across the bow, the whole bit."

She heaved a massive sigh. "Friday afternoon we got a call from the Coast Guard that the boat had blown up and sunk with all hands. Not a trace. They say the explosion was so loud it woke everybody in Gig Harbor, which was the better part of five miles away. Supposedly a fuel leak. They recovered two

... parts of two ... bodies. Brought them back here."

She was having trouble maintaining her facade now.

"One was Nicky . . . Dental records. No question. The other body was female. That's all they could say for sure without something to compare it—the remains—with."

"And Heck didn't think it was them?"

"Nicky's for sure. Even Heck couldn't dispute that. Heck didn't think she was on board, though."

"Any particular reason?"

I sensed that I'd asked the wrong question again.

"Guilt. It had to be the guilt. Heck felt guilty for not listening to me about that little bitch. I think he was punishing himself for being so damn stupid. I think he needed somebody to blame. He needed to feel he was doing something. First he couldn't face Nicky's illness; then he couldn't face his death. As long as he kept this ridiculous thing going, he didn't have to face the facts." She swallowed. "So childish.

"What I really think is that my son is dead, and my husband may well be a vegetable for the rest of his life, and that none of that macho bullshit is going to bring either of them back to me."

"So there was nothing tangible about his suspicions?"

"There was the missing money and the mortgage on the boat."

"I thought Heck refused to mortgage the boat."

"He did. That's where it gets sticky. Nicky mortgaged the boat during the two weeks before they left on the honeymoon. Never said a word to Heck or me. Very out of character for Nicky. Five hundred and seventy-five thousand dollars. He also cleaned out his trust fund. Another three hundred fifteen thousand. Altogether that's the better part of a million dollars missing."

"Missing?"

"Thin air." She snapped her fingers. "The bank said they couldn't tell us anything. Some privacy law. Just that the accounts were no longer active. Nicky was over twenty-one, and it was a joint account with Allison. Right now, their deaths are officially accidents. We need a court order to get the bank records."

"So, if it wasn't Allison on the boat, who was it?"

"Heck hung around the terminal for weeks, pestering everybody. Eventually he became convinced it was some wharf rat he'd seen hanging around the marina while they were working on the *Lady Day*."

"That's all? Wharf rats come and go. Heck knows that. Doesn't sound like much to me."

"When he couldn't stand hearing that from me anymore was when he moved aboard. It was ridiculous."

"Why call me, then?"

She was ready for this one.

"I've been asking myself that for days, and I think

I've finally come to an answer. It's because I need this finished. I need some sense of resolution, of closure. If this wild goose chase turns out to be the last thing Heck ever does, so be it, but it needs to have an end. I need to feel I've done everything I can."

I understood completely. This need for closure was what kept me in business. It permitted those who were faced with disaster and guilt a cushion of hope and allowed those who were left behind to eventually turn the page and get on with their lives.

I thought she was finished, but she suddenly continued.

"And because there's just too many questions left, Leo, even for a pragmatist like me. Where's the money? Nicky could have had whatever he'd wanted. All he had to do was ask. And . . . there's her . . . that bitch. I don't know how to—" She shrugged. "Then there's the ATM card."

I waited.

"On the day of the accident, just before midnight, Heck took five hundred dollars in cash out of the company account with his ATM card."

"So?"

"He never used the card. Not once. He liked to go into the bank. He had a card for the better part of ten years, and in all that time, that morning was the first and only time he'd ever used it."

"Where did he do this?"

"That's another thing. First Avenue. By the market. What could he be doing in that neighborhood at that time of night?"

I decided the question was rhetorical and stood mute.

"Finally," she intoned, "there's the pictures."

"The pictures?"

"I just noticed them a few days ago. I was shuffling through all of our recent pictures, sort of feeling sorry for myself. That's when I started looking for you. I probably could have lived with the rest of it, if I hadn't gone through those damn pictures. They pushed me over the edge."

"What about the pictures?"

"All the pictures we took over the couple of months she was around. Heck had become quite the cameraman. There must be thirty or forty shots she's in, and you know what, Leo? There's not a single good picture of her. Not a single frame where her hand isn't somehow in front of her face, or where she isn't half covered by somebody's shoulder or by her own hair. It defies the law of averages. It had to be on purpose. The pictures were the last straw. I had extra prints and negatives made."

She opened the drawer in the nightstand, took out a pale green paper bag with interlocking silver rings woven into the pattern, and held it out to me. I walked over and took it from her hand.

"Those are his notes and all the stuff he took out

of the apartment. He's been a man possessed, Leo. He hasn't done anything else but investigate for the past few weeks. You'll have to go through all that stuff. I imagine he's just been running in circles. There's also keys to the *Lady Day* and to Nicky's apartment."

Again, she anticipated my question.

"Heck wouldn't part with the apartment either. I'll pay the power company so you can see in there. I let it lapse, hoping if he couldn't see, maybe he'd give it up."

She rose, folding her arms over her ample chest.

"Can you help me, Leo?"

"I don't know, Marge. I can promise you I'll try, but I think I should tell you up front that things are generally just the way they seem to be. The cops are pretty good at what they do. There are damn few insidious plots. People generally die in bed or get killed by the people closest to them."

"I understand that, but I need to feel that I've done everything possible. Will you help me?"

"I'll see what I can do."

"Do you need some money, a retainer or something?"

"What I'll need," I said, "is to get with your attorney."

"Why?"

"We need to follow the money. The money is the only tangible thing we've got here. Even when there are other leads to follow, it's still best to follow the money. If your attorneys aren't up to it, I know one who is."

"For what we pay them, they'd better be up to it," she snorted.

"Can you get him down to your office on a Saturday?"

"In his jammies, if I insist."

"Insist."

"What time?"

"One," I said, heading for the door.

"You'll bill me later?" she persisted.

"Then I'm working for you?"

"So it would seem."

"Then you can count on it."

She gave me a smile thin enough to pass for a scar.

4

IT WAS A CLEAR CASE OF PREMATURE JOCULARITY. From the second he'd figured out that I wasn't there to lease a yacht, he'd dropped the jovial sales facade and moved with practiced speed from simply insolent to downright unpleasant.

I'd spent an hour and a half in Vito's, down the hill from Swedish, nursing a coffee and going through Heck's notepad, as the late lunch crowd came and went. Heck had covered a lot of ground without getting much accomplished. The yacht leasing agency had seemed as good a place as any to start.

"Do I have to call security?"

"Easy there, Scooter," I said, showing a palm.

While his right hand danced above the phone, he used his left to jab at the pale blue business card on the counter. Each word punctuated by a jab.

"All questions about the accident need to go to our attorneys."

The embroidery on his pink Ralph Lauren pullover said this was a Chipper, not a Scooter, but what the hell? He was a compact little fellow, about thirty, with a pitted face, a fair hair-helmet so stiff it appeared to be shellacked, and a pair of the smallest feet I'd ever seen on an adult.

"You must have an earwax problem," he added.

"I told you, I don't want to talk about the accident. I just want to have a few words with the person who leased them the boat."

"Same answer, bub. The bossman himself leased that one, and he's not talking to anybody, so beat it."

"Why don't we ask him?" I suggested.

"Why don't you shag your ass back out that door?"

"I'll tell you, Scooter, I'm not much impressed with your idea of customer service."

"That's your problem, dickwad."

I leaned forward on the counter and beckoned him closer. When he declined, I spread out, letting my forearms push a pile of glossy brochures off onto the floor. They fanned out over his little feet, which began doing something akin to the Ali Shuffle.

"How clumsy of me."

He got louder. "All questions about the—"

I interrupted him by walking around to the open side of the sales counter.

"—the accident—" he stammered.

"You say that again, Scooter, I'm gonna mess up your hair."

He turned toward the phone, dialing finger poised. I stepped closer.

"I wouldn't," I said quietly. He replaced the receiver with a bang.

"Come on man," he whined. "I don't want any trouble. We had a whole meeting about this crap. I'm sorry about those kids, but it's my ass if I tell you anything. Mr. Richmond said—"

"Then call Mr. Richmond," I suggested for the third time.

"I told you, man, he hates being bothered if it's not an emergency."

"Trust me, Scooter, as far as you're concerned, this is an emergency."

As he turned to the phone, he betrayed himself with the slightest of sneers. The buttons clicked.

"If you're calling security, my friend, I'd suggest you reconsider. I'm self-employed. I've got nothing better to do than wait outside for you for the next couple of weeks. Unless you plan on this being your last day on the job, and then like moving to another state, you'd better be calling this Mr. Richmond."

His shoulders visibly sagged as he depressed the button and redialed. After half a minute of apologetic mumbling and kowtowing, Chipper returned the receiver gingerly to its perch.

"He'll be right down."

"Thanks," I said, leaving the business card on the counter. It was identical to the one I'd found with Heck's notes. I turned on my heel and walked back out the door toward the afternoon sunshine of the marina.

"Fuck you very much," he shot at my back.

I repaired to the nearest bench to catch a little sun and admire the view. From the northwest, the gleaming monoliths of downtown Seattle appeared to be under attack from giant insects. These days, the Port of Seattle completely surrounds the spot where the jagged Duwamish River empties into Elliot Bay. A swarm of bright orange loading cranes stood sentry, seeming to ring the downtown core like modern engines of siege.

This had been the original Seattle. A hundred years ago, Doc Maynard and his cronies had simply called those bootsucking tidal flats the Sag. Prior to the regrade, that area had been the only place our founding fathers could, at low tide, get down and walk on the beach. The contemporary Doc Maynards called it the Gateway to the Pacific Rim.

I was pulled from my ruminations by the sound of leather soles on the cement behind me. Richmond was a big, florid man, flushed with the good life. His hair was wet, combed straight back. He wore a sport coat over a pink shirt and grey slacks, penny loafers. No socks, no tie. After unbuttoning the double-breasted blue blazer, he sat heavily next to me on the bench, his bulk springing the central steel support slightly.

"Chipper says you threatened him, Mr.—"

"Waterman. Leo Waterman." I offered a hand. Without hesitation, he took it in his oversize mitt and moved it up and down, eyeing me.

"Waterman's a rather famous name around here. You any relation to Wild Bill Waterman?"

"My father," I admitted.

"Hell of a character, if you don't mind me saying," he said.

"So I understand," I said.

Predictably, Richmond had a story.

"I remember one year, it was just after the war, late forties, early fifties, some time in there, he led the Candidate's Parade down Fourth Avenue dressed up like Mahatma Gandhi." He slapped his knee. "He was leading this mangy old goat on a leash. Everybody loved it. It was swell. I'll never forget it."

Neither would anyone else. Seattle was like a reformed drunk, pious and sober, but secretly nostalgic for its wild youth. I'd heard all the stories so many times that the line between how I remembered him and the stories I'd been told was forever muddled, leaving me with a blurred image of the old man that was, I suspected, more apocryphal than real. I changed the subject.

"Nice name—Chipper."

"Yeah, if you're a beaver," he said, studying the water.

"Nasty little fellow."

He shrugged. "He's my Helen's third attempt at connubial bliss. If I don't keep him working, they'll move back in with us."

"I wouldn't really have hurt him," I confessed.

"Too bad."

We sat in silence gazing out at Elliot Bay, still and unbroken in that brief lull between morning and evening breezes. I watched a bufflehead. The small diving duck flicked beneath the surface, stayed an eternity, and then popped back to the surface twenty yards from where it went under.

"I'm sure you understand why we can't talk to anybody about the accident," he said finally.

"How's about off the record?"

He looked at me like I'd just hawked a lunger onto his shirt front.

"What's your interest in this, anyway, Waterman?"

I fished in my pocket and produced a business card.

"Working for?" He pocketed the card.

"The Sundstroms."

"Then how in hell can it be off the record?" He spat disgustedly, beginning to rise.

I laid it out for him. The missing money. Heck's suspicions, the whole unlikely tale as told to me, culminating with the truck hitting Heck. He settled back, resting his arms along the top of the bench, rocking slightly.

"You're being straight with me?" he said.

"I've told you the story just like it was told to me."

"So your interest in this has nothing to do with litigation?"

"I don't do insurance work. I can't guarantee

anything about what the Sundstroms might do later, but right now this is about peace of mind."

"And the Sundstroms don't think it was an accident?"

"They don't know what to think."

"That makes three of us."

"How so?"

"I've got half a million invested in that vessel. Just had it completely refurbished. Brand new twin Cummings three-seventies. New water, propane, satellite dish. The whole works, inside and out. I checked that boat out myself. You know, if you want something done right . . . Five of us took it up through the San Juans to Vancouver. Some of the best men I've got, been with me for years, went over every inch of it. I've been in this business for thirty years. Believe me, *Risky Business* was leaking nothing."

"Sometimes, with boats—"

"And she wouldn't take on any crew, not even a pilot."

"You offered?"

"Hell, I insisted, but she didn't want to hear about it."

"Why'd you back off?"

"Don't think I haven't asked myself that one."

"And?"

"First of all, that particular boat was damn near foolproof. We try to set them up that way. If you're going to lease boats to the public, they'd better not be rocket science. Everything electric. Directions for everything. Hell, you've got about fifty thousand pounds of boat, with less than four-foot draft. It's not easy to fuck up in a fifty-two-footer. Motor during the day; put up at night; don't hit anything too hard. Not much to it. It had every kind of safety gear in the world. VHF, radar GPS, depth sounder, autocompass, autopilot—the thing was loaded. Hell, it had a Whaler with a fifty-horse. Like I said, pretty much idiot-proof. Even Clarence could have gotten the thing down to Baja without a problem."

"Clarence?"

He jerked a thumb back to the rental office. "Chipper."

I smiled. He continued.

"Then their credit check came in. Golden, even without the Sundstroms, who as you're probably aware could buy this whole damn marina and then some. The kids had more than the boat was worth sitting in the bank, which makes your tale of the missing money even more interesting."

"It was sitting in the bank when they leased?"

"Seafirst. Downtown branch."

"What day was that?"

"I don't know offhand. But we can find out."

I rose with him as he pried his bulk from the bench. I'd been so engrossed in our conversation that I hadn't noticed that Chipper was standing thirty feet behind us, midway between the leasing office and the bench, slapping a black, polished fish billy into his palm.

Richmond sighed again. Chipper hopped from foot to foot.

"Should I call security, Dad? Or should we handle him ourselves?"

Richmond winced.

"Get the Sundstrom file. Make a copy of the lease agreement and of their credit report and bring them out here," he growled. "And put that thing back in my desk before I have Mr. Waterman here floss your teeth with it."

Chipper, although visibly crestfallen, scurried to oblige.

"And you wonder why some species eat their young."

"You said she didn't want to hear about a crew."

"Yeah. Didn't seem to me the Sundstrom kid cared much one way or the other, but the girl didn't want any part of it."

"That didn't set off any bells for you?"

He chuckled. "Now there, Waterman, just when I was beginning to think you were a man of the world," he chided. "How many married men you know are running their own lives?"

I thought it over.

"Exactly zero," I said.

"Then you see my point. If I refused to lease to every guy with a wife jerking his chain, I'd still be renting rowboats and cutting herring plugs."

"Point taken," I said. "What was she like?"

He thought about it.

"Intense," he said after a while.

"How so?"

"Well, you know, Mr. Waterman, we get quite a few folks who think the ocean is just a big wet freeway, that they can just sail or motor up to Alaska, putt around the icebergs drinking margaritas, and then putt home in time for Letterman. The fact that you might have to know something, or could very well get your ass killed, never occurs to them. That's when I come down to the office and have a little talk with them. I can almost always put the fear of God in them. By the time I get through running down my list of possible disasters, they're usually begging for a crew of six and beefed-up insurance coverage. Not this one, though. She never blinked. Never budged an inch. Just kept smiling at me and saying no thanks."

"And him?"

"Just the opposite. Wishy-washy. Sort of along for the ride. I didn't know he was sick then, but it makes sense now."

We were interrupted by Chipper's reappearance. He handed the boss a sheaf of papers, then stood behind the bench, rocking on the balls of his feet, as Richmond handed them over to me.

Richmond started to speak and then stopped. He turned to Chipper.

"Who's minding the store?"

"There's nobody—"

"Go back inside."

Reluctantly, Chipper complied, walking backward, keeping us in view.

"Thanks," I said, indicating the papers.

"Same stuff I gave the Coast Guard. You might as well have it too."

"What did the Coast Guard think?" I asked.

"Hell, she'd been on the bottom for an hour when they got there and down for nearly forty-eight hours before they brought anything up. Between the fire, the tides, and the crabs there wasn't a hell of a lot left other than the engines. They've got what precious little they recovered down at Pier 50, if you're interested."

"Still," I repeated. "I'd like to thank you again on behalf of my clients for your cooperation. Most folks would just have blown me off."

"Don't worry about it. Fucking lawyers just end up with the money anyway," he said. "If the Sundstroms wanted it, all they had to do was ask. God knows I feel bad about their boy."

"I think Mr. Sundstrom did."

"How so?"

I told him of finding his attorney's business card among Heck's things.

"Chipper," was all he needed to say.

A strained silence settled over us like a heavy dew.

"Where were we?" the big man asked, massaging the bridge of his nose with a thumb and forefinger.

"The happy couple."

"Oh yeah." He started to rise, springing the

bench. A thin smile crossed his lips as he stretched in the sunshine.

"Just between you and me, I know this isn't nice, but when something like this happens you get a chance to think. I remember thinking at the time, you know, it being a honeymoon cruise and all, I remember looking at the Sundstrom kid and thinking he better enjoy it while he still could, because with this little honey it sure as hell wasn't going to last."

"What wasn't going to last?"

"You know—the heavy breathing," he said, stopping and thrusting his big hands into his pants pockets. "With her, it just seemed to be something she could turn on and off like the smile. Hell, by the time they'd signed the contracts she had Chipper there running out for latte and tripping over his dick."

He shook his head and turned to leave.

"At least he didn't have far to fall," I offered to his back.

5

I REACHED THE TOP OF THE SECOND TIER of concrete
stairs in time to watch the forward ranks of a low,
leaden fog bank as it rolled swiftly across Elliot Bay and
back toward the city like an advancing gray brigade,
enveloping any and all in its widespread, opaque
arms. Unconsciously pulling my green canvas jacket
tighter about me, I headed for the shelter of the car.

I recrossed the Magnolia Bridge and slid north
on Fifteenth, toward Ballard, Seattle's Scandinavian
enclave. Fighting the car windows back up just in
time to dart across both lanes and jump off on the
Nickerson exit. Running purely on memory, I wound
right, up Emerson, then through the tricky chicane
down toward Fisherman's Terminal. Memory failed
to suffice as I pulled into the crowded lot. What
had once been a greasy spoon and a bait shop had,
I supposed predictably, evolved into a fair-sized shopping center and restaurant complex. An art gallery
—"Afishionado." Cute. The Wild Salmon Fish Market. A café.

I felt older than my father by the time I wove my way through the commercial claptrap to the Fisherman's Memorial. I'd read about it, but never seen it before. Twin granite blocks, rough on top, framed a central obelisk. The plaque on the right held the dedication—1988.

Dedicated to the men, women, their families and the members of the fishing community who have suffered the loss of life at sea.

On the left, the names. From the turn of the century to the present. Better than five hundred, I estimated. The central granite column was decorated at the bottom with an encasing bronze fish ensemble: a prominently whiskered sturgeon winked benignly at the tourists, while at the top stood the mythic fisherman, seeming even harder and more weathered than the dull metal of his body, inexplicably facing landward as he pulled his resisting bounty from the sea.

The last of the day's tourists hurried toward warmth as I threaded my way down to Dock 7. A maze of masts, booms, supports, antennae, and cables multisected the backdrop into crazed segments, thin against the sky like the lifeless remains of a drowned forest. As I stepped out onto the stout timbers, I felt strangely unbalanced and began walking gingerly as if on the high wire, hoping that no one would notice my discomfort. I could make out the *Lady Day*'s black transom a third of the way down. I eased cautiously down the dock, staying in

the middle, feeling the ominous presence of the
black water in spite of having five feet to spare on
either side.

Berthed now among less impressive craft, some of
which were converted pleasure boats, the *Lady Day*
seemed larger than I remembered. Signs of recent
work were everywhere. A fresh coat of black covered
everything in sight. Four fancy, rectangular crab
lights had been mounted halfway up the rigging.
Brand-new, bright orange balloon floats hung from
the sides, protecting the freshly painted hull. The
skiff was tied off on the port bow, making room for
the massive purse net that lay heaped in the stern
like some captured beast.

Working outward from the boat, I began to look
for signs of life along the dock. Out of season, and
late in the afternoon, most of the boats were buttoned up tight. Every third craft or so had a For Sale
by Owner sign.

Six berths down from the *Lady*, I came upon
another Limit Seiner—the *Haida Queen*, Ketchikan,
Alaska, docked bow in, two crew members straining
mightily in opposing directions on a pair of pipe
wrenches as they struggled to break loose the
threads on a piece of corroded plumbing. The older
of the two, gap-toothed, his matted hair held in
place by a red bandanna, explained that they were
down in the lower forty-eight only for repairs and
knew nothing from nothing. The younger guy, his
right eye reduced to a slit by an enormous purple

bruise, kept his mouth shut and his one working eye glued on Red Bandanna.

At the far end, out where the dock forms a long T, two yellow-clad figures—a guy and what must have been his son—meticulously wound miles of mended monofilament onto the gill net drum. Struggling to keep my feet clear of the rapidly disappearing net, I spent five minutes dancing the Highland fling, ascertaining that, as near as I could tell, neither of these two *se habla*'d any known Indo-European language.

I'd worked my way halfway back on the other side before I spotted an open hatch on *Ocean Spirit*, a green-and-white wooden forty-five footer in serious need of work. Checking the deserted dock, I followed boat etiquette and lustily called out to those on board. The two net winders stopped what they were doing and gawked, but there was no response from aboard the *Ocean Spirit*. When further half-hearted shouts got no results, I stepped on board and found an older guy in a short-brimmed black cap and greasy striped overalls sitting on the top step staring glumly as a pair of electricians worked below-decks.

"I yelled," I said when he looked my way.

"I heard ya."

"I was wondering if you had a minute."

"With these two sons a bitches"—he poked a thick finger down below—"a minute's worth about sixty bucks. If I could find any experienced hands, I'd do it myself. These bloodsuckers—" He interrupted his tirade. "Wadda you want?"

"I'm working for the Sundstroms."

He marinated this message for a minute.

"Damn shame about those kids," he said finally.

"I'm trying to get a line on some young girl who's been hanging around the terminal for the last couple of months."

He rose from his perch, dusting off his palms. He was even wider standing up. He closed most of the distance between us.

"You said you were working for Henry Sundstrom?"

"I am."

"He knows you're down here, then?"

I told him about Heck. The bad news seemed to relax him.

"You know Henry was down here a few weeks back, asking about the same thing." When I didn't respond, he continued. "I'll tell you the same thing I told Henry. I usually don't pay no attention to the wharf rats. They come; they go. They're all the same to me. Most of 'em ain't worth salt. But little Norma, her I remember. Never seemed to have enough clothes on, always shivering, walking around hugging herself, little nipples looking like they was gonna poke a hole in her shirt."

He waved her memory away.

"Not enough sense to get in out of the cold, if you ask me."

"Seen her lately?"

"Nope."

He quickly poked his head down the hatch.

"You don't need to replace all that, Abdullah—just redo the connections and junctions and then use the old cable."

"No meet code," came the response.

"Son of a bitch," he fumed. "Got all these damn codes made up by hummers downtown who ain't never sailed anything more than a goddamn rubber ducky. Stuff's so damned complicated it's gotta be installed by an engineer, none of who I understand a friggin' word they're sayin'. How the hell do they expect us to stay in business? How in hell do they—"

He ran through a number of rhetorical queries as he raved, waving his stubby arms. When he cooled down, he remembered I was there.

"Go see old Wendy on the *Biscuit*."

"The what?"

"The *Biscuit*. It's an old tub out on Dock 10. Low number, one or maybe one-A. Way the hell out the end, anyway. Ask Wendy about the girl, she'll know. She's kinda like the den mother hereabouts. Whatever's goin' on around here, she'd know about."

He directed a stage whisper down the hatch.

"She may not be an engineer, but at least she speaks the goddamn language."

Momentarily satisfied, he turned back to me.

"I shoulda thought of her when Henry asked me,

but I was too busy watching my life savings disappear." He checked the sky. "Better hurry, she goes home before dark."

He dismissed me with a pat on the shoulder, turning away. A torrent of gripes and grouses preceded his broad back down the stairs.

"Goddamn it, fellas—"

The *Biscuit* was more like a dumpling, a congealed mass of water-soaked dough bobbing listlessly among the flotsam, seemingly held together only by forty coats of white paint. A single bulb glowed yellow in the front window. I banged on the hull with the heel of my hand.

My legendary record for anticipating women remained unblemished. I'd expected something salty, maybe a maritime version of Mammy Yokum. Trim and elegant, she was more like Celeste Holm than Granny Clampett. Her long gray hair in a French braid, she was immaculately clad in a yellow cardigan with wildflowers embroidered on the yoke, freshly pressed jeans, and matching blue Keds. She hopped nimbly out onto the dock.

"Yes?" she said, smiling.

"Are you Wendy?"

"I am. Wendy Kroll. How can I help you?"

"I'm trying to get a line on a young girl who's been hanging around the terminal for the past few weeks. Her name—"

"Norma?" she anticipated me.

"I think so."

"Oh Lord, what happened to that poor thing now?"

"You haven't seen her lately then?"

"I've been worried to death."

"Any particular reason?"

She mulled the question over.

"I'm afraid Norma just may be one of life's victims, Mr.—"

"Waterman. How so?"

"That poor child wasn't all there, Mr. Waterman. Nowadays they don't call it retarded any more. I don't know what the current term is. You had to talk to her for a while to see it. On the outside, she seemed fine. Always happy and smiling. She made a little money running errands, doing odd jobs. Folks kind of felt sorry for her, invented things for her to do. If you caught her at the right moment, though, or brought up the right subject, this blank look would come into her eyes. She'd go off somewhere by herself and you could see that she just wasn't all there."

"Any idea what her last name was?"

"Whatever."

She saw my confusion.

"I swear that's what she always said. Whatever. Whenever I'd ask her, she'd say, 'Whatever. Norma Whatever.' And then she'd laugh and laugh like it was the greatest joke in the world."

"When was the last time you saw her?"

"It was about two weeks after—" She pursed her lips. I waited.

"It wasn't Norma's fault, Mr. Waterman. She was just eager to please. It was that animal. He's the one who should have known better. I wanted to call the authorities, but Norma kept saying it was her fault. All her fault, my fanny," she sputtered.

"What happened?"

When thoroughly confused, ask general questions.

"I made my usual stop at the ladies' room in the terminal office on my way down to the *Biscuit*. So I won't have to go back before lunch." She gestured toward the boat. "The *Biscuit* doesn't have a head. She was more of a hobby for my Marty. That's . . . was my husband. Forty-four years. I come down every day to do maintenance. You'd be surprised how much needs to be done on an old scow like this. It's nice and quiet down here, too," she added as an afterthought.

Putting an index finger to her lips, she looked back at the *Biscuit* with new eyes. "You know, it's funny, Mr. Waterman. I never used to like it down here. It always seemed so cold and damp to me. But now somehow I can feel more of Marty here than anywhere else. I think it's because he spent so much time here in those last years before . . ." She looked back to me, surprised, as if I'd been the one speaking.

"Listen to me prattle on. A sign of old age, I'm afraid. Anyway, I heard this sobbing from inside the ladies' room. The door wasn't even locked. There was that poor child sitting there, pants down around her ankles, just bleeding up a storm. At first I thought she had, you know—" I indicated that I did. "But then I could see that it was more than that. She was hurt."

"And?"

"I took her right to my doctor. She didn't want to go, but I insisted. I practically had to drag her." I waited. "She'd been used terribly, Mr. Waterman. She was just raw everywhere down there. Dr. Conger wanted to call the authorities, but Norma simply wouldn't hear of it. Kept saying it was all her fault. That she'd gone on board with him willingly. Dr. Conger said there was no way we could press charges without Norma's testimony."

She leaned closer, whispering.

"Doctor also said it wasn't the first time, either. Said she was terribly scarred down there. Internally."

"Any idea who—"

"I know exactly who. Norma told me. And don't think I didn't let him hear about it. You know what that pig did, Mr. Waterman? He laughed in my face. Called me a dried-up old hag and laughed in my face. Put me off the boat."

"Which boat?"

"The *Haida Queen*. It's over on—"

"I know the boat."

I described my earlier encounter with the two deckhands.

"Not those two. They're just the hired help. Buster is his name. He's the mate. He doesn't do anything. Just sleeps all day while the other two work. A big ox. No, a pig."

"Approximately when was this?"

"I can tell you exactly. I just got the doctor's bill the other day."

She skipped back on board, went below, and reappeared with a white business envelope.

"Tuesday, September twenty-sixth," she said after extracting the contents. "So this happened the night before, the twenty-fifth."

"And you haven't seen her since about two weeks after that?"

"That's right. I'm sure of the time because I brought her a sandwich every day for lunch after that. She came over every day at noontime. We talked. She hardly ate. Always fed most of her sandwich to the gulls. I gave her Marty's old red Pendleton coat to wear. Then"—she shrugged—"one day, she didn't come any more. I've been quite concerned."

"Any idea where she came from?"

"Up north. That's all she'd say. Up north."

"That covers quite a bit of ground."

"I guess it does. But Norma had a way of not answering questions."

"Did she share anything else personal?"

"She said she'd recently found her momma and that her momma was better now and had a real important job. She also said that a ship was coming to take them all to the promised land."

"You have any idea what she meant by that?" I asked.

"Just what she said, I guess. That she'd seen her mother and they were all going away on a ship."

"Nothing more specific?"

"Norma tended to be a bit vague."

I was beginning to feel rather vague myself.

"Did she live down here somewhere?"

"Oh, no. There's no living on board anymore. She had a room in the city. Rode the Metro bus down here every morning."

"Any idea where in the city?"

She shook her head. "You might ask that pig, Buster. Norma said he drove her home . . . afterward. A real gentleman, that Buster."

She drew the collar of her sweater close around her throat.

"You wouldn't by chance have a picture of her?"

She shook her head sadly.

"Any obvious identifying marks?" I asked, trying not to lead her.

"Just that big smile," she said wistfully.

I collected a full description, wrote it in my notebook.

"Thanks," I said.

"You will let me know if you find out anything, won't you? I've been so concerned about her."

I said I would. It was a lie. I'd come back only if the news was good, and with the Normas of this world, the news was never good.

Red Bandanna and Shiner had wrestled the pipe apart and were in the process of installing new stainless steel fittings.

"Buster around?" I asked.

"Told you, we don't know nothing about no girl," Bandanna said.

"Mind if I ask Buster personally?"

"No, but Buster sure as hell will," he smirked.

"Why don't you rustle him up, and we'll ask him."

"Listen Bub, you don't want no parta Buster. On a good day he's mean as a shark, and right now he's sleeping one off. I was you, I'd get up the road. He gave Rob here that eye for just whuppin' him at pool last night. Do yourself a big favor and take a hike."

"Still need to talk to Buster, I'm afraid."

The picket-fence smirk got bigger.

"Afraid's what you oughta be. But since you ain't, you just stay right there. I'll fetch him for you. I surely will. Don't go anywhere now."

Bandanna headed below decks. Shiner fixed me with his one good eye. "Mister," he said.

I looked up. He underhanded the pipe wrench my way. End over end. I stepped back and let it hit the dock at my feet, then retrieved it, stashing it in my jacket pocket, handle out.

Bandanna reappeared. His yellow teeth jack-o'lanterned as he eased back against the rail, lighting a cigarette, folding his arms. Might as well get comfortable for the show.

Buster burst out of the hatch, his head swiveling to find me. Moving quickly around the skiff in my direction, he exhibited amazing dexterity for a man of such proportions as he stepped deftly over a maze of pipe, wire, and fittings. Wendy Kroll had been wrong. Buster was neither an ox nor a pig. Buster was a buffalo. One of those genetically obese men whose fifty-pound layer of fat belied the two hundred pounds of rock-hard muscle beneath. The chili-bowl haircut and ruddy cheeks lent almost a cherubic quality to his face, as long as you didn't look at the eyes. Squeezed nearly shut by his cheeks, red with sleep and alcohol, his eyes showed all the humanity of rusted ball bearings.

Insisting on an audience with Buster had been a major miscalculation. Pumping adrenaline began to give me that lighter-than-air feeling. I cured my stupidity and reckoned how having such an easy time with the Bo Peeps and Chippers of this world must have given me delusions of grandeur ... I should have known better.

I silently thanked the kid for the comforting weight of the wrench tugging at my pocket. My reading of Buster said that, without the wrench and the element of surprise, my best chance would probably be to assume the fetal position and hope that

Buster either lost interest or ran out of gas sometime before he pureed my kidneys. While the prospect of hitting another human being with a four-pound pipe wrench was repugnant to me, this alternative was even less attractive. I took a firm grip on the handle.

Buster hit the dock at a lope. The front panel of his bib overalls hung down in front, the buckles banging off his massive thighs. No shoes. Curled yellow toenails. I spread my feet for balance. Unless I was mistaken, Buster was going to turn out to be a man of few words; there wasn't going to be any prefight chitchat.

He covered the distance in six quick strides; four feet from me, he cast a porcine sneer up at the deck of the *Haida Queen*, making sure his audience was in place for the main event. I chose that moment to bounce the wrench off Buster's wide forehead. The loose parts of the heavy wrench gave a muted clank. The shock waves of the blow rocketed down my arm, numbing my elbow. He staggered back, clutching his head. Before he could recover, I roundhoused the wrench, catching him full in the temple with the flat side. He rocked once, reached out to me, and fell gracefully onto his side, unmoving.

"Damn," breathed Shiner.

I reached down and checked the pulse in Buster's thick throat. Strong and steady. His eyelids fluttered like fallen leaves, then were still.

Bandanna had bumped himself off the rail and

now, cigarette gone, ashes clinging to his shirt, stared openmouthed. His gaze went from the wrench at my side to Shiner, who was now brandishing the other wrench, and back to the tool in my hand.

"You better get your stuff," I said to the kid.

Bandanna settled back against the gunnel, mouth set, arms akimbo.

"Nobody ever whupped old Buster before. Least not that I seen."

"Nobody has yet," I said. "Buster just got careless. I couldn't whip him with a baseball bat."

Bandanna seemed to agree.

The kid was traveling light. A long olive-green duffle bag and black ghetto blaster were all he hit the dock with. I tossed the pipe wrench in the water. Buster moaned, fluttering his eyelids constantly now, his extremities beginning to twitch as he came around.

Grabbing a double handful of Buster's coveralls, I rolled him, one revolution at a time, over the edge and then toed him over the side. As I'd hoped, the freezing water instantly revived him. He emerged from the darkness sputtering and coughing, frantically clawing at the smooth hull of the *Haida Queen* for a purchase.

"He can't swim," blurted Bandanna.

"Even better," I said.

I watched as Buster slapped the green water into foam. Wedged in between the hulls of two boats, he had no choice but to wallow over toward the dock. He thrashed his way toward me, his eyes now wide with fear. The second his sausagelike fingers managed a grip on the dock, I stomped them hard. He involuntarily let go, and quickly slipped beneath the oily surface, leaving only a striated ripple expanding on the surface. Instinctively, I stepped back to the middle of the dock.

After what seemed like minutes he breached like an orca, blasting up and out of the water, getting both forearms up on the dock, whooshing great gulps of air, reaching blind for where he thought I should be. The wrench had put a jagged split in his forehead. A thin solution of blood and seawater rolled down between his eyes, dripping off the tip of his nose onto the timbers. He used one hand to wipe the hair and water from his eyes. His sodden coveralls were floating away behind him, leaving him naked but for a yellowed T-shirt that had floated up around his neck.

I drew back one foot.

"No. No swim," he gasped.

"The girl."

"What girl?" he wheezed.

I kicked him in the head. He lost his purchase and slid back toward the water. Only by the immense power of his hands did he maintain a grip. I walked to the edge, resting the sole of my shoe on the fingers of his right hand.

"Norma," I said quietly.

"All I did was—" I put some weight on my foot.

"Don't even start with me, Buster. I'm afraid of what I'll do. Just answer my questions. When you drove her home, where did you take her?"

His eyes were open again. His lips were beginning to turn blue. His teeth chattered like discolored castanets.

"I'm not fffffrom here. I ddddddon't—"

I increased the pressure of my foot.

"Try harder."

"Bbbby the market," he stuttered.

"Which market?"

"The fffffamous one."

"Where by the market?"

"Rrrright accross the street. I llllllet her out right under that Lllllllive Girls sign. She said she could wwwwwalk from there."

I put all my weight on his fingers. He began to shake.

"You sure?"

"Swear ttttttttto GGGGGGod," he ratcheted out.

As the kid and I started down the dock, Buster began yelling at the net menders for help. His luck was no better than mine. They turned a deaf ear to his cries for help, mending ever faster as he flailed his arms.

"Try Latvian," I yelled back.

I nudged the kid toward the north. The smell of fried foods drifted out over the pavement, mixing with the seawater and diesel fumes that swirled about us as we walked along the face of the Chinook's Restaurant.

"How's your English?" I asked.

"I'm from Hoboken," he said.

"Then I'm pretty sure I know where you can find a job."

6

SINCE THEY INHERITED THE HOUSE and became slum-
lords, the Boys were seldom hard to find. In the old
days I'd have started in the alleys down by Pioneer
Square, kicking appliance boxes, waking drunks
under the Viaduct, passing out promises and dollar
bills until I got a line on one of them. These days,
there were only two real choices. If it was early in
the month and they were flush, they were at their
favorite watering hole, the Zoo, playing snooker and
bending their elbows. If not, they were back at the
house, playing cribbage and pouring their own. The
only real differences were the price of the liquor and
the distance to bed.

I doubled-parked on Eastlake for long enough to
poke my head into the Zoo and ascertain that the
Boys were presently not holding down their deeded
stools. I backtracked up Lynn and then turned left
onto Franklin.

Like most downtown middle-class neighborhoods,
the Eastlake area had found that the dramatic rise

in property values was having a profound effect on the composition of the area. The widening gyre of yuppies that spread relentlessly outward was being shadowed by an equally insistent wave of faceless bistros, bakeries, and fern bars, which now nipped hard at the old neighborhood's heels like a pack of wild spaniels.

Franklin, between Lynn and Louisa, was a block in transition. What in a less pretentious era had once been simply called two-family houses had been gutted and resurrected as trendy condos. Most of the single-family dwellings showed the typical outward signs of recent cash infusion: restored gingerbread railings and facings, colorful stained glass door panels, and pastel two-tone paint jobs, all designed to recreate a revisionist sense of a nonexistent past.

Here and there the block was dotted with the actual remnants of the past, standing in mute rebuttal. Unembellished, overgrown, views blocked by their taller, newer neighbors, they persevered as insistent reminders of the street's humble origins. What new and old alike shared was an abysmal lack of parking. A combination of gridlock, astronomical parking rates, and the gnawing fear that they might never find an open parking space again had forced most of the residents onto public transportation, relegating their cars to occasional weekend use. This left the two curb lanes perpetually packed. What remained in between was a clogged little capillary barely wide enough for a single vehicle.

I gunned it down the narrow lane, sprinting for the Boys' driveway about two-thirds of the way down. Since none of the Boys had been permitted a driver's license in recent decades, parking was not generally a problem. To my surprise, two cars were parked in the driveway—a green Explorer and a gunmetal-gray Accord. I slipped the Fiat against the curb, blocking the driveway.

Twenty-seven-oh-four was a psoriatic three-story neocolonial, its white weathered facade in a constant molt, shedding old paint like unwanted skin. Just outside the front door, the Speaker's omnipresent sandwich board leaned crookedly against the wall.

Today's missive read "Ozone-Schmozone." I vowed not to ask.

The sound of the opening door had no visible effect on the three guys staring blankly at a black-and-white TV in the front parlor. Each flicked a glance my way, then unconsciously tightened his embrace on the bag-shrouded bottle he guarded like a Doberman.

I continued down the long central hall toward the kitchen in the back. I got about halfway down before George looked up from his cards, forced a focus, and broke out in a wide grin. Slapping his cards on the table, he rocked to his feet.

"Leo!" he shouted.

I'd interrupted the evening cribbage marathon among George, Ralph, Harold, and Nearly Normal

Norman. I was, as usual, greeted like a visiting dignitary. It was hugs and handshakes all around.

"Whose cars are those in the driveway?" I asked.

"They belong to the kids across the street," said George.

George Paris had to be the better part of seventy. A former banker, he'd drunk himself out of half a dozen jobs, two marriages, and eventually into the streets, without ever looking any worse for wear. His thick mane of slicked-back white hair always reminded me of a boxing announcer. Since Buddy's death, he'd become the de facto leader of this little band.

"We rent 'em the space," said Harold Green, his softball-size Adam's apple bobbing furiously as he spoke. Year by year, Harold was in the process of disappearing right before our very eyes. His gaunt frame lost a few more pounds every year. A former shoe salesman, he looked to be made of old, distressed leather.

"Seventy bucks," blurted Ralph.

"Each," amended George.

"Seventy bucks," Ralph said again.

"We got it, Ralph," sighed George.

Ralph Bastista had, years before, been a minor official with the Port of Seattle. Ralph was, as George liked to point out in moments of extreme unpleasantness, perhaps the only guy in history to drink himself out of a civil service job. Twenty years of uninterrupted debauchery had exacted a terrible toll on Ralph, unlike George. His round pleasant face and agreeable manner belied a startling lack of functioning gray matter. Whoever it was said life doesn't take place in a vacuum hadn't spent much time trying to give Ralph instructions. Ralph was, however, renowned as the finest flopper in the Pacific Northwest. Whatever his other failings, Ralph could still spot a tourist in a rental car a block away and be bouncing off the fender in the wink of an eye. Many an out-of-town visitor, visions of exploding insurance premiums numbing his brain, had silently thanked God that the old guy was miraculously unhurt as they slipped him fifty bucks and sent him limping on his way. The Lord provides in mysterious ways.

Little or nothing was known of Nearly Normal Norman's background. Different days produced different stories. My inquiries as to his family's state of origin had on successive attempts been met with Rhode Island, Indiana, and Sri Lanka. While his vast store of esoteric knowledge suggested a formal education, Norman was less than forthcoming with any usable facts. A pair of the most seriously unhinged eyes since Rasputin coupled with a heavily muscled six-foot-six frame precluded insistent inquisitiveness from all but the most seriously addled.

"Nice crowd out in the parlor."

"They're all right," commented Harold quickly.

"They got no bugs. They don't steal things or cause no trouble. That's all we ask, Leo. We just give 'em a roof over their heads for a while. No questions asked. If they wanted a fucking sermon they'd go to the Mission. If they fuck up, they work it out with Norman," added George with just enough zing to let me know that he didn't want to hear any jokes about the boarders.

"And pizza," said Ralph.

"Yeah, we give 'em pizza too," agreed George.

"We give everybody pizza," Ralph said with obvious pride.

When I looked confused, they pulled me over to the rear door. The entire back porch was hip deep in empty Domino's boxes.

"Summer Special," said Harold. "It was Ralph's idea. He found the first handful."

I looked to George for confirmation. He shrugged.

"Believe it or not," he confirmed.

"There's a coupon for a free small pizza in every box they deliver."

"So you guys buy one and then—" I started.

"We don't buy squat," said George. "The solid citizens, they don't give a shit; a small pizza ain't worth crap to them. They throw the coupons out with the box when they're done. We just go out after dinner and liberate the coupons from the containers."

Experience had taught me that liberation meant scrounging, and container meant dumpster.

This talk of food had touched a nerve in Norman,

who exited to the porch and began digging through
the collected boxes in search of a snack.

"How's it going, Norman?" I asked.

"There used to be a hippopotamus on Madagas-
car the size of a dog," he said without interrupting
his forage.

George shrugged. "He's into animals lately."

"What does Domino's think of this loaves-and-
fishes program of yours?" I asked.

"After a few nights, they wouldn't deliver anymore," said Ralph.

"That was until we sicced Mr. James on them,"
added Harold.

"He said the coupons were an implied contract."

"And?"

"And he called the main office and threatened
them. Threatened to get the media involved. You
know, discrimination," George continued.

Out of the corner of my eye I could see that
Norman had extracted from one of the lower boxes
a fossilized triangle, upon which he was now munch-
ing contentedly. I looked away.

"But by then we were attracting a pretty big
crowd," Harold said.

"We had forty-three for dinner last Friday," Ralph
bragged.

"The neighbors went ballistic," said George with
obvious pride.

"Old lady Tollifer up the street caught Big Harvey
taking a dump in her rhodies and called the cops."

"The jalapeños are murder," said Ralph with a wink.

"So you gave it up?" I asked.

"Hell no," said George. "The coupons are good till the end of the month. We started having them delivered directly to the parks."

"Closer to home for the folks anyway," said Harold.

"I'll bet Domino's liked that."

"They lost corporate sphincter control," said George. "Claimed they didn't have to deliver except to an address."

"Mr. James fixed that too," said Harold.

"Get this Leo, you'll love it," said George, pulling me closer. "This guy James is a genius. He goes down to regional headquarters the next day with a camera crew from one of the local channels. Seems he's been to the movies lately with his grandkids and seen Domino's pizza delivered to a sewer grate in one of those movies about the mutated turtles."

"Teenage Mutant Ninja Turtles?"

"Right. Anyway. Right there in front of God and the cameras he asks the regional director how come if he's willing to deliver pizzas to anonymous amphibians in aqueducts, he's not willing to honor his contracts with some of the city's less fortunate citizens. Says if they'll deliver it to a grate, they damn well better deliver it to a park. The skunk about drops his teeth."

"So?"

"Coupons are good till the end of the month," said Harold, waving a sheaf of coupons as thick as his wrist.

"Jesus," I said. "How many of those things have you got?"

"We been getting about twenty a night just here in the neighborhood. If you count all the other people we got looking in other neighborhoods, we been averaging about sixty a night."

"Is this what Ralph and the Speaker were doing at my apartment last week? They wanted to tell me about the pizzas," I guessed.

"We don't go near your—" George started.

The hangdog look on Ralph's face stopped him cold. He began to scream.

"What the fuck is the matter with you?" He waved himself off. "Never mind, I know the answer to that. How many times have I told you—"

Having made my point, I bailed Ralph out.

"You guys want to make a little cash looking for something other than pizza coupons?" I asked.

"You got work for us?" asked George enthusiastically.

"Wadda you need us to find?"

"A girl," I said. "Maybe not actually find her, but at least find out where she's been living. Maybe find a neighbor or a roommate."

"We'll find her, Leo," said Ralph. "Where is she?"

"If he knew where she was, you dumbass, he wouldn't need us to find her," shot George.

"I know where to start," I said.

"That's what I meant," said Ralph.

They waited like waifs at a toy-store window.

"Down by the market. She had somebody let her out across the street from the market. Somewhere you can walk to from the market."

"Lot of places to stay down by the market," said Harold with considerably less enthusiasm.

"Terrible neighborhood," muttered George. "Even the cockroaches are perverts. The place even makes me nervous."

Out on the porch Norman was using his thumbnail, attempting to pry an outsize piece of congealed cheese from the inside of one of the lids.

"Cockroaches used to be four inches long," he said between bites.

"We'll find her," said the ever-affable Ralph.

"I've got a hundred and fifty a day to donate to getting a line on her. You divide it up however you want."

I fished in my wallet and came out with seventy-three bucks. I threw it on the table.

"We'll find her," they all agreed.

"Got a picture?" George asked.

"Nope, just a description."

"Let me get my notebook and the map," he said.

While the Boys sat at the kitchen table and mapped out a plan of attack, I used the yellow dial phone on the wall to call Rebecca. Rebecca Duvall, in addition to being my lifelong friend and sometime

social companion, was also the chief forensic pathol-
ogist for King County. I tried the office first and was
not disappointed. Rebecca lived at home with her
aged mother. Having known her mother for all my
life, I could understand why Duvall worked late
whenever possible.

"Pathology."

"Rebecca."

"Leo," she said. "I can't talk right now. I've got
my hands full of something."

"Something?"

"Someone," she admitted.

"How's about dinner? I need to pick your brain."

"You really should try not to use that unfortunate
phrase with pathologists."

"I'll keep that in mind. How about it?"

"I've got about another hour here," she sighed.

"I'll pick you up at eight."

"Sounds good. Where?"

"No idea. You choose," I said. "Pasta?"

"No pasta. I've been doing brain sections all day."
She thought about it for a moment. "Let's try the
Blob. We threaten to stop every time we drive by.
Let's finally do it. Hillary said it was surprisingly
pleasant inside."

"This is the same Hillary who epoxied six kinds
of macaroni to her apartment walls and then painted
over it. Random texture, I believe she called it."

"Don't start, Leo. She says the interior decor is
nice."

"Okay, okay. Sure, what the hell. Eight."

"Eight-thirty. And Leo—if you can manage to be less than totally obnoxious, you may get to pick more than my brain. Mom's out of town for the next couple of weeks."

"Should I consider this to be an offer?" I asked.

"You should, at best, consider that to be a possibility, and wear your new clothes."

"What for, I—"

"Remote possibility," she amended before she hung up.

As was the case with nearly any event, including such things as sunrise, the upcoming search for Norma had proved sufficient occasion for a drink. The Boys passed a bottle of peach schnapps around as they formulated battle plans. If they noticed my departure, they didn't let on.

7

I'M SURE AT ONE TIME IT MUST HAVE HAD A NAME, some proper noun to lend substance to the otherwise-ethereal concept floating about the mind of its creator. The Casbah, maybe. Or Shangri-la. Something Eastern and whimsical. Everybody I knew always just referred to it as the Blob.

Just as every family must have its black sheep, every city must have its architectural monstrosity. This was Seattle's. Somewhere out there, laboring long into the night at some menial task, was the defrocked city employee who'd allowed this to happen. Permits had been granted; inspections had been passed; and, in the end, heads had most surely rolled.

Attached like a tick to the base of Queen Anne Hill, it looked like a resort swimming pool turned upside down. The white two-story structure meandered aimlessly over nearly half a block. Shapeless, formless, a series of stark stucco humps, bumps, and mounds, punctuated here and there by small porthole-like windows, it was seemingly the product of chance rather than design. Frank Lloyd Wrong on acid.

The attached lot was half full when Rebecca and I pulled in a little after eight-thirty. For a town where, on a Friday night, you needed a reservation at a Denny's if you wanted to avoid a half-hour wait, this was by no means an encouraging sign.

"Funny, but I don't see Hillary's car anywhere," I said as I opened the car door and helped Rebecca out.

Rebecca tried to change the subject.

"You look great. Is this the first time you've worn it?"

The *it* to which she so casually referred was my new Sunday-go-to-meeting suit. Back in August, after months of complaining about my unimaginative taste in clothes, Rebecca had dragged me to the down-town Nordstrom for a complete refitting. The result had been a navy double-breasted Joseph Abboud blazer, a pair of taupe Corbin trousers with a highly mysterious reverse pleat, a John W. Nordstrom Signature Series dress shirt with a Manhattan collar and French cuffs, into which I could fit my new fourteen-carat gold Haan cufflinks, a burgundy-ground woven Facconable tie, and a pair of Salvatore Ferragamo loafers into which I could slip my cashmere-socked feet. It was a hell of a deal. For little more than three months' rent and utilities, I was now the proud owner of a completely coordinated ensemble that, until tonight, I had been far too intimidated to wear.

"Too bad Hillary's not here to see it."

"Hillary's away this weekend at a Vedic astrology seminar."

"Of course." I tapped my forehead. "How could I have forgotten?"

"Hillary's very artistic."

"Do you by chance remember the last restaurant she recommended?"

"You mean that—"

"Right. Up in Wallingford."

"It was called 'Healthy Pleasures,' as I remember."

"What I remember most was how my jaws eventually went into vapor lock from the chewing."

"Roughage is good for you."

"If you ate at that place twice a week, you could pass wicker furniture."

"Stop it, Leo. If you don't want to eat here—"

I stopped. With Mom out of town, I wasn't about to be drawn further into another round of the great Hillary debate. Hillary was Rebecca's childhood friend, who since her most recent divorce had rocketed into the New Age. Each new week brought a fresh incarnation of Hillary. Hakomi therapy, rebirthing, Rolfing, Voice Dialogue, Wildwoman workshops, hypnotherapy. You name it, Hillary was spending Bill's money on it. I'd always figured that a woman who was working so hard at finding herself could at least have the common decency to first get lost.

Using Rebecca's elbow for leverage, I mumbled

an apology and steered her toward the nearest
ground-level swirl, which I presumed to be the
entrance. I pulled open the ornately steel-strapped
door and followed Rebecca in.

The interior was a pleasant surprise. Red terra-
cotta tiles led off in all directions. Here and there
the walls had been professionally painted with grape
arbors, palm trees, and desert scenes. A series of
cleverly placed dividers had been used to divide the
hodgepodge interior into a series of connected but
intimate dining areas.

The reservations kiosk was personed by a swarthy
guy with a Zapata mustache. His black hair gleamed.
He looked like the short dark half of Hall and
Oates. I'd never gotten them straight. He was wearing a stiff formal shirt with a pattern woven in, no
collar.

"Two?" he asked.

I looked around. We were alone in the lobby.

"Two," I confirmed.

"You hab reservations?"

"Yes, but we're going to eat here anyway."

Smiling broadly, Duvall hip-checked me.

"Smoking or nonsmoking?"

Guys I knew had enlisted with fewer questions
than this.

"Nonsmoking, please."

He came out from behind his pulpit.

"Right this way," he said with an elaborate
flourish.

His black pants were too tight. The little black zipup boots replete with four-inch Cuban heels made him wobble as if on ice skates. He led us on a circuitous path through most of the sparsely peopled restaurant, finally coming to a halt at an isolated little table in the back bar.

Either he'd taken offense at my reservations joke or these people were taking the concept of a nonsmoking section to a whole new level. With its stunning view of the back wall, this table would have been perfect for Bartleby the Scrivener. I, on the other hand, had been thrown into better places.

Figuring I'd used up my obnoxious coupons picking on Hillary, I was, however, prepared to be agreeable about it.

"I think you better handle this," I whispered to Rebecca. "I seem to be having one of those days."

Duvall could always be counted on in a pinch. Like myself, she dined out alone quite a bit. Astute single diners quickly come to realize that table allocation is a highly relative business. Left to their own devices, headwaiters will generally try to make it seem as if they've been holding this lovely table next to the garbage chute just for you.

Without a word, she turned on her heel and went back into the main dining area. "How about this one?" she asked as nicely as possible, indicating a table beneath the northernmost porthole.

"You would be very hoppy with this table," our

host reiterated, gesturing back toward the isolation chamber. "Is no smoking."

"We would definitely be hoppier with this one. We'll take our chances with the smoking," she said firmly.

He wasn't a bit hoppy about it, but for want of an alternative, went along with the program.

Before he could skate off, we ordered cocktails. An unblended Margarita, no salt, for Duvall, a Jack Black on the rocks for me.

"I don't think he liked you," she said.

"Today, he'll have to take a number."

I quickly changed the subject.

"Is this your mom's yearly pilgrimage down to her sister's?"

"Two fabulous weeks with Aunt Rhetta in beautiful Lincoln City," she confirmed. "I put her on the bus this morning."

"Didn't say she was never going back down there?" I asked.

"That happens every year. They'll be threatening to murder one another by Wednesday. As I understand it, it's all part of being sisters."

Rebecca was an only child, the product of an alcoholic, short-lived relationship between her mom, Letha, and an abusive merchant marine. Throughout grammar school, Rebecca had always been the ragged little girl who knew the answers to everything but wasn't a pain in the ass about it. Her mother had worked three jobs to get Rebecca through medical school. As if in penance, Rebecca had never married, choosing instead to see her mother through old age. Letha, for her part, was taking full advantage of the fealty. She was older than mud but healthy as a horse.

"What did you want to pick my brain about?" Rebecca asked.

"Nick Sundstrom."

"Are you sure, Leo? Before dinner? You tend to get a bit queasy."

"Nothing graphic. Just the basics."

"What's it to you?" she asked.

I told her about it. Rebecca listened in such a way that I always felt I was the only one on her desert island at that moment. When I'd finished, she reached over and patted the back of my hand as it rested on my glass.

"I remember when you got fired from the boat. You were so sad. It was like somebody shot your dog. Except you didn't have a dog."

"I wanted one, though."

"I know you did," she sympathized.

As if on cue, our drinks arrived. We sipped and twirled. Rebecca picked up the slack. "I didn't do the work personally, but I oversaw. Andy Tsukahara did the actual work, such as it was."

"Such as it was?"

"There wasn't much to work on. Less than ten percent of either of them. Virtually no soft tissue.

What there was had been burned and contaminated by seawater. It was pretty much either dental records or throw the I Ching."

"No doubt that it was the Sundstrom kid though."

"None. The family had a lifetime of dental records."

"And the other one?"

She shrugged.

"Female. Under thirty. Childbearing years, but never had children. Malnourished at an early age. Between five-two and five-four, about a hundred pounds or so. A little thing."

"How can you tell all that from so little?"

"We recovered the pelvis. In a woman, you can tell a lot from the pelvis. Age, size, whether or not she's given birth, all of that."

"I've always had great respect for the pelvis."

"I know you have, Leo. It's one of the things I've always most admired about you."

"But no way to confirm an identity on her."

"Compared to what? Show me a history, and I'll tell you if it matches. Give me a couple of blood samples, and in two days I can tell you whether they were related. Give me something for comparison. With this one, we had nothing. We ran the wife's social security number through the national database and got nothing."

"Nothing?"

"Zilch. Not so much as a flu shot."

"Isn't that a bit strange?"

"Not really. The database isn't complete. Lots of rural areas aren't on-line yet. She could have just fallen through the cracks."

The waiter arrived with our menus. We took our time picking out a couple of esoteric Greek dishes that we thought we might be able to share.

"What about where she worked before she got married?" I asked after the waiter had left with our order.

"You'd have to ask the cops about that."

"Fat chance," I said, downing the remains of my drink.

Most private operatives can count on minimal support on those cases that the authorities deem to be dead ends. I, however, was the exception to this rule. My ex-wife, Annette, was presently married to Captain Harry Monroe of the SPD, who, I'd been given to understand, had issued a standing directive to the effect that anyone assisting me in any way could expect to spend long periods on the aptly named graveyard shift in South Seattle. I suspected it was probably a result of my failure to provide Annette with an appropriate warning label. As a result of Harry Monroe's unceasing efforts, my niche in the formal investigative hierarchy was only slightly lower than whale shit.

"I'll make some calls on Monday for you, see what the boys in blue have come up with. What would you do without me, Leo?"

I ignored her.

"Any idea who's handling it for the police?"

"None," she said. "They probably handled it the same way we did. Somebody junior doing the actual work, somebody senior covering their asses. The Sundstroms being as prominent as they are, SPD will want to have their ducks in a row."

I caught the waiter's eye and ordered another round. The drinks arrived with our dinners.

"What we need to discuss now, Mr. Waterman, is how you're going to make all this information gathering up to me."

"You mean dinner isn't going to do it?" I asked innocently, never looking up from my plate.

"Hardly."

"What about my undying gratitude?"

"That and a buck will get you on the bus."

"Have I told you what a pretty dress that is?"

"It's a Donna Karan."

"Stunning."

"Stop changing the subject."

"No. I mean it."

"If you play your cards right, you can wear it later."

"Promises, promises."

"You owe me big time."

"I don't know if I can perform under such pressure."

She gathered up her purse.

"Look at it this way, Leo, you're the first live one I've seen all day."

I mulled this over as I threw bills onto the table.

"I'm pretty certain I can compete with the dead."

"I love a confident man."

8

"I MIGHT HAVE TO AGREE WITH YOUR MARK," CARL SAID.

"Client," I corrected.

"Whatever," he sneered. "Either the shooter is the Stevie Wonder of point-and-shoot photography or Little Miss Tasty Trim here really didn't want to have her mug immortalized."

His opinion tendered, he sat back and fired up a fresh Winston. Since I'd arrived a half hour ago, he'd smoked half a pack without ever stubbing one out. The glowing embers of butts smoldering in the bottom of the oily crystal ashtray could have barbecued a pork chop. A pall of dense, drifting smoke that by now filled the upper half of the small room was slipping steadily into my pores, glazing me like carcinogenic ham.

I fanned the air around me in a pathetic attempt to see better. Predictably, my discomfort cheered Carl considerably.

"Smoke bothering you?" he asked.

"Perish the thought, Carl. Not me. I try to suck

up as much secondhand smoke as I can. Especially right after breakfast."

"Tsk tsk," he chided. "Wadda you want, to live forever, Leo? You becoming one of these fucking yuppies, joggin' all the time? Livin' on nothin' but ginseng root and no-fat yogurt. Pushin' out these little turds look like rabbit pellets."

Carl's laugh honked like an air horn.

"Is that it, Bud? Have they finally worn you down? And here I had you figured for the last of the old-time hard-livin', hard-drinkin' Damon Runyon characters. This is quite a disappointment." He finished with an exaggerated shrug. "I guess I'll have to write it off as another blow to my already shattered idealism."

I wasn't going to let Carl get me going. Carl liked nothing better than a good argument first thing in the morning, or any other time of the day or night for that matter. Carl Cradduck made casual conversation a contact sport—as if he were on stage, playing to the very last row, always exaggerated, larger than life, challenging the unwary to jump into the scene with him. I stayed put. If I humored him even the slightest bit, we'd be here squabbling indefinitely. No matter. He started in on me anyway.

"And will you look at these threads," he said, twisting the sleeve of my blazer between his thumb and forefinger.

'Ooooh. Nice material," he said in a thick Central

European accent. He looked down at my feet and clicked his tongue again.

"And will you get a load of the little Eye-talian ballet slippers. Gotta be three hundred if they're a fuckin' dime. And what have we got here?" He showed me his palm. "No, No. Don't tell me."

He motored over, pulling up my pant leg, and pawed at my left sock.

"Ho, ho, ho," he chuckled. "Really—you shouldn't have. No need to dress for me, Sherlock. Although I do appreciate the thought. We're strictly informal around here, or have you forgotten?"

I hadn't known him when he'd had legs. I'd only met him afterward—the summer after that ill-timed Christmas dinner at his sister's. After the accident. That white instant when a couple of drunken teeny-boppers failed to negotiate a hard left-hand turn, putting themselves under the ground and him into the chair forever.

He'd been running a little photo lab in South Seattle when I blundered in one morning looking for an instant development job on some grounds-for-divorce shots I'd just taken over in West Seattle. His New York accent and caustic manner had quickly gotten my attention. He'd made no move to take the roll of film I'd proffered. He'd sat there in the chair and looked at the little yellow role as if I'd been trying to hand him a dog turd.

"It's a Saturday," he'd said, as if I'd insulted him.

"I'll pay extra," I stammered.

"Goddamn right you will," he agreed, motoring over, snatching the film from my hand, humming toward the darkroom in the rear, leaving me to stand alone in the small deserted shop.

My bored gaze was stopped cold by a picture high over the counter. A Vietnamese grandmother in full stride, ancient arms and legs made limber, fear-infused with sudden strength, pumping desperate for escape, a full yard from the building, connected only by the single greedy tongue of fire that now consumed both the thatched roof of the hut and the last remains of her long white hair. In that moment, as I stood in the store, the old woman's deeply furrowed face took its place among the gallery of deathbed, funeral-parlor images that I unwillingly drag behind me like the rusted remains of wrecked cars. I looked away.

Carl Cradduck in Korea and Vietnam for the *New York Times*—in Beirut for *Newsday*. Hundreds of other war shots of such graphic anguish as to at once capture and repel the eye. Carl with Robert Kennedy, with Martin Luther King, Jr., for the *Atlanta Constitution*. Carl with about everybody I'd ever heard of. A ton of awards. A couple of plaques. Carl nominated for two Pulitzers for photography.

As his sister Annie was his only living relative, he'd stayed on after he got out of the hospital. I'd asked him once, years ago, why he hadn't gone back to

New York after the accident. His answer had been short but less than sweet.

"The city's too tough on gimps," he'd said. "I go back there, I end up on a creeper sellin' pencils. Here, amongst the yodels, at least I got a chance."

Carl Cradduck had made the most of his chance. In the last fifteen years he'd used his technical wizardry and twenty-four-hour, seven-day-a-week service to pull himself from the small photo shop in South Seattle to a preeminent position as the area's most sophisticated electronic surveillance specialist. C&C Technical was on the cutting edge of the assault on privacy. If you wanted to surreptitiously watch anybody do anything and then record it for posterity, Carl Cradduck was your man.

He still lived in the tiny four-room apartment behind the store in beautiful downtown Lake City. I'd asked him about that once too, a few years back, right after the grand opening of the new offices.

"You ought to find some new digs, Carl," I'd said. "Something befitting your elevated station in life."

He'd set me straight in a hurry.

"This fucking chair is my digs, Peeper. I can roll around in it here. I can roll around in it in some fancy-ass house down on the lake. Don't make me no friggin' difference. Either way it's me and the chair. This"—he patted the chair—"is my universe. Might as well be right here." End of discussion.

I'd shown up unannounced at his back door first

thing on Saturday morning. With Carl Cradduck, the hour was never a problem. As nearly as I'd ever been able to tell, he didn't sleep. No matter what ungodly hour I showed up, he was always up, seemingly waiting for me. Perfect for a guy in my line of work.

I heard the hum of his electric wheelchair before the door opened. Carl wasn't surprised to see me. Carl was never surprised by anything. He was a wizened little guy, all vein and tendon. Whole, he wouldn't have topped five foot six or so; in the chair, he gave the impression that perhaps he too might be part of the chair's electronics. His left hand rested on the control panel for the chair. His right hand, beneath the black-and-red checked blanket covering his lap, would be holding the .765mm auto I'd given him after he'd been burglarized in 1989.

Without a greeting, he U-turned the chair in the hall, leaving the door to me. I followed him down the wide hall to the kitchen, where I tossed the four packs of photographs onto the yellow Formica table.

"What makes you think she was trying not to be photographed?" I asked, squatting by the table's edge, trying to duck under the smoke.

"It's obvious to anybody with a triple-digit IQ, Leo. You just gotta open your fucking eyes."

I looked again. Nothing jumped out at me. The table full of photos looked to my unseeing eyes to be a typical collection of all-American family photos.

Some bad, some better, some a total waste of film. Nothing special.

"There was this philosopher, some Frenchman, I don't remember his name, who said that after a certain age people become responsible for their own faces."

"Camus," I said. "Albert Camus."

Carl was rolling now.

"The guy was right, you know, which by the way is pretty fucking amazing for a Frenchman, since they're the biggest assholes in the universe, bar none. Back about sixty-seven—"

He stopped himself, not wanting to seem bitter, as if even that admission was more than he cared to share. His photos were great because they were honest. Knowing Carl Cradduck had taught me that honesty was at best a double-edged sword. Honesty neither makes excuses nor feels pity. Carl liked to say that self-delusion, not baseball, was the national pastime. The fact that Carl Cradduck tolerated me was in some odd way far more affirming than the often-forced affection of my extended family.

"Anyway," he continued, "if you know what to look for, you can sometimes put the people back into the pictures. That's the secret, Leo. It's like them oldtime Muslims were right. You remember? From those old Ripley's *Believe It or Not* books. How the people there in North Africa used to be shit-scared of having their pictures taken. They thought

it would rob them of their souls. What's interesting
is that in a way they were right. Photography does
have this way of taking the people out of the pictures. You know what I mean? What you got to do,
if you want to make sense out of pictures, is put the
people back into the pictures."

"What do these pictures tell you?"

"Everything," he said.

My face earned me another sneer, followed by a
resigned sigh.

"For starters"—he tapped the collage of photographs laid out before him—"most of these images
are your typical stagey tourist shit, right?"

He didn't wait for an answer.

"But look at the number of misfires. It's unbeliev-
able. I could maybe understand this many blottos if
the photographer was one of those rat bastards who
likes to sneak up on people in the bathroom, but
these things are staged. Theoretically, everybody's
supposed to be looking right at the camera, showing
off their crowns, right?"

I had to agree. Nicky, Marge, and Allison most
certainly were posing.

"Look at the spacing in most of these shots. Look
at the fuckin' body language. The body language
alone ought to tell you everything you need to know.
These three look like they got a broom up their
collective ass."

At second viewing, a certain amount of discomfort
was indeed obvious. I checked for bristles.

"Also, look how you can tell that they're way the hell inside each other's personal space. Look how close together they're standing. Only Japs and politicians get that close to their fellow citizens. Look at the facial expressions in this series."

He pointed to a group of four shots of Nicky, Marge, and Allison in front of the teahouse in the Japanese Garden at the Arboretum.

"The older broad here"—he pointed to Marge—"who, I'd like to mention, is sporting an absolutely bodacious set of warheads, looks to me like she'd rather be having a high colonic."

He held the first picture close to his thick lenses and smiled at me.

"Correct me if I'm wrong, Leo, but old Warheads here, she don't like Little Tasty Trim at all, does she? Lemme know if I'm gettin' warm here."

I didn't give him the satisfaction of an answer.

"Fuckin' A," he said.

"How can you tell all that from just looking at a picture?"

"Notice how the kid is always in between the two muff. Which, I'd like to mention, would not be a half-assed bad place to be. Not a single shot of the two snappers side by side, and notice how Hooters here"—he tapped Marge's chest—"is always slightly inclined away from Little Miss Tasty." He tapped Allison this time.

"Tight unit," he murmured.

He was right about the body language. If you

looked closely, Marge seemed to keep her body slightly angled away from Allison, as if being blown off center by a persistent wind.

"So, that probably makes Warheads and the boy mother and son. Am I right?"

I admitted that they were.

"Fuckin' A."

"And Little Tight 'n' Tasty here is the fiancée or maybe the daughter-in-law, then. Right again, huh?"

My face must have spoken for me. He picked up and then replaced several photos, bringing each up to within an inch or so of his glasses.

"Look at the color tones. Good lens. Real warm skin tone. Little Tasty's got quite the tan. Probably got great little tan lines. Late-afternoon sun behind the camera just like it says in the manual. Everything nice-a-nice. Gives a nice rosy glow to the skin. Almost looks like there was a red filter on, which there wasn't. Buuuut—"

He drew it out.

"Look at the kid."

I studied the picture for whatever Carl saw, but came up blank.

"Look how sallow he looks compared to the wool. A definite yellow-green cast to him. I'd say the kid's probably not well. Jaundice maybe, or some kind of liver disease."

"Cancer," I said.

"How old?"

"Twenty-two."

"A bitch," he said with feeling.

We studied the pictures in silence for a long moment.

"It's all there, Leo," he said finally. "I'll tell you somethin' else about this particular series. Helen Keller was really struggling to get a picture of her. He or she was working like a dog at it."

"How can you tell?"

"See those strained looks? Those are the expressions of people who have been posing for quite a while—doing the amateur shuffle. You know, a little to the left, a little to the right."

He threw his short arms left and right as if doing the Charleston.

"You do that for a while and everybody comes out looking like they're takin' a shit."

He tapped Allison's half-hidden face.

"The tight unit had plenty of time to get ready. We got this one with her hair over her face. Number two where she's got one side of her face behind his arm, and a third where she's looking the other way, for Christ's sake."

He lined the three stills up on the table top. He picked up the negatives from the bottom of the envelope, holding the thin brown strips carefully by the edges.

"Watch," he said. "I got fifty says they were taken in this order."

He tapped the three photos again. "One, two, three. Wanna bet?"

"No way."

I'd played in card games with Carl. He had a nasty habit of going home with everybody's folding money.

One after another, he held the strips up to the light.

"That's why there's three or four in every series. The photographer can tell he's not quite getting her and keeps pushing the button."

I must have looked dubious. He continued.

"Bingo," he said. "Here they are. Right in a row, one, two, three."

I took the negative and held it to the light. Carl was right. The three photos were indeed sequential.

"Where's my fifty?"

"I didn't bet."

"You don't have to take the bet. That's life's little joke, Leo. You're playin' whether you know it or not."

He pointed down at the table.

"Look at the one with her hair in the way," he said. "Look at her hand."

"What about it?"

"It's on the outside by her ear, like she's moving the hair in rather than out of her face. If she were moving her hair out of her face, her thumb would be on the outside and up. You try moving hair out of your face that way. You'll poke out your fucking eye, is what you'll do. And speaking of poking, I'd sure like to wet a finger in that one."

When I ignored him, he began to paw through the photographs again.

"How many pictures we got here?" he asked no one in particular.

He counted up one row and across, then multiplied.

"Fifty-six," he said, answering his own question. "You remember back to those thrilling days of yore, before no-fault divorce, when I had the little shop down on Michigan and you used to bring me all those motel-room specials you used to take?"

I admitted I remembered.

"Even under those circumstances, you bein' the worst photographer on the planet, bad light, people diving under beds, you still used to get usable shots of them, didn't you?"

I nodded.

"Why?" he asked.

"I always figured it was by virtue of my great cunning and dare."

"No, Shamus, it's just a numbers game. That's why I sold you that autowinder. If you take enough shots, something will come out. Watch the pros. They'd never admit it, but half the time they just keep burning film until luck takes over. They know that if they get enough prints, they'll stumble on something good when they get in the darkroom."

"So what do we do?" I asked.

"We?" he chucked.

"Okay, you."

"Well, Leo, I'll tell you. You're a lucky bastard on two counts. First off, there's your timing. Just a few years ago, this would have been a first-class pain in the ass. Woulda cost you a fortune. Now"—he snapped his fingers—"it's a piece of cake. Actually," he chuckled, "it's a piece of software. Adobe Photoshop. Hell of a fuckin' program. Do everything except milk your lizard for you."

I poked him back on track.

"So the computer will do it?"

"Only in the hands of a master, my friend, which is where you get lucky on the second count. You have me," he said expansively. "For"—he waggled a thick finger—"a nominal price, of course."

"Of course," I agreed. "What needs to be done?"

"First, we pick out the best of this crap."

He took his time as he poked through the collage of prints covering his worktable, eventually selecting six, piling the rest.

"Then?"

"In the old days, I'd have had to take the negatives into the darkroom, adjust the focus and the distance from the camera so they more or less matched each other, cut the damn negatives by hand, and then patch them back together. The twist would have come out looking like Marge Schott that time of the month."

"But with this software—"

"Now, I'll just scan the pictures into the hard-drive memory and do all the editing right onscreen."

"And then we'll have a picture of the girl?"

"No, then we'll have a composite of the girl."

"But it will be a likeness."

"All composites look like Karl Malden," Carl corrected.

He sensed I was losing my patience and moved along.

"Then we run it through the digital enhancer, which smooths out the rough edges and gives us more or less a finished product."

"More or less?"

"More like"—he waggled a hand—"an average of a good likeness. You've got to understand, Leo, when you digitize something, you tend to lose the character along with the rough edges. The same process that keeps everything from looking like Leona Helmsley also takes some of the human element out of it. My assistant, Mark, says it makes everybody look retarded. It ain't real nice, but the kid has a point. What you get is a homogenized version of the image."

Before I could ask another question, he continued.

"But we can adjust the picture, pixel by pixel, until we get it right."

"Really?"

"You just have Warheads tell me what needs to be fixed. More chin, higher cheekbones, anything. We'll eventually get it right."

Confidentiality being the cornerstone of my

business, I felt a need to put an immediate stop to Carl's assumptions regarding Marge Sundstrom.

"For your information, Carl, the woman in those pictures isn't—"

He cut me off.

"Forget it, huh, Shamus," he snapped. "It's in the pictures, just like it was in your face when I started talkin' about her tits. I just hope you're gettin' some of that, Leo. Be a terrible waste otherwise."

Before I could deny all, he began to laugh at me. His laugh, created on the inhale, honked like a wedge of Canada geese as he reveled in my discomfort.

"You better stay the fuck out of poker games, Leo. Just have her make corrections, and we'll come up with a workable image."

"Like one of those Identikit pictures the cops use?"

"Better. Way better. Those Identikit drawings are more like caricatures. The cops have to show those things to a shitload of people before they get somebody to make an ID. Lots of the citizens just can't make the mental leap from the drawing to a real face. We won't have that problem. We'll end up with a photo, instead of just a fuckin' drawing."

"How long and how much?"

"I'll need the weekend and two hundred."

"Now and two and a half," I countered. "I want to be up and running on this by Monday morning," I said.

"Three," he shot back. "Don't forget my fifty."

"That includes all the changes we might have to make?"

"Fuckin' A."

"Deal."

9

H. R. MCCOLL DID A HELL OF AN IMPRESSION OF CHEERFUL.
Thirty-five years of kissing well-heeled asses had
provided the senior partner with an impenetrable
veneer of unctuous affability as slick and stout as any
Willapa Bay oyster.

Just this side of sixty, he was a tall man. His sharp
cheekbones were framed by a shock of thick white
hair, shaved nearly bald on the sides, worn in a short
Marine brush cut on top—all bones and angles in a
dark gray wool suit. The deep purple tie and matching pocket hankie added a slight contemporary
touch to his otherwise conservative attire.

"Let me set your concerns to rest, Marge." The
resonant basso profundo held a nearly incantatory
assuredness. For punctuation, he leaned back in the
chair, crossing his ankle over his knee, exposing a
well-controlled two inches of light gray sock.
Smooth—the patient parent assuring the frightened
child that the bedroom closet was free of ghosts.

"I can assure you that we are doing everything

humanly possible. I'm sure you understand. This is not nearly as simple a matter as it might seem."

"I don't see why not," Marge shot back. "We *are* the next of kin. There's no question about that. At the moment, there's no money involved. All we want is an accounting for the funds."

I wondered how long it had been since the senior partner of the august firm of McColl, Moody and Cole had been called to a meeting at a client's office on a Saturday afternoon. His easy grace suggested that this was a service that he regularly provided to his corporate clients. I knew better. McColl, Moody and Cole specialized in asset retention. They had so perfected the mechanics of the international banking system as to make it nearly impossible for any governmental body to keep track of the considerable sums with which they were routinely entrusted. They didn't launder money; they had it dry-cleaned.

From Carl's, I'd headed home for a shower and a change of clothes. My appointment to meet Marge at the Sundstrom office wasn't until one o'clock. After steaming the nicotine out of my skin for a half hour or so, I dressed in a pair of clean jeans, a burgundy chamois shirt, and my dress Nikes. I made myself a couple of grilled cheese sandwiches, washing them down with a Barq's root beer, and was in the process of rounding up some random clothes to accompany my Sunday-go-to-meeting outfit to the cleaners when the phone rang. It was Marge.

"Finally," she huffed.

She seemed to be waiting for either an apology or an explanation.

"Are you there?" she asked finally.

"I'm here."

"I've been trying to get a hold of you since yesterday evening."

"Here I am."

Her dissatisfaction was palpable.

"We're still on for this afternoon?" she said finally.

"One o'clock," I confirmed.

"Howard McColl will be there."

"The great man himself?"

"In the flesh."

"I figured for sure he'd send a junior partner."

"Don't think that worm didn't try," she said with obvious satisfaction. "First he wanted to do lunch. Just the two of us, of course. Then, as soon as he realized that wasn't going to happen, he offered to send everyone in the firm except the cleaning lady— and himself of course—until we finally had a little chat regarding retainers. Speaking of which, I've decided that I'd feel better about our relationship if I gave you a retainer. How much would—"

"No thanks," I interrupted quickly.

"If we're going to have a business relationship—"

I nipped this one in the bud.

"Because then, sooner or later, you and I would be having our own little chat about retainers, and I don't work well that way."

The phone company was right; you could hear a pin drop.

"One o'clock, then," she said after another strained silence.

"See you there."

I dropped the bundle of clothes at the cleaners and tooled down over the hill, arriving at the Sea Sundstrom offices on Western Avenue about five minutes early. McColl was already ensconced in the red leather chair closest to the desk, somehow managing to look like he'd been born to occupy that particular seat. Patrician presence, I supposed.

Marge handled the introductions without rising. McColl stood reluctantly, brushing my outstretched palm with a limp, dry hand. I dragged a flowered wing chair across the room, settling for a spot on the other end of the low polished table that served as a desk. This was the president's office; the sign on the door said so. It was a woman's room. Vaguely floral. Decorated with flair and care, functional but flattering.

"Your rights are not in question, my dear," Mc-Coll said. "The problem lies in the next of kin named by your—"

Something in Marge's expression produced an instant edit.

"—in Ms. Stark's next of kin."

"She named some aunt in Wisconsin," Marge said.

"Who does not and, as nearly as we are able to ascertain, has never lived at the address of record.

For that matter, we have thus far been unable to procure even a single document confirming the existence of this Miss Audrey Danielson, let alone secure a release."

"So what's the problem then?" I interjected. "No aunt. No money. No problem."

"Would that it were that simple, Mr. Waterman."

McColl pinned me with a pitying glance that suggested that although the problem was manifestly not simple, I most certainly was.

"I don't want to hear it, Howard," Marge said. "I don't care what it takes. Get it done. I want whatever paperwork is necessary to grant us access to that account ready by Friday."

"I don't know what this person"—he cast me a disgusted look—"has been telling you, but it can't possibly be—"

"Do it, Howard. If your firm can't manage it, I'll find one who can."

"Marge," he started. The concerned parent again.

"Mrs. Sundstrom," she corrected quickly.

"Of course. Of course. I forget myself. Excuse me. Believe me, I'm every bit as upset about our lack of progress as are you."

"Somehow I don't think so," Marge snapped.

"Listen to me, please. This is a bureaucratic nightmare. Death certificates haven't even been issued yet in this county. We'll need a certificate of qualification, letters testamentary. These things take time."

"Pull strings, Howard. It's what you do best. Do

it. Call in whatever favors you're owed. Press some flesh. Grease some palms. I don't care how, just do it, just do it. If it costs money, send me a bill. The firm seems to be quite efficient at billing."

"I shall assuredly do my—"

"By Friday."

"Mar—Mrs. Sundstrom, believe me, I and the rest of the members of the firm sympathize with your most grievous loss, but this is no time to—"

He reached out to pat her hand, which sat motionless on the desk. Before he could make contact, she eased the hand back into her lap.

"I got your card. Very thoughtful. By Friday, Howard."

He uncrossed his leg and sat back hard against the chair like a spoiled child denied a second helping of dessert. After a short interval of staring into space, he pulled a hand through his close-cropped hair, leaning forward toward Marge again as he absent-mindedly ran his cupped hands down both sides of his nose.

"You do realize of course, don't you, that if—and I acknowledge this possibility only with the greatest skepticism—but if your suspicions are indeed correct and there has been some willful misappropriation of these assets, access to these accounts will almost surely lead only to a dead end."

Marge looked to me for confirmation.

"You're talking numbered Swiss accounts. That kind of thing?" I said.

"Most certainly," he breathed. "As you so astutely put, Marge, that is precisely what we do. It's never been easier to obscure funds. Never. The emergence of the third world has created a massive underground banking system that makes the fabled Swiss seem positively effusive. If—"

He held up a bony finger.

"If that is indeed where the funds have gone. That will most surely be the end of the matter right there. Neither mine, nor any other firm"—he sent a paternal, forgiving glance toward Marge—"can be of any help from there."

"I understand," I said. "From you, all we need to know is where the money went after it left the Seafirst Bank. You get us into the records. We'll have to see where, if anywhere, that leads and then take it from there."

He levered himself from the chair and spoke directly to Marge.

"This isn't going to be easy, and it isn't going to be cheap," he intoned gravely.

"Well then," Marge said sweetly, "that's something we'll all have in common, then, won't we?"

The rebuff had no discernible effect. He bid Marge a courtly good-bye, sent a dismissive nod in my general direction, and was gone.

"A charmer," I commented when the sound of his heels had faded.

"He's always thought so. Howard always wants to

have business meetings when he knows Heck's out of town."

"Probably because he has a genuine interest in your assets."

"A woman's greatest asset is a man's imagination," she said without a trace of humor.

Her tone made me doubly glad I hadn't taken her retainer.

I filled her in on what I'd been doing, complete with all the details. About Richmond's conviction that his yacht was sound. About Allison's refusal to take on a crew. About confirming that a wharf rat named Norma had, as Heck insisted, disappeared about the same time the *Risky Business* had gone down. About sending the Boys out to see if they could find where she'd lived. About leaving the pictures with Carl and the probability of getting a workable likeness of Allison Stark.

She listened in silence, no questions, clasping and unclasping her hands on the desktop as I spoke as if the fingers were a pair of bellows pushing air in and out of her lungs.

"Doesn't amount to much, does it?" she said when I'd finished.

"On the contrary. Nothing I've found discredits Heck's idea either. That, in itself, is pretty interesting considering how far-fetched this whole conspiracy thing is."

She considered my assessment.

"Do you think your friend can really make a picture out of those snapshots?"

"Let's find out," I said, pointing to the slim black phone on her desk.

She passed it over. I dialed Carl's home number.

"What?"

"Can we come over and take a look at the picture?"

"Why?"

"Why what?"

"Why come over? I already seen enough of you and them silly clothes for one day. Where's the nearest fax machine to you?"

I held the phone to my chest and spoke to Marge.

"Is there a fax machine here?" I asked.

"Right over there," she said, pointing to a gun-metal-gray unit about the size of a portable type-writer sitting on the bottom shelf of the wall unit at the far end of the office.

It occurred to me that I was going to have to do something about my abhorrence of technology. I was rapidly becoming a dinosaur.

"Got one right here," I said into the mouthpiece.

"Say hello to Warheads for me," he said.

"Yeah, sure, you can count on it, Carl."

"Well?"

"Well what?"

"What's the fucking number?"

Marge anticipated my question. I repeated the number into the mouthpiece as Marge gave it to me.

"Use something dark. Magic Marker, something like that. The fax ain't real good with light lines. Just give me a shape. I'll take care of the rest. Send it back corrected when you're done."

I started to hang up, but heard him shout into the receiver.

"You screeched?"

"How in the hell are you gonna send it back without my fax number, you fucking moron?"

"You may have a point," I admitted. "Okay, what is it?"

He told me and then hung up in my ear.

By the time I'd stood and returned the receiver to its cradle, the fax machine emitted its first trilling ring. Then another, followed by a short series of electronic squeaks and beeps, silenced by a single soft click.

Allison Stark came out of the machine neck first. Right in front of my sneakers, she emerged into a red plastic basket. The machine clicked off. I tore the image off, carried it back across the room, and set it on the desktop in front of Marge. Her breath caught in her throat. She looked away.

She smoothed the sheet and looked again. The picture was of a narrow-faced young woman with a Prince Valiant hairdo. Just above shoulder length. Long bangs. Her slim lines were accentuated by large almond-shaped eyes that didn't seem to be focusing anywhere in particular. The nose might have been too narrow on a bigger face, but it worked just fine here. As Carl had predicted, there was a certain blankness to the expression, as if she had just risen from a long sleep.

"Well?" I said.

"More than I dared hope. Amazing, almost— remarkable really."

"A good likeness?"

"Close . . . close . . . not quite right, but close," she said, more to herself than to me.

"What needs to be changed?"

Marge Sundstrom spent a long minute studying the image, running the tip of one scarlet nail over and around the outlines of the face.

"First the lips, I think," she said. "She had thicker lips. Particularly the lower lip. She had that pouty look. You know those collagen-injected lips. I know she had them done."

I picked a red felt-tip pen from a cup on her desk and handed it to her.

"Fix 'em," I said.

She began to trace an outline.

"No, no," she said disgustedly. "I was never any good at art."

"Try again."

I pulled a pink Kleenex from the ceramic dispenser on the desk and handed it to her. She wet the Kleenex with the tip of her pink tongue and rubbed out the red ink. The image came off with the ink.

"Shit," we said in unison.

I called Carl.

"Send another one."

He didn't require an explanation.

"Make copies, you idiot. Faxes aren't fast." Click.

They seemed pretty quick to me, but I took his word for it. This time, I used the Xerox machine to make five copies. On the third try, Marge was satisfied with the lips.

"That's as good as I can get them."

"What else?" I prompted.

"Too fat in the face. She needs to be more . . . gaunt. The little bitch never ate anything. I don't think I ever saw her take more than six bites of anything. It got so if I ordered anything more than cottage cheese, I felt like such a sow. I couldn't even enjoy my meals."

I handed her the fourth copy. Still muttering, she shaded in the cheeks. "Like that," she said.

I faxed both pictures to Carl and then took out my notebook.

"While we're waiting, tell me about all these stories she used to tell about her background."

"That rubbish?"

"Most likely not all of it," I said. "Liars usually mix up a little truth with the lies. It not only sounds better that way, but it's a hell of a lot safer. Gives them a few verifiable details to throw around. Lends an air of authenticity to the lies. You probably never thought about it, but liars have to be careful about what they lie about. If they go around long enough telling people they graduated from the University of Illinois, sooner or later they're going to run into somebody else who either went to school there or who lived in Champaign. At that point, they'd better have at least some basic geography down."

"I see," she said dubiously.

"Start at the beginning. Give me whatever personal history you can remember. Try to recall those things that she seemed most credible about."

Marge heaved a sigh and started.

"Wisconsin. Born and raised in Madison, Wisconsin. Only child. Her father was a doctor, of course. According to her, she had the perfect childhood. Big house, picket fence, tree swing. The whole ball of wax. Parents killed in an airplane crash when she was fourteen, but you know that already. Very convenient. Brought up by this aunt—the one she named as next of kin. Went to the University of Wisconsin on a small insurance settlement. Had all these summer jobs there. River guide, aerobics instructor. During the school year she worked part time in a pizza parlor to make ends meet. When the insurance money ran out, she had to drop out and went to work selling timeshares. She—"

Marge stopped.

"Timeshares," she repeated. "She knew all about timeshares."

"You're sure?"

"I'm an expert, Leo. Heck was such a sucker for

those things. We've owned three over the years. I had to stop letting him go out by himself when we were on vacation. He kept coming back with a new timeshare every time. Allison knew timeshares inside and out."

"You know where she sold them?"

"Supposedly at Chelan. Over east at the lake."

"Anything more specific than that? Last time I was over there, every third person was selling time-shares."

"Afraid not."

We were interrupted by the soft click of the fax machine. By the time I reached the far side of the room the picture had dropped into the red plastic basket. I took it directly to the copy machine and made five copies.

"The lips are right," Marge said after squinting at the new picture for a full minute, "but the face is too thin now. She looks emaciated. And . . . I don't know . . . there's something wrong about the eyes."

She picked up the marker and began to doodle, defacing and destroying three of the copies to no end except to litter the floor around her desk.

She worked hard on the fourth copy, working the shape of the eyes, rounder, bigger, smaller, giving her an Asian visage, then wide-eyed with surprise. Finally, in a fit of pique, she crossed out the right eye, then quickly looked at the picture and back at me.

"It's the eyelids," she said. "She needs heavier eyelids. She had those eyes men like that always looked like she was half asleep."

"Fix them," I said, handing her the last copy.

It only took her about thirty seconds to make the changes.

"There," she breathed. "God, that's close now, even with the red marker."

She held it at arm's length.

"If he could do something about the expression . . . I don't know . . . just, you know, put some life in it, we'd be pretty close."

I took the image and scrawled across the bottom. *Lips fine. Face too thin now. Do eyelids like this. Can you fix blank expression?*

I fed the paper into the machine, dialed Carl's number, and waited as our copy went through the box. I was on my way back to Marge when the machine clicked again. About face.

Yours or hers?????? was printed thickly on the page.

"That was quick," Marge commented.

I crumpled the page into a ball and lofted it toward the basket. It rimmed off, joining its brethren on the floor.

"Just Carl being cute," I said apologetically.

I picked up my notebook.

"What else?"

Marge waved me off.

"Oh, I don't know, Leo. After a while, I stopped

listening to her. It was just so much garbage. It always sounded to me like some bad TV show. That's all I can remember right now."

"Was she working when she met Nick?"

"Selling real estate."

"Where? For who?"

"Leschi. Not Windermere, but something that sounds like it. It's right in that same little complex with Daniel's Broiler. I dropped her at her car there once."

She ran me through a long list of vague deals, both residential and commercial, that Allison supposedly had in the works.

"It's a place to start. Real estate requires a license. A license requires documentation. Documentation requires a background."

Marge hadn't heard me. She was somewhere else.

"Maybe we should just stop all of this, Leo," she sighed.

"All of what?"

"This . . . this wild goose chase. All of it. I'm beginning to think, I don't know, maybe we're just grasping at straws here. This is all just so off the wall. You said it yourself. This is like some comic-book plot. Maybe we . . . I don't know," she said finally. "I'd better get down to the hospital."

"I think we've just started. I think it's not going to take all that much to discredit Heck's conspiracy theory. We've got a line on a paper trail here. We've almost got a picture. I think we ought to keep at it."

Two images arrived. Across the first Carl had written: *I focused the eyes for expression. Eyelids okay? How's the face for width?* The second was identical without the writing.

I placed both of them facedown on the desk in front of Marge.

"But listen, Marge. This is your party. If you want to quit, we quit. Any time you think this is too painful or too expensive or too whatever you just say the word, and—"

As she listened to me, she turned over the pictures on her desk.

She pulled a loud breath into the back of her throat.

I stopped talking and watched the blood leave her face and then surge back with a vengeance.

"That's her. That's perfect. God, that's amazing that he could do that. That's her," she repeated.

I walked behind and looked over her shoulder. The benign face of the first picture had taken on an almost spiteful look—a gaze that said, "You should get so lucky, fool." It was easy to see how the boy had become entranced. Allison Stark was a stunner.

"Well," I started. "What do you want to do?"

There was no hesitation this time.

"Seeing her again—I'm sure now. I need to know. Stay at it," she said.

Marge got to her feet.

"I have to go. Heck's been restless. He had a

rough night last night. Call me if you need anything or if you find out anything."

She reached into the top small drawer of her desk and drew out a blank sheet of letterhead. She wrote, *Thanks for everything. If there's anything I ever can do to repay you for your excellent work, please call.* Signature and phone number.

She strode across the room, fed it into the fax machine, and pushed the redial button. "I have to get down to Heck," she said as she slipped into a full-length red wool coat and headed for the door.

The fax was doing its thing again. I wandered over and retrieved the message. *How about a shot of those hooters? Use the copy machine.*

Marge looked at me quizzically.

"Carl says you're welcome," I said, pocketing the page.

10

WAS THAT THE SOUND OF MY MOTHER RUNNING? Or was she dancing? I strained to hear. The thin clicking of her heels faded slowly, now a dull echo in distant rooms, on lower floors, nearly silent. Then . . . still. I relaxed again and drifted. Without warning, she was back, dancing flamenco furiously in the hall outside the door to my room. The rhythm left me reeling. I'd never seen her either run or dance. I'd never seen her any way except moving between tasks at her unhurried gait. Her great sense of purpose left little choice but to imagine her having been born busy. The organized had no need to hurry, her cadence seemed to say. Running would be somehow confessional. No running.

And dancing? Dancing was the province of savages, of those with no self-respect—worst of all, those without enough to do. Every aspect of her being decried the squandered moment, the lost opportunity. The very sound of her incessant feet, sensible heels tapping the meter, served as a cautionary tale of perpetual motion to the idle, the slackers, the self-satisfied. Dancing, too, was pretty much out of the question.

I'd never seen her any way except fully and properly dressed—no chenille robes, no pink curlers. She materialized from her room each morning at precisely 6:30 A.M. like Dracula risen from the grave. Reanimated. Rejuvenated. Eternal. The spitting image of the day before. Hair perfect, tasteful jewelry in place. When I was young, I'd imagined that she slept that way, fully dressed, standing up like a horse in its stall, emerging the next morning as an exact, unrumpled reproduction of the previous day. In those days, my life had been timed by the clicking of those metronome heels on the oak floors of our house.

My old man used to call her the Drum Major. On those occasions when the business of influence peddling allowed him a night at home, he and I would curl up in the study and, warmed by a fire in the grate, lit by the blue glow of the oversized television set, eat the contraband Hershey bars he'd secreted in his pockets. Plain for him, almonds for me. He had radar. His extra years of practice had blessed him with an even more delicate and refined ear than mine for the tapping.

"Better hide those wrappers and wipe your mouth, son," he'd say as we watched the Russian bears on "The Toast of the Town." "Here comes the Drum Major."

I'd cock an anxious ear but hear nothing. He was always right, though. A minute or two later, I would pick up the staccato cadence of her approach. Once an hour or so, she'd poke her head in to confirm her worst fears concerning our wastrel evening and, most importantly, to make sure the old man wasn't polluting my system with any of the accursed junk food. My mother was a health nut long before it was chic.

"You're not feeding that boy a bunch of trash, are you? You know he has nightmares if he has too much sugar."

"No sugar," the old man would say.

"I want him off to bed right after this program."

"One more show."

"No, I want him—"

"You're letting a draft in," he'd reply.

The heels would then recede. Louder than before. Angry.

"Son," he'd always say as she stalked away, "for the life of me, I will never understand why anybody who's having so precious little fun here on earth is so damned intent on living forever."

I never had an answer.

We'd wait for the sound of the stairs. The groan of the fourth step. Once she went upstairs, she didn't come back down until morning, when the unremitting parade of progress would begin anew.

She began each day at the kitchen sink with a crystal pitcher of ice water and a colorful pile of pills and capsules the size of a modest cow fritter. She got her rest, avoided sweets, abhorred grease, and was still in possession of her girlish figure when she gamboled into the grave at fifty-nine, the victim of a massive cerebral hemorrhage. The old man, who was ten years her senior and had for better than thirty years started each day with a jelly doughnut and a cup of Irish coffee because he claimed they contained the four basic food groups—caffeine, sugar, grease, and alcohol—lasted another seven years. Go figure.

I awoke with a start. Dark volleys of raindrops, driven horizontally by a blustery wind, clicked rhythmically onto the window above my bed, brittle, insistent with their still-frozen centers. I sat up and checked the street. Out on Fremont, the icy rain was bursting and dancing, forming a moving carpet of frozen mist six inches above the black glistening pavement. Mary Sloan's white VW Bug, parked in perpetuity half a block north, rocked slightly on its aged springs as if cowering under the violent onslaught. In spite of the protective windowpane, I found myself squinting into the abrasive wind. So much for Indian summer.

After liberating my favorite pair of blue sweats from bondage in the bottom of the hamper, I headed out to the kitchen to make coffee. Mechanically, I opened the fridge. Nada. It all came back to me. Knowing that I was going to be shepherding Tony Moldonado, I'd purposely allowed myself to run out of everything even remotely perishable. This, of course, included milk for my coffee. Shit. It was either head to the store or do without. As if to assist me with the decision, a fresh barrage of sleet ratcheted against the front windows of the apartment, rattling the ancient sash. I opted for the suffering.

I padded over to the front door, and pulled my *Sunday Times* in from the hall. The story of my aborted evening was plastered across the front page: "Four Dead in Fiery Southcenter Crash." Rebecca and I had planned dinner and a movie. We'd managed neither; her beeper had put a stop to any such foolishness. I had watched her thin face take on added weight as she held the receiver to her ear.

"Fifteen minutes," she'd said into the receiver and hung up.

"Bad?"

"Sounds like it. Traffic accident. Three, maybe four dead."

"At least you'll look good," I commented weakly.

"Doesn't sound like it's going to matter. Lock up for me, will you, Leo?"

I'd promised I would.

Rose Moldonado had, as usual, messengered her check over as soon as Tony arrived home. I'd plucked it from my mailbox as I'd sulked home last evening. The money had proven small consolation. I'd moped around the apartment, waiting for it to get late enough to go to bed.

On two separate occasions I'd picked up the pale green bag full of the stuff Heck had collected, and twice I'd failed to muster up the initiative to do anything useful. Pulling out the collection of bills and receipts, gazing absently at the dates and amounts, stuffing them back in, finally lobbing the bag back onto the kitchen counter in disgust. The sack's wrinkled countenance still gazed speculatively at me from the counter. After freeing the sports section from the paper, I used the bulk of the Sunday edition to intern the insolent bag.

The Sonics were still undefeated at home. Ten and zero. Eighteen and two overall. What else could a serious sports fan ask for? Coffee, that's what. Maybe a fresh onion bagel with some . . .

The phone interrupted my imaginary breakfast.

"Jew wann guess who'z at Jazz Alley tonight?"

"Fidel and the Modal Marxists?"

"Not fonny, Leo. Jew shouldn't joke like cat. De man is a tyrant. What he has done to my country ees—"

"You got any coffee, Hector?"

"Chewer. Go on, guess."

"Milk?"

"No till you guess."

"Gene Harris Quartet."

"Dey left Thursday. Jew know dat."

"You got sugar too?"

"Why don' I yost creek it for you. Save jew de walk."

"Who's playing?"

"Benny Carter."

Now he had my attention.

"Let's go."

"Second show?"

"For sure."

"Jew tink we chould call?"

"Second show. No way."

"Coffee, milk, and sugar. Dat's it? No eggs? No toast?"

"I'll be right up."

"Don' sweat. I got some groceries for old Mees Bandon. I drop eet by."

"What a guy."

"Jew focking right."

He hung up. I returned to the Sonics. After a slow start, Shrempf seemed to be settling into his niche with the team. Averaging nearly ten boards a game for the past week and a half. Ricky was in a slump, though. Couldn't throw it in the ocean. Shooting less than 40 percent for the past five games. Must be injured and keeping it to himself. Bad news. Above all else, we needed a healthy Ricky Pierce.

The doorbell interrupted my research. Hector dangled three small plastic bags out from under a huge cardboard box of groceries. I plucked them from his fingers.

"Thanks."

"I come by nine-fifteen or so."

"I'll be ready."

Between the Sunday paper and the coffee, I was

able to stretch my morning into early afternoon. The front section. Arts and Leisure. The Classifieds. Weekender. The weekly TV guide. Travel. I attacked the paper one section at a time, careful to keep several sections always restraining the recalcitrant green bag. It was nearly one o'clock when I finally reached for and then discarded the fashion section. Much to my chagrin, I was forced to face the realization that, Sunday or no, I was going to have to at least try to accomplish something.

An hour later, freshly scrubbed and showered, I grudgingly guided the Fiat east on Northlake, along the ship canal, sliding up to Pacific, crossing over the Montlake Bridge on my way down through the deserted Arboretum. I babied the car along the narrow lanes, radio off, listening to the intermittent hissing and cracking as the undercarriage caught, dragged and discarded an unending series of small windblown branches while the narrow tires popped legions of fallen pine cones.

From under the arch of trees at the south end of the park, I briefly emerged into the light, darted across Madison, and slalomed my way down through the high-rent district to Lake Washington Boulevard, where the heavy south wind whipped the green surface of the lake into a humped and hollowed froth of small rolling whitecaps, rioting simultaneously in all directions, driven by the wind to lurch in a self-destructive chaos of foam and frenzy. I turned on the wipers.

Although the rain had stopped, the airborne mist created by the disintegrating waves showered down on the little car and veiled the distant arcs of both of the floating bridges as I wheeled into the waterfront parking lot. A large U-Haul truck was backed in against the far curb, its mouth open, tonguelike ramp licking the golden, leaf-covered ground.

In one sinuous motion, I stepped from the car into a puddle that nearly reached the top of my sock. Before I could recover, icy water filled my left shoe, running down between my toes and under my foot. A real day killer. I swore, briefly considered turning around and going home, and then swore again for good measure.

Using the car for leverage, I vaulted my way onto a small island of pavement. I realized now that the even yellow carpet of leaves was a cruel ruse. The storm had turned the lot into a single large puddle, then used the wind-blown leaves to hide its dirty work.

Intent on avoiding further puddles, I kept my eyes glued to my feet as I squooshed across the lot. Walking blind, I was nearly bowled over by a gray-shrouded desk being wheeled along the sidewalk on a dolly. The double doors to the real estate offices had been propped open by a couple of chrome folding chairs. Another desk on a dolly fell into line behind the first. I stepped aside and let it pass. It followed along in the exact wet tracks of its predecessor, like a trailing circus elephant, joined trunk to tail. Windlass Real Estate was on the move.

"Don't just stand there like a bump on a log. Take that box of files."

Like many well-maintained women, her age was hard to guess. Somewhere between forty and fifty-five. Wasp-waisted, well-fed, a natural blond about five-eight. Big blue eyes, pretty face. Her manual-labor ensemble consisted of a purple hooded U-Dub sweatshirt, a crisp pair of new 501s, a pair of Nike Airs, and a clipboard. Matching purple earrings, of course.

"Time's a wastin', my friend," she chided.

When I failed to move, she looked up at me for the first time.

"I'm sorry," she said after perusing me from head to toe. "You must be here about the phones. I should have known. You're obviously not one of the movers. My apologies. This whole move has just got me dizzy."

She used the clipboard to point toward a morass of phones, wires, and connectors heaped in the front corner of the office, nearly covering a flattened patch of sienna carpet where some heavy piece of furniture had rested until quite recently.

"We need at least the main line to be up and running by tomorrow."

She watched with mounting disbelief as I shook my head.

"I was assured by the company—"

I redoubled my head-shaking efforts. It worked.

"You're not here about the phones either, are you?"

"I'm afraid not."

She placed the heel of her free hand against her creamy forehead.

"Sorry again."

"No problem."

"What can I help you with?"

"Allison Stark."

"I've already . . . I'm sorry . . . Are you with the police?"

"I'm a private investigator, working for the Sundstrom family."

We were interrupted by one of the movers, a dark, heavyset guy with a thick Stalin moustache and a five-day growth.

"We're gonna take this load over and be right back."

"How many more loads do you figure?" she asked.

He scanned the single large room. Half a dozen metal desks, twenty assorted chairs, the pictures and posters on the walls, and a bank of file cabinets were all that remained.

"Next load be the last, easy."

"Okay."

She watched as the workman, unhurried by the inclement weather, ambled back toward the truck.

"This should have already been over," she said to his broad back. "First they're two hours late. When they finally get here, they move like they're on Thorazine. I've never seen—"

She sighed deeply.

"Please excuse me, Mr.—"

"Leo Waterman."

I pulled a business card from my jacket pocket and handed it over. She studied the card, checked the other side.

"May I keep this?" she asked.

"Please do."

She slipped the edge of the card under the metal retainer on the clipboard and then stuck out her hand. I took it in mine. We shook. She held on to both my gaze and my hand.

"Nancy Davies," she said. "I'm the broker here. This . . . er"—she disengaged our hands and swept her free arm over the interior—"this mess is more or less mine."

"My pleasure," I said.

"I'll tell you the same thing I told the police, Mr. Waterman. Naturally, I was shocked to hear of her accident. The death of anyone so young always comes as a shock, but there's no point in pretending to a lot of grief. That's not my style. I barely knew the woman. Other than the day I hired her, I probably saw her a total of three times. She was one of my junior sales associates for a little over a month. She came and went as she pleased, which in her case was mostly went. She graced us with her presence maybe a couple of days a week. Two residential sales. A new listing or two. Several other offers. Playing at real estate rather than being a real player, if you know what I mean?"

"I'm not sure I do."

"We get a lot of day trippers in this business, Leo. You don't mind if I call you Leo, do you?"

"Not at all."

"How nice. Anyhow, real estate has a certain ease of entry, Leo. You pass a little test, they give you a little license. We get a lot of people new to the workforce who have no idea what a tough racket this is. People who think they can take weekends off, who think listings are going to fall from heaven, people who have no idea what they're getting into, how hard you have to hustle to make a living. Sometimes they're just trying to show hubby that they can make money too or maybe pay for that car or cruise that hubby won't spring for. They come; they go. They show up at my doorstep with a license—if I've got desk space and they feel right to me, I'll give them a try. There's very little expense to me. Associates pay their own phone bills."

"Then Allison Stark felt right to you?"

She paused to consider.

"Depends on what you mean by felt right. I wouldn't want to give the impression she was cuddly or anything. Nothing like that. Allison Stark was not a person who was going to bring out the maternal instinct in anybody. She seemed competent. That was enough."

She stepped in closer. The musky aroma of a bit too much Obsession hung in the surrounding air.

"You ask more probing questions than the police."

"Thanks," I said tentatively.

"I say that because, when I think about it, I'm usually pretty right-on with my first impressions. Not always, but most of the time. I had her figured for a real shark."

"And you were wrong?"

"Yes and no."

She folded her arms across her chest and measured her words.

"I had this feeling that there was more to Allison Stark than met the eye. There was some quality about her . . . a lack of vulnerability maybe."

"Can you be more specific?"

She thought about it.

"I guess it was just the size of the discrepancy between how she looked and the feeling she gave off."

I waited.

"She was a cute little thing, but—I don't know—hard is maybe the closest word. You only had to look in her eyes. There was nothing soft about Allison Stark. Always immaculately groomed. Expensive clothes. Nothing but the best shoes and accessories. Everything perfect. A very pretty package, but very

remote. Self-contained. Almost like she was manufac-
tured. Very skilled at keeping her distance. Now that
I think about it, that's why news of her accident
seemed so unreal."

"Why's that?"

"Well . . . I guess it's because she just didn't seem
at all like a victim to me. She seemed like someone
who happened to things rather than someone who
had things happen to them, if you know what I
mean."

"A predator rather than prey."

"Exactly," Nancy Davies agreed. "That's it precisely."

"So I guess she never talked about her background?"

"Never. Absolutely nothing personal. Just how
she'd been selling condos over in the eastern part of
the state. I figured anybody who could make a living
in that racket would surely survive in residential real
estate."

"But she didn't?"

"Yes and no again."

She sensed my frustration.

"I hate to keep answering like that, Leo, but, like
the man says, that's the way it is. Considering how
little she worked at it, her two sales were quite
remarkable. She just didn't work at it."

"Any idea why?"

"None. I figured maybe she had some kind of
independent income and was just using the job as a

supplement. Something like that. Whatever it was, she had some other agenda besides selling."

"And that was okay with you."

"In a flat market like this, I was willing to put up with it. In better times, I'd have gotten on her case about it. But hell, as it was, she was outselling a couple of the people who've been with me for years. People who work their butts off."

"When did she quit?"

"Never. She never did quit. She just stopped coming in altogether."

While I mulled this over in silence, Nancy leaned back against the window, resting her hands on the sill behind her.

"Married?" she asked with a smile.

Noticing that she'd taken me offguard, she widened her smile.

"I was once. But not for a long time now."

"I didn't mean to embarrass you."

"You didn't," I lied.

No matter. She ignored me.

"I hope I wasn't being too pushy for you. Twenty years of selling makes a person a mite forward."

"No problem. I bang on quite a few doors myself."

"Spoken for?" she persisted.

"Depends on who you ask," I hedged. "Sort of, I guess."

"Don't tell me you're one of those types who breaks out in a cold sweat and runs for the weeds at the very mention of commitment."

"Actually," I countered, "it's more like the other way around."

"She's the one who's scared?"

"No. What she is, is smart."

This new admission brought forth a deep-seated chuckle from her.

"How romantic. That sort of makes you the knight errant in pursuit of the unattainable lady, doesn't it?"

"God, I hope not."

"I can see now how come you're more accustomed to being the pursuer than the pursued. No wonder I upset you."

Denial wasn't going to work, so I quickly changed the subject.

"So, I assume that she had a real estate license."

"Absolutely."

"Do you have a copy?"

"Absolutely. It's the law."

"Could I see it?"

"Why?"

I told her the part about the missing next of kin, the aunt in Wisconsin, leaving out everything else. Her pale blue eyes filled with mirth as I wound my tale to a close.

"I don't believe a word of it," she said when I finished.

"It's my story and I'm sticking to it."

She again treated me to her throaty laugh.

"Anyway, it's almost true," I added.

"Close enough," she said, walking over to the file cabinets.

She rummaged through the files in the top drawer, finally pulling out a clean orange folder. From the folder, she extracted a photocopied real estate license. She surveyed the wreckage of the room.

"They took the copier in the first load."

I pulled out my notebook.

"I'll just write it down."

She handed it over. I wrote down everything that I could imagine to be useful and handed it back.

"Did the cops ask for the license?"

"Nope. They just asked about her employment history. I was no help there, I'm afraid."

"No letters of reference or anything like that?"

"Not worth the effort. Warm body. Current license. I'm covered. They either sell or they don't. Hello. Good-bye."

I handed the copy over; Nancy returned it from whence it had come.

"Thanks," I offered my hand again. Again she took it.

"Anything else?" she asked speculatively.

"Not unless you can think of something else."

"We've already covered that, haven't we?" she grinned.

"I believe we have."

She rolled open the top drawer on the nearest desk, pulled out a business card, scribbled something on the back, and handed it to me.

"I'm moving the office over to Magnolia. Closer to home. Better rates. A more fluid area. I put the new address on the back. In case you need anything else."

"I appreciate it."

I was halfway back to the car before I remembered my wet foot.

11

"PACIFIC FIRST FEDERAL."

"Paul Waterman, please."

"May I tell Mr. Waterman who is calling?"

"Mr. Waterman."

I'd confused her.

"That *is* who you asked for, isn't it, sir?" she tried again.

"No. I mean . . . yes, it is. Tell him it's his cousin Leo Waterman calling."

"One moment please, Mr. Waterman. I'll try Mr. Waterman."

Two years my senior, Paul was the sole issue of the other branch of the Waterman family tree. As the only child of my Uncle Dan and Aunt Helge, Paul was my closest living relative on the paternal side of the family.

My father had, over the years, arranged a series of increasingly more responsible and thus increasingly more lucrative city jobs for his little brother Daniel. For his part, Uncle Dan, unlike my mother's brothers, had quelled the grumbling about cronyism by proving an adept if not particularly imaginative city administrator. By the time he passed away, back in the late seventies, he'd risen to the rank of city water commissioner and, within the corridors of power, become a force to be reckoned with.

Paul had been born old. Somehow sensing this quirk of fate, his parents had always dressed him accordingly. They'd trussed him up in scaled-down madras sport jackets, knit ties, miniature trench coats, and worst of all, those terrible little porkpie hats that made him look like a midget FBI agent. Paul and I had spent a great deal of our childhoods sequestered together at the mandatory social functions required of public officials. Invariably, before consigning me to the children's section of whatever gala we were attending, my mother's last words were always the same.

"Go find Cousin Paul, and I don't want to hear that you've been picking on him again. Do you understand me, young man?"

I'd reckon how I understood, and I'd mean it. I really would. I'd mean it all the way until I got my first look at his dour little face. From then on, it was all downhill.

They say time heals all wounds. They're wrong.

Predictably, Paul had become a banker. These days he was submerged among the legions of VPs over at Pacific First Federal. His specialty was commercial real estate. He called me two or three times a year, keeping his foot in the door, waiting for the day when he'd be able to broker the property in my trust fund. He hit the line affable. The strain was palpable.

"Leo, Leo. To what, pray tell, do I owe the honor of a call from you on this fine Monday morning?"

"Desperation. I need a favor."

"Now, how did I know that?"

"Must be that prophetic streak of yours."

"Indeed." Paul took the offensive. "Still playing detective?"

"Sure am," I replied, determined to keep cool.

One of the ways in which Paul exacted his passive revenge on me was by also calling several times a year to let me know about insider employment opportunities to which he was privy, in the vain hope that he could induce me to take some steady but servile position, thus confirming his long-held reservations concerning my genetic deficiencies.

Experience had taught me what came next, so I was prepared.

"You know, Leo, I've been meaning to call you. Honestly. I was just thinking of you. I flew down for a seminar in the Bay Area last month. On wills and trusts. Incredibly interesting. They had a speaker from a big firm in New York. A fellow named Wrigley. I forget his first name. From what he told us about recent court decisions, I believe that we might actually be able to break that trust of yours. What do you think of that?"

"Interesting," I replied, as noncommittally as possible.

I resisted the temptation to tell him, as I had so many times before, that I had no desire whatsoever to mess around with my trust fund, that the old man's instincts had been right on the mark, that forty-five was, if anything, an optimistic estimate of when to give somebody like me a substantial amount of folding money.

"We could double, maybe triple the income on the principal."

"You don't say."

"I do. According to Wrigley—"

"Can you check a real estate license for me?" I interrupted.

"Check it for what?"

"Validity, I suppose. And anything else you can find out."

"Like?"

"Where it was issued. Where the holder took the real estate test. When. Other places where she's worked. Stuff like that."

"What's in it for me?"

"I'll let you take me to lunch at your fancy club and run all this trust-busting stuff by me. I promise to sit through the whole thing. How's that?"

"You mean it?"

"I swear."

"You'll wear a tie? They won't serve you at the club without a tie."

"Oh God."

"Everything has its price, Leo."

"Okay. Okay."

"You at home?"

"For another hour or so."

"Be back at ya."

We hung up together. I went back to the paper-work. Twice, I'd persevered through everything Heck had collected in the fancy green bag. Every phone bill, electric bill, and rent receipt. Nothing. Or almost nothing. Nicky Sundstrom had personally signed every credit card receipt. Allison, it seemed, paid strictly cash. Even for the rent. I'd called their building super to see if I could get a line on one of her personal checks. No such luck. The one occasion when Allison had done the actual paying, it had been in cash. The super remembered. Nobody had given him cash in years. Dead end.

First thing this morning, I'd started in on the long-distance numbers. Thirty-five long-distance calls to fourteen different numbers. All Nicky's calls, it turned out. Medical specialists. Marine electronics suppliers. Marge's mother. Not one long-distance call attributable to Allison. The girl was either frugal or careful, or both. Another trail to nowhere.

I sorted the bills and receipts into their various categories. Credit card receipts in one pile, gas receipts in another, a third for the phone, and so on down the line. Then I arranged each pile chrono-logically. I had just finished stuffing each group into labeled business envelopes and was preparing to return them to their home in the bag when the phone rang.

"Waterman Investigations."

"This is just soooo tawdry, Leo. Even for you."

"What's that, Paul?"

"This whole thing with this license. You've embarrassed me again."

"Embarrassed? You're a banker. For most of human history, they stoned people for doing what you do. They called it usury, tied them to stakes, and pitched rocks at them. Nobody can embarrass a banker."

"Hardy-har-har."

"So, what's the matter with the license? It's not valid?"

"Oh, it's valid all right."

"Then what's the problem?"

"The problem is that this particular license was issued to one Rosalee Weber, that's Rosalee with two *e*'s but Weber with one *b*, of Lakeside, Washington, on October eleventh, nineteen eighty-eight. She works and has always worked for Shore Properties Inc. of Lakeside, Washington. Your mythical Allison Stark appears nowhere in the state files."

"Thanks Paul, I'll—"

"Uh, uh, uh," he clucked. "There's the matter of our agreement."

"I said I'd do it, and I will."

"When? I want a firm commitment."

"Don't I always keep my word?"

"Only when you used to threaten to punch me."

"See."

"When?"

"How about early next week? Right now I need to follow up on what you just so graciously gave me."

"I'll be in touch," he said ominously.

"I have no doubt. Thanks again."

"Ta ta."

I disconnected and dialed information for eastern Washington.

"What city please?"

"Lakeside. Shore Properties."

"Just a minute, please."

After a brief interval, a disembodied, mechanical voice droned the number. I listened to it twice, just to be certain, hung up, and dialed again.

"Shore Properties." A woman's voice.

"Ah've lost your durn address," I drawled.

"We're located at four-fifteen Front Street. Right across from the Key Bank."

"Thank y'all."

"Is there—"

I replaced the receiver in the receptacle. No sense pressing my luck. Shore Properties existed. It was open for business. I called Marge. I got the machine at home, then tried the office. They patched me through.

"This is Marge."

"It's Leo."

Her relief was audible.

"Thank God. I was afraid it was the hospital. Every time the phone rings, I jump out of my skin."

"Heck's bad?"

"He had another bad night, Leo. His vital signs were bouncing all over the place. They took him back to the ICU."

"Anything I can do?"

"He seemed to settle down a bit early this morning."

"If there's anything I can do—"

"My mother's flying in this afternoon."

"Good."

I heard her sigh again.

"How's it going?" she said.

Her tone was different. The question posed more as a conversational filler rather than from genuine interest.

"You sure you want to hear this now?" I hedged.

"I could use the diversion."

I told her about the real estate career and the bogus license, sticking strictly to the facts, omitting Nancy Davies's intuitions concerning Allison as well as the prickly sensation that kept running down my back whenever I thought about the elusive Miss Stark.

"What do you think, Leo?"

"I'm withholding judgment until I get back from Chelan."

"When will that be?"

"If I hurry, and get real lucky, I can maybe make Lakeside right before things close for the day. That way, maybe I can come back tonight. If I miss it, I'll stay over and do business in the morning."

"I'll be at the hospital every day from lunch on."

"I'll keep in touch."

I called the airport. Horizon flights to Wenatchee at nine, eleven, three, five, and again at nine. Since I was too late to make the eleven, any sense of urgency would be wasted effort. An hour in flight, the time wasted picking up the rental car, and the forty-mile drive from Wenatchee to Lake Chelan. Unless the folks at Shore Properties worked unusually long hours, I wasn't going to make Lakeside before the close of the business day.

I cleaned up, packed an overnight bag, and called Rebecca at work. Wrong again. It seemed she had the day off. I rang the house.

"It's me," I said.

"I tried to catch you last night." Her voice was slow with sleep.

"Hector and I went over to Jazz Alley and caught Benny Carter's second show."

"You dogs. I'll bet he was great."

"Incredible."

"If you had a single shred of decency, you'd take me tonight."

"The Sundstrom thing. I've got to run over to Chelan."

"Lovely. This time of year, that area has a certain lunar charm."

"Doesn't it though."

"'Tis twice the pity, sir. I have tomorrow off."

"Well then, fair lady, why don't you join me on my quest?"

"To Chelan? This time of year? Are you daft?"

"Undoubtedly, but it's part of my charm. How's about it?"

"You wound me, sir. What would you have me tell my sainted mother? That I've decided to spend the night in some rural hostelry with an intermittently employed private dick who—"

"Intermittently employed, but boyishly handsome," I interjected.

"—who, as is his ilk, will almost certainly grope and fondle me in a most unseemly manner."

"Tell her that this time I kinda figured on skipping the groping and fondling part and moving right into the cross-dressing and spanking."

"Deviant."

"You've noticed, eh?"

"Degenerate."

"Flight's at three."

"Pick me up at two."

12

"IS YOUR ORANGE JUICE FRESH-SQUEEZED?"

"Most likely it was at some time or other, honey."

The pink plastic tag read, "Hi, My Name's Wynona. Please Let Me Serve You." Rebecca's question only served to deepen the overlapping pockets and pouches that made up the weathered satchel of Wynona's face. When Duvall stuck her nose back into the menu, Wynona shot out a massive hip, parking the green-and-white receipt book impatiently on the heavily starched half-acre ledge.

"You want the juice, dearie?"

"I'll have wheat toast, dry, and some decaf with two Equals. You do have decaf, don't you?"

Directing her bored gaze my way, Wynona ignored this last query.

"What about you, sport? You want the self-denial special too?"

"No," I said quickly, "I'll have the Paul Bunyan Breakfast."

"Good choice," she said, sending a short glance at

Duvall and then back to me. Returning her pencil behind her ear, Wynona rustled off toward the counter.

"After this, I don't ever want to hear any complaining about the restaurants I choose," Rebecca said.

"I liked the name. 'Ruth's Snack and Yak.' Lyrical, don't you think?"

"I think this place should have an attached angioplasty clinic."

"When in Rome, my dear. Not even the mop is fresh-squeezed in a place like this. Especially not the mop."

Rebecca was not what you'd call a morning person. Under the best of circumstances, she greeted each new day like one of those cute reminders from the dentist, and Lakeside, Washington, at nine o'clock in the morning was several miles east of the best of circumstances. As with my previous attempts at levity, the mop joke elicited little more than a feral sneer.

She brought her water tumbler up for microscopic inspection.

"What clever ploy have you hatched for sweating the info out of the poor unsuspecting rubes over at the real estate agency?" she inquired, absently turning the scratched burgundy tumbler slowly before her eyes.

"I kinda figured I'd march right in and just ask 'em."

"Rife with your usual Florentine complexity."

Rebecca now produced a monogrammed hanky, with which she began to meticulously scour the rim of the glass.

"What if we're not the first people over here asking questions?"

"I think we are."

"How come?"

Hygienically unsatisfied, she set the glass back down without drinking.

"SPD never asked to see her real estate license. I can't see any other way they'd get to here," I said.

"I think you're right."

"Have you been holding out on me?"

Rebecca arched an eyebrow.

"I rather thought I'd given my all."

"Indubitably, my dear, but to the point."

"I asked a few questions Saturday night between autopsies. Bill Bostick was hanging around, looking professionally concerned, hoping to provide the public with information and get his picture taken."

"How is old Peerless these days?" I interrupted.

"Same old same old. The ultimate spin doctor."

"My old man used to say Bostick was a white guy trapped inside the body of an even whiter guy."

This engendered Rebecca's first thin smile of the day.

"According to the photogenic Billy B, the state and the SPD are just going through the motions. As far as they're concerned, it's death by misadventure

—period. Unless and until they see something new that gets their attention, it's going to stay that way."

"Why didn't you tell me on the way over?"

"I was waiting until you cleared your account. Any further charges would have put you over your limit."

Our breakfasts arrived. Between measured bites, Duvall treated me to a running commentary not only on the well-known effects of cholesterol and saturated fats on the pulmonary arteries but on the various scraping and grinding tools used to remove the glutinous buildup thereof. For my part, I made it a point to use the last of the oiled toast to sop up the dregs of my eggs.

It was a little before ten as I guided the rented Taurus through town. Lakeside was strictly a one-story town. Typical western layout. Two one-way streets in opposite directions wound north and south along the south shore of Lake Chelan, making up the ten-block business district. What wasn't real estate offices was either fast food or minimarts. Perpendicular to downtown, a truncated series of side streets headed west into the high desert, randomly losing interest and petering out among the withered sage and juniper. And this was the civilized end of the lake. Fifty-five miles to the northwest, Stehekin was justly famous for being sufficiently remote as to be reachable only by boat.

As promised, Shore Properties was on Front Street, diagonally across from the Key Bank. A red neon sign shone OPEN from the front window of a cedar A-frame. The attached gravel parking lot was empty except for a battered bronze Subaru station wagon.

Nancy Davies's movers could have cleaned this place out in fifteen minutes. The shiplap cedar-paneled walls were decorated haphazardly with out-of-date calendars and yellowed pictures of the lake. Two gray metal desks, one on the left, one on the right as we entered. The one on the left presently was home to a small copy machine, a coffeemaker, a hotplate, and a fair collection of basic foodstuffs. A one-person operation.

Rubbing her hands together, a woman emerged from the back room. About thirty, she was tall enough to gracefully carry the extra twenty pounds and pretty enough for it not to matter. She wore a long denim skirt with a line of silver buttons up one side and a blue-and-yellow plaid blouse held close at the throat by an oversize cameo. Her long, brown hair was pulled straight back, tightened into a pony-tail by four blue retainers spaced evenly along its conspicuous length. She looked up for the first time.

"Oh." She instinctively brought one hand up to her throat. "You startled me. I haven't had many people stop by, particularly not this early in the morning."

"We wanted to get an early start."

"Well, that's sure the only way to get the jump on the summer season around here. Everybody wants to wait till spring, and then they're all bent out of shape when all the choice dates are spoken for. This is sure the smart way to do it. I'm Rosalee Weber. How can I help you folks?"

"I wanted to ask you a few questions, if I may."

A cloud shaded her face.

"About property?"

"Not exactly."

"Who are you with?" she demanded.

"I'm from Seattle," I said.

"From the bank?"

"No. I'm not."

"From the board?"

"I just had a few questions."

"I don't have to answer any more questions." She pinned me with a level gaze. "I've cooperated fully. I've agreed to a payment schedule, and by God I'll live up to it, but I will not, I repeat, I will not be hounded by you people. You go back and tell them that."

"I'm not from the bank or the board or anyone else you know."

She was cautious now.

"Are you here about property?"

"Not exactly, I—"

She waved at me dismissively. "Then I don't have time for you. I don't mean to be impolite, mister, but my dance card is full. I've got more than I can handle already. Anything you're selling, I haven't got the money to buy. So, if you don't mind, let's not waste each other's time, okay?"

She gestured toward the door, then turned her back on me.

"Nice work. You've got her eating out of your hand," Duvall mumbled from behind me. I tried again.

"I wanted to ask you about a former employee."

Inexplicably, I suddenly had her undivided attention.

"Who?"

"Allison Stark."

Her relief was apparent.

"We've never employed anybody by that name."

"You're sure?"

"Positive."

"Perhaps Mr. Weber would—"

"Listen, mister, before you travel too far down that road and make an ass of yourself, Mr. Weber is my father. Okay? This is his business. Has been for twenty-three years. I've worked here full time since I got out of high school. Every year we hire three or four new salespeople to work the busy season. Usually it's four. It's not like they're hard to keep track of. Soon as Labor Day rolls around they're out of town like they were shot out of a cannon, never to be seen again. In case you haven't noticed, Lakeside isn't exactly Gotham City this time of year. And I'm telling you we've never had any Alice."

"Allison."

"No Alice, no Allison. No anything. Okay? So, if you'll excuse me, I'm a little backed up here at the moment."

She sat down heavily at her desk and began leafing through her oversize Rolodex. I slipped a folded-up copy of Carl's composite photograph out of my coat pocket, smoothed it out on the edge of the empty desk, and crossed the room.

"Could I just get you to take a look at this picture for me?"

Glowering at me. "And then you'll go away?"

"I swear."

She snatched the picture from my hand.

"I don't have time for this foolishness, mister."

She cast an exasperated glance at the paper in her hand. In an instant, she went black and white. She slid back into her chair as if pressed back by a giant hand; her button eyes remained glued to the picture as it slowly waffled its way to the floor. From deep within, a single contraction convulsed her body, snapping her like a whip. Throwing both hands over her mouth, she stumbled pell-mell toward the rear of the building, darting into the lavatory, slamming the door behind her. I opened my mouth and then closed it again. Rebecca was not so kind.

"She's putty in your hands now."

Neither the door nor the distance was sufficient to muffle the anguished sounds of her violent retching. The toilet flushed a couple of times, but the heaving ground on unabated, coming in waves for what seemed an eternity. I started back. Rebecca stopped me with a small wag of her head and went herself.

Tapping lightly on the door, she stepped partially inside.

"I'm a doctor," I heard her whisper before she softly pulled the door closed behind her.

The toilet flushed again. The gagging went on— straining, dry and empty-throated now, then ceased, replaced by muffled talk and tears.

Rebecca reappeared briefly, stepped back into the far room, gathered a handful of paper napkins, and reentered the bathroom. More running water and talk. I retrieved the offending picture from the floor and pocketed it.

They came out together. Rosalee Weber was the color of oatmeal, her eyes unfocused, the front of her blouse soaked and dark. A wayward line of brown vomit clung stubbornly to the hem of her skirt. The smell of vegetable soup trailed in her wake. Guiding her with a hand on the shoulder, Rebecca eased her to her chair.

Seated, Rosalee used both hands to wipe imaginary hair from her face and then gave a final snuffle.

"Please excuse me," she said to the room. "Nothing like that's ever happened to me before. I don't know what came over me."

I kept quiet. No matter. She read my mind.

"It was that face. I never expected to see that face again."

She slid out the bottom drawer of the desk, took out a box of tissues, and blew her nose.

"What did you call her?" she asked.

"Allison Stark."

"She called herself Rachel Gandy when she was here."

"When was that?"

"This past summer . . . back before . . . before . . ."

She began to sniffle again and then, in stages, worked into a full cry; the cries turned to wails; her heavy body pulsed to the sobs as if some inner wall of collected reserve had suddenly crumbled. I fidgeted and waited.

"I'm so sorry," she said, scraping herself back together. "I thought I was past all of this. I thought I'd put it behind me. I've worked so hard to put this all back together. Sorry." She dabbed her swollen eyes.

"No problem," I said.

"Nobody would listen to me."

"I'll listen, if you feel up to telling me about it."

Nodding, Rosalee Weber inhaled deeply and then began her story as if she were going to have to tell it in a single breath.

"She showed up right around the first week of April, just about when we begin to take on new people for the summer season. She'd met my dad over in Seattle. They'd been at a survivors' support group together. You know, for people who've recently lost loved ones. So they could talk and support each other." I nodded, understanding. "My mom had passed away last January. I mean, it wasn't a surprise or anything, she'd been real sick for quite a while, but Dad was devastated. He—" she snuffled once, caught herself and continued. "Anyway . . . he'd been going over twice a month for these support groups that his doctor recommended. That's where they met. Rachel lost her husband in a car accident a couple of months before, and you know they'd got to talking and Dad told her how we hired in the spring and she told him how she was in the business before she got married, so he ended up offering her a job. And then in early April, there she was on the front steps."

"Where did this support group meet?"

"Providence Hospital, over in Seattle."

"What then? You hired her?"

"I thought she was a bit uptown for around here, but Dad really liked her—her being from Wisconsin and all." She read my face. "Dad's family was originally from the Madison area. We've still got people back there on his side of the family—aunts and uncles."

"Can you remember anything else about her Wisconsin background?"

She shook her head. "That was between Rachel

and Dad. Wisconsin was way before my time. We went back a couple of times for the holidays when I was little, but I don't know anything about it."

"So she signed on—" I led her back.

"Right around the beginning of April. You could see right away that she knew what she was doing." She shrugged heavily. "She turned out to be one of the best salespeople I'd ever seen. Maybe a bit too strong at the close for my taste, you know, pushy, but nobody complained so I—we let it go."

Rosalee finally came up for air.

"Anyway, by the time Lake Vista came around, she was so far ahead of all the other new hires that we just naturally put her to work on that."

"What's Lake Vista?"

"That's the new condo project over on the east side of the lake. Ninety-six custom units. It was Dad's baby. He got in on the ground floor. He put a lot of his own money into it. Dad helped line up the other investors and everything. Vista was going to be his big one. We had a sales exclusive on it."

Rebecca's eyes told me that she'd also noticed the change in tense.

"And Rachel was selling the condo units?"

"Between her and Dad they sold fifty-three of the units, which was just incredible in what everybody said was a flat market."

Her eyes welled again, but she surprised me and carried on.

"Dad was just aglow. It was like he'd been reborn.

I hadn't seen him that happy since before Mom got sick. The Lake Vista project was the best medicine in the world for him. It gave him hope again. He kept saying how this was the one that was going to lift us up to a whole 'nother level. No more small-time for us, all of that kind of stuff. How he already had a start on an even bigger project. How he was going international."

She was winding down, beginning to sniffle again. I poked her.

"And then?"

"And then . . . it was a Monday. Right about at the end of August. Things were beginning to wind down for the season. Dad went over to Seattle for a stock-holders' meeting. To tell them the good news about how far ahead of projections we were and all that. He was like a little kid. Bought himself a brand-new suit and everything."

She cleared her nose again, hurrying now.

"A couple of hours after he left . . . she . . . Rachel . . . she comes in and tells me that she got a call, you know, with a job offer and what with the season winding down how she's gonna take it, but that she's gotta get there instantly if she wants the job. She asks me to pay her off so she can leave right away."

"And?"

"Well, what was I going to do? She knew I could sign checks. I'd paid her before. It was the end of the season. I paid her off. I sat right here and watched while she took it across the street and cashed it. Thirty-eight hundred bucks and change. She came out, got on the airport shuttle, and I never saw her again until you—"

She waved a hand in my direction. This time, she prodded herself.

"Anyway, Dad came back the next morning just walking on air. He was everybody's hero. Then . . . you know, when he got finished with his story, I just sort of casually mentioned that Rachel had moved on."

She shuddered at the memory.

"It wasn't like it should have been such a big surprise or anything. Rick and Loretta had already given notice. She wasn't the first associate to just up and leave. I shouldn't have . . . he . . ."

She looked up at me as if for a dispensation. I had none to offer.

"I'll never forget the look on his face—the pain and hurt. He screamed at me. Swore. He never swore. Called me a bitch. Said I was a goddamn liar. In my whole life he'd never talked to me like that before. For a second I actually thought he was going to attack me, but he just ran out the door, across the street to the bank."

She found a hidden cache of strength. Her tone got stronger.

"He looked twenty years older when he came back from the bank. Never said another word to me. Just picked up his briefcase and headed out the door. I never—" Another tissue. "He . . . to make a long story short . . . the Lake Vista escrow account was empty."

"How much?"

"Four hundred ninety thousand in down payments and deposits."

"You called the cops." I made it a statement.

"My dad signed the transfer. He was an officer of the corporation. It was his responsibility. And there was the note."

I didn't want to ask, but did anyway.

"Note?"

"He left a note. He said it was all his fault. That he took full responsibility. That he'd made a bad investment and lost all the money. Didn't mention anybody else. He was that way. He wouldn't blame anybody else for his problems. He just took all the blame on himself."

"Handwritten?"

She nodded, twisting a wadded-up tissue in her big hands.

"He took eighty Valium."

"I'm sorry." It sounded inane, but I said it anyway.

"It was probably better that way," she said. "At least it was over for him. He didn't have to be around when they auctioned off the house, the cars, Mom's furniture, everything. I don't think he could have stood that. It would have broken him. They even sold his and Mom's clothes to a secondhand store in Wenatchee."

"And Rachel Gandy?"

Rosalee Weber sat up now, placing both hands flat on the desktop.

"That was later. After the auction and the suits and the settlements, when things started to slow down a little and I had time to think about things, that's when I got back to wondering about Rachel Gandy. About the timing of it all. How Dad had looked that day when he found she'd gone. How he'd run right over to the bank. How happy he'd been up until that morning. How terribly alone he'd been since my mother passed away. Then I started to think about how much time he and Rachel had spent together out there at Vista in the models. Day and night for months, just the two of them out there together. It started to add up. That's when I started to wonder. She had him to herself. He was so lonely. It would have been so easy for a woman like her. He was country, just a small-time, small-town guy, you know, it would have been no problem for her. So I started asking some questions."

"And?"

"Most people around here wouldn't even talk to me. Lots of folks around here had money in the project. Far as they were concerned, if I wasn't going to have the decency to do what Dad did, I should have at least left town. I kept at it though, and eventually I ran down a couple of the original construction guys, electricians, who said that on a couple of nights, back in late July, when they'd stayed late to finish up projects, the model was lit up long after closing time, that it sounded like there were people in there. Music, laughing. Sounded like a party. The second time it happened, they knocked to see what was going on. They thought maybe it was kids, you know. According to them, my Dad answered the door, and she, Rachel, was in there with him."

"Interesting," I offered.

"And her file. She took it with her. After I talked to the electricians I went back to see if, you know, maybe I couldn't get a line on her. Gone. Her license. References. The whole thing. Gone."

"Did you run your suspicions by the local authorities?"

"They didn't want any part of the idea. Still don't. They've got their villain. Twenty-odd years of doing business in this town, and now they spit on him. Took his picture off the wall over at the Rotary. You can still see the light spot on the wall where it hung for all those years."

For the first time, anger began to push sadness aside.

"I'm still a hundred and seventy thousand in the hole, but I'm going to pay off every last dime of it if it takes the rest of my life. And when I do, I'm going right back in there and hang his picture up where it was. Then I'm gonna put this town in my rearview mirror once and for all."

"I believe you will," I said earnestly.

"Do you know where she is?" she demanded.

"No. I don't even know who she is."

"Where did you get that picture?"

I gave her the abridged version. The missing aunt story. No sense raising any false hopes in her. As she'd said, her plate was already full. When I'd finished, she was quiet for a long time. Rebecca shuffled uncomfortably behind me.

"Then it's finished. Good. And I don't mean good she's dead. I won't allow myself that sort of bitterness. I wasn't raised that way. Dad wouldn't want that. I mean good, I can stop wondering, thinking that maybe this is all just some sort of bad misunderstanding. Part of me kept thinking that maybe she was going to walk back in the door with the money or something. Isn't that stupid?"

"It's not stupid. I'd say it was a pretty natural reaction to all you've been through."

Self-conscious now, she gazed down along the length of herself.

"What a mess I am. I'd better change my clothes. I keep some clothes . . ." She gestured awkwardly toward the rear of the building.

I put a business card on her desk.

"In case you think of anything else. Or maybe just want to talk or something."

She nodded absently.

"Thanks," I said.

She started back. Rebecca and I found our way out.

"Why didn't you tell her what's going on?"

"Because I don't know what's going on."

"But you've got a feeling, don't you? I can tell."

"What I'm thinking is too ugly for words."

"She lives back there, you know," Rebecca said, as I accelerated out onto the two-lane highway. "There's a little Hide-a-Bed. Her clothes are all in back there hanging on a rope. And all her shoes."

We passed the forty miles back to the airport in silence.

13

I REMEMBER NEXT TO NOTHING OF THE PLANE RIDE from Wenatchee to Seattle and even less about the drive home from the airport. Later that evening is mostly blank too, as if the proximity to the recorded message had so tainted the memories and sensations as to make recall impossible.

A flat, professional voice I didn't recognize. No name, no number.

"Mr. Waterman, I have been requested to inform you that Henry Sundstrom died at nine seventeen last evening. Services for Mr. Sundstrom will be held at eleven o'clock A.M. on Wednesday, November eighth, at Gethsemane Lutheran Church, nine hundred eleven Stewart Street in Seattle. In lieu of flowers, the family requests remembrances to the American Cancer Society." Click. Hiss.

I poked the play button hard. Listened again. Same message. Then again. Tomorrow. Eleven in the morning. Oh, goddamn. I pounded the offending phone with the flat of my hand, sending the receiver down toward the floor, where it bounced twice, then danced just above the surface, spinning on its spiral spring. Feeling foolish, I first bent to retrieve it, then, as rising blood burned the tips of my ears, instead used my forearm to sweep the rest of the phone from the table; a muted tinkle announced its arrival on the carpet where it lay motionless, its tightly curled neck now arched like a fossil bird.

I paced the apartment, breathing hard, the air in my lungs suddenly cold. As I passed each window, I pushed back the curtains and raised the blinds. Spears of sunlight herded the newly airborne dust into illuminated schools of swimming crystals. After several complete circuits, the apartment was awash with the kind of slanted late-afternoon light so favored by Dutch painters, but Heck was still dead.

These days, every death sets me adrift. Even the smallest change in my delicate web of connectedness is enough to loosen my slim purchase, to set me bobbing about like airborne dust. The phone began to make insistent noises. I blocked it out. Surrounded by a crystalline moat of floating slurry, I stood in the single remaining shadow at the center of the apartment and wept.

Much later, when the receding light had allowed the dust to settle, I resurrected the phone and dialed. Marge's home number got me the maid. Mrs. Sundstrom was unavailable at this time. When charm, reason, and guilt failed to elicit further data,

I called the Sea Sundstrom offices. Same deal. Mrs. Sundstrom was not available. No, they did not know where she could be reached. No, they had no idea when she would become available. Click.

I tried McColl's office. Mr. McColl was away from his desk at this time.

"That's kinda vague, don't you think?"

"Excuse me, sir?"

"That phrase—'away from his desk,'" I said testily. "There's a pretty wide range of possibilities in 'away from his desk.' People serving lengthy prison terms could be said to be 'away from their desks.' Technically speaking, the dead are 'away from their desks.'"

"They are indeed sir," she said evenly.

I was supposed to go away now. I wasn't in the mood. A lengthy silence ensued.

"Well?" I said finally.

"Well what, sir?"

"Well, where is old Howie?"

Rather than lightening the atmosphere as I'd hoped, my cavalier use of McColl's first name had precisely the opposite effect.

"I'm sorry, sir. I only know where *Mr.*"—heavy emphasis on the Mr.—"McColl is not."

"Which is . . ." I countered.

"At his desk," we said in unison.

Another silence.

"Howzabout a hint, then?" I suggested.

"A hint as to what, sir?"

"Well, maybe a hint as to approximately which end of the 'away from his desk' spectrum Mr. McColl might be closest to. I mean like has he left the country or something, or is he just off takin' a leak?" Click. Hummmmm. . . .

GETHSEMANE LUTHERAN CHURCH WAS PACKED to the rafters. They had come, nearly seven hundred strong, to pay their respects, packing both the surrounding parking lots and the pews. Arriving a half hour early had gotten me a seat in the third row of the balcony. I could make out the families up front. Marge was hunched between her parents on the inside and the ever-attentive H. R. McColl, who occupied the aisle seat in the front row. Her extended family of aunts, uncles, brothers, sisters, nieces, and nephews filled the better part of six rows on the left-hand side of the church. On the right, about an equal number of solid Sundstroms strained the seams on seldom-worn suits. I recognized few others. Martin Henry and Artie Klugeman from the old days at the marina sat together center left. A cadre of minor political figures were hard up behind the Sundstrom contingent. The rest were strangers.

I absently crushed and twisted the small pink program that I'd been handed on the way in. Thanks from the families. Address for remembrances. According to the wishes of the deceased, no funeral home viewing. No graveside service. Closed casket. Cremation. Coffee reception to follow. Lutherans always had a coffee reception.

What Lutherans were was *not* Catholic. Where the Catholics poked presumptive spires toward heaven, the Lutherans built square brick earthbound sanctuaries. No miracles, no saints, no gothic arches. Instead, a rock-solid house of worship. A wine-red carpet bisecting twenty-five double rows of light oak pews leading to an unassuming altar covered today with black vestments. The light poured in, not refracted through stained glass but rational and clear, through high sets of twelve-panes fifty feet tall. I reluctantly moved my gaze to the front, where the draped coffin rested slightly to the right of the simple altar. A single blaring note from the massive pipe organ signaled the start of the service.

"EXCUSE ME." AN ELDERLY WOMAN STOOD at my left shoulder.

I stared dumbfounded at the rest of the people in my pew, who now inexplicably wanted out. The church was filled with whispers and moving bodies. I focused out over the church. The front rows had emptied. A solid line of mourners shuffled toward the back of the church. The service was over.

"I'm sorry," I said, quickly stepping out into the aisle. They filed past me.

Downstairs, the crowd seemed to be evenly

divided between those turning left for the reception and those heading out onto Ninth Avenue. I waffled.

"That you, Leo?"

He was small, indigenous, and leathery, with thick gray hair and a wide, expressive mouth that broke into a smile as I turned. He read my confusion.

"It's me, Rudy," he said.

"Jesus," I stammered.

"Naw, just old Rudy." The grin got wider.

I stuck out a hand. Rudy filled it with a fist. His roughened fingers were contorted nearly into a ball. I held on.

"Hands are about gone. Arthur-itis, big time," he said. "Too damn many years pullin' at them froze-over nets."

Struggling to recover, I released his hand.

"You look great," I said with conviction.

"Us old Aleuts, we just dry out like racked salmon."

"You hear from Angel?" I asked.

"Moved up to Sitka to be near the grandkids back around eighty, eighty-one, someplace in there. Went overboard crabbin' in eighty-five."

"Oh," I managed.

"It's how he woulda wanted it."

I nodded unwilling agreement.

"You ain't goin' in to pay your respects?"

"I was . . . I thought maybe . . . I've been . . ." I hedged.

"She done good by him, Leo."

When I didn't respond, he went on.

"She got him in off the water, Leo. You stay out there on the water you end up like me and Angel. You either go down or you end up so stove up you ain't good for no kind of work. She got him off the water. Made him into a big man."

"He was already a big man."

"You know what I mean."

I nodded again.

"You going in?" I asked.

"I'll see her later."

"Oh?"

"I work for them. Her now, I guess. You know, in the warehouse . . . Foreman. Heck . . . he was . . . you know how he was."

"I know."

"I don't know how he found out about my hands, but he did. Tracked me all the way to my sister's place down in Ukiah. Wouldn't leave. Wouldn't take no for an answer. I been there damn near nine years now. You go in and pay your respects. She's had a lot of sorrow, what with the boy and all. She'll be glad to see you."

"I'll go," I promised.

"Gotta run. Gotta loada fish to get out there. Damn near everybody's down here today. Fish don' wait. Nobody's mindin' the store. Nice to see ya again, Leo."

"Nice to see you too, Rudy."

We stared at each other for a long moment before he turned and walked out the door with that crabbed sideways waddle that old fishermen never lose.

I headed in to pay my respects. I didn't get far.

Four strides into the reception room, my elbow was pinned by H. R. McColl.

"Ah, Mr. Waterman," he said. "I was hoping I'd see you here. Beautiful service, didn't you think?"

"Beautiful," I lied.

He applied pressure to my elbow in an attempt to turn me back toward the door. I held my ground. He tightened his grip.

"My office will be handling Mr. Sundstrom's affairs," he said, levering his gray eyes at me. "If you'll submit time and expenses to date, I'll instruct payable to cut you a check immediately." He leaned in closer. "And, of course, a handsome bonus for your stalwart efforts."

He tried to turn me again. I looked down at his hand on my sleeve.

"Please take your hand off my arm," I said.

McColl checked the room around us without removing his hand.

"Let's not have a scene, shall we, Mr. Waterman?"

"The only scene we're going to have, McColl, is the scene where I beat the shit out of you right in front of all these people if you don't take your hand off me."

H. R. McColl released my elbow and stepped back one pace.

"Raymond," he said quietly.

Raymond stepped forward. Nice dark blue three-piece suit. Shaved head, glistening like a giant black egg. Probably forty-five by now. Six-two, probably two-forty in what passed for his prime, no more than a couple of biscuits from three hundred now.

"Show this gentleman to his car, Raymond. Firmly but quietly, please."

"Hi, Ray," I said.

"Leo," he replied.

For once, Mr. McColl was taken aback.

"You two are acquainted?" He directed the question at Ray.

"We're acquainted," Ray confirmed.

Ray Townsend had had a short, flamboyant career back in seventy-seven as a third-string offensive guard on the original, expansion Seahawks. An eleventh-round choice out of North Texas State, he'd demonstrated so little athletic acumen and so much heart that he'd become the guy the fans chanted to see when the score had gotten out of hand. An entire generation of Seattle football fans had forever etched in their brains the image of Ray Townsend the wedge-breaker, obscene in tight football pants, limbering downfield after a kickoff. Images of the fearsome plastic-shattering licks he'd absorbed, but most of all of the strange, good-natured determination that dragged him immediately back to his feet and propelled him inevitably forward, toward the next crushing blow. Coach Jack

Patera had been every bit as unmoved by Ray's ability to absorb punishment as he had been by the incessant chanting. Ray hadn't quite lasted that first year.

Unable to generate any interest whatsoever in his services as a football player, Ray used his local notoriety to start his own private security firm. Initially, the business had taken off. Townsend Security's yellow windbreakers had been everywhere. Once in a while I'd see Ray himself on the tube, opening the car door for some visiting rock star or waiting in the wings for some long-winded politician. A couple of years later, when the whole local economy sank in the last big Boeing bust, Townsend Security went down with it. To his credit, Ray had done whatever it took to support a wife and four kids. When I'd first met him, he was working as a collector for a small-time Portuguese loan shark named Gregorio Enos.

"We went to thug school together," I said. "Thug U."

"Remove him," McColl sighed.

Ray shot me an exploratory gaze. I cut him no slack. He turned to McColl.

"Won't be quiet if he don't wanna go, Mr. McColl."

"And I definitely don't wanna go," I added quickly.

"Remove him now, Raymond," McColl fumed.

"Excuse me, Mr. McColl, but you pay me to

prevent the kinda ugly scene we're gonna have here if me and Leo get to rollin' and scufflin' about the floor. Leo here ain't some wino or college boy, sir. He's good. Not near as good as he thinks"—he pinned me with his most serious stare—"but he sure as hell isn't gonna go quiet."

"If you're not up to the task, Raymond, I know of a number of people who are."

"That's entirely up to you, sir. I may get him out. I may not. Either way, they ain't gonna be a whole piece of furniture in this place by the time we get done. I'm not sure that's what you got in mind, Mr. McColl. But"—spreading his feet for balance, he rolled his thick shoulders—"you say the word and we'll get down to it."

Ray now treated me to his most baleful and terrifying scowl.

McColl turned and checked the crowd while he thought it over.

"Perhaps you're right, Raymond," he said finally. "You and I shall have to discuss this at length at some later time." It was McColl's chance to glare.

Ray reluctantly returned his gaze. McColl dismissed him with a wave.

"Go see to Mrs. Van Curen, Raymond; it appears she could use some assistance in getting to her car."

With a nearly imperceptible bob of the head, Ray Townsend waded off through the crowd. McColl regrouped. Without turning back my way, he said, "Surely, Mr. Waterman, you can't expect to continue this little charade of an investigation, now that Mr. Sundstrom is gone. I assure you that as Mrs. Sundstrom's close confidant I shall advise most strongly that we terminate this little sham of yours immediately. It's all rather moot now, don't you suppose?"

"Not to me it's not. Nothing's ever been less moot."

Ray Townsend came by leading an aged hawk-faced woman nearly buried beneath a mound of dead mink, smiling earnestly as he steered her out onto the street.

"You'll have to excuse me while I pay my respects," I said.

Marge saw me coming. She disengaged from a small group of well-wishers that included her parents and pulled me over to an unoccupied area beyond the refreshments. She looked tired and drawn, her eyes slightly unfocused as if sedated.

"Leo. I was afraid you hadn't gotten the message. I'm so glad you could come. Heck would have wanted you here."

"I'm sorry," was all I could think to say.

"He—" she started.

"Please," I said.

We embraced as if among the assembled throng only the two of us fully understood the magnitude of the collective loss.

"I'm going to Wisconsin later this afternoon," I said into her shoulder.

Her hug tightened. Finally, she released me,

looking uncomprehendingly into my eyes as if I had suddenly been speaking in tongues.

"That all seems so . . . I don't . . . now."

"I understand," I said. "I'll call you when I get back."

"Oh, Leo—" Her eyes filled. "I don't know if I want to."

I took both of her gloved hands in mine.

"I want to," I cut her off.

Her eyes gave no indication that she'd heard me. Her mother was suddenly at her side, whispering in her ear. When Marge turned her dull eyes that way, I slipped off through the crowd.

Ray Townsend was puffing on a butt in the parking lot around the corner from the front door.

"Hope I didn't spoil your gig, Ray."

"Lotsa other gigs, Leo. Don' sweat. Son of a bitch is a pain in the ass anyway. I let him, he have me standin' out on his lawn holdin' a lantern when I ain't drivin'."

He flicked the butt to the pavement and retrieved his handkerchief from the hood of the gleaming black Acura Legend he'd been leaning against. He put a massive hand on my shoulder, leaning in close. His breath held the asphalt-licorice odor of Sen Sen.

"You remember that time you and me duked it out down by where the Kingdome is now? By the old Burlington tracks there, when I was workin' for that fuck Enos?"

"It's not something I could forget, Ray; I still have to shave around some of those places."

"I'da kicked your ass, you hadn't kept hittin' me with that pipe."

"It was a bolt," I corrected. "A real big bolt."

"Heh, heh, heh," Ray said, unconsciously rubbing his cheek. "Can't recall, though, for the life of me, Leo, just what in hell it was we was fightin' over."

"I don't think it was over anything much at all, Ray. I was young, just starting out, mostly serving process. As I recall, old Enos was still holding some grudge against my old man. About the time he figured out who this punk was that had just slapped a subpoena into his palm, he suddenly decided that the sins of the fathers ought to be visited upon the children, so he sicced your big ass on me."

"That surely was a wang dang doodle."

"I mostly remember them yarding us both up to Providence afterward, us laying side by side in emergency, and how I wasn't up and around for a couple of weeks."

He chuckled again. "I 'member, Leo, how when I got home and looked in the mirror, my head was all swollen up. They had my face all stitched up with this maroon thread. I looked like a big black baseball."

"Those were good days, Ray."

"They surely were, Leo. They surely were."

Ray and I were beginning to sound like Sam and Ralph, the sheepdog and the coyote in those old

Warner Brothers cartoons. Just a couple of good old boys punching in for another day of madcap mayhem. It was definitely time to go.

"Later, Ray."

I shook his hand again, ducked between cars, and started across Ninth Avenue.

"Later, Leo," he growled to my back.

14

CARL HAD FIRST OBJECTED ON BOTANICAL GROUNDS.

"It's too fuckin' green."

"Chlorophyll is the essence of life on the planet," I assured him. Scientifically thwarted, he'd taken a more cultural approach.

"Oh, yeah. Me and Sam Spade a thousand miles from home, surrounded by about a million cheeseheads. Be still my heart."

"They won't harm you. They'll all be out pruning their shrubs." Next, he'd tried the old business excuse.

"I *am* in business, ya know, Leo. What am I supposed to tell my customers—Come back in a week or so, I'm goin' to Wisconsin to get my bratwurst polished?"

"Mark can handle things while you're gone."

"Fuckin' kid will steal me blind."

From the far end of the counter, Mark piped up. "I already steal you blind."

I knew I had him when he then slipped totally out of character and went trolling for sympathy.

"Right, so I'm gonna roll through a couple of major airports so the citizens can gawk at the freak. Right? Sit in my little chair on the plane, in the aisle"—he jabbed a thumb back over his shoulder—"in the back, right next to the shifter, listening to the white-knucklers tooting 'Stairway to Heaven' on their sphincters."

"It's a short flight," I countered.

"And what then? You gonna load me and the chair on the roof of some rental car, tool us over to the university?"

"There's a company in Madison that'll rent us the same kind of van you've got. Lift, hand controls, the whole ball of wax. You can drive."

This was my trump card. Carl enjoyed nothing more than terrorizing the citizenry in his specially equipped Chevy van, ignoring any and all traffic laws, parking in places that would make a UPS driver blush. I was banking that the prospect of having an entire new state at his mercy would be more than he could resist.

"No way. It'll be a piece of shit. Cheap. No way they'll have a—"

Mark jumped in. "Exactly the same equipment you've got, Carl. I talked to them myself this morning. I explained that you were a discerning consumer."

"A discerning consumer, huh. Those were your exact words?"

"Actually, pain in the ass were my exact words."

By 9:00 A.M. Thursday morning, Carl and I had found our way to West Lake Street in Madison, Wisconsin. We watched as the blue-clad janitor slid back the bolts on the smoked-glass front doors of Alumni House. An insistent, swirling breeze moved my hair about. Carl fidgeted with the buttons on his chair, bumping over the uneven stones, rolling three feet forward then three feet back.

"This is a hell of a reach, Leo."

"I know."

"I can't believe this is all you got. Most of all I can't believe I let you talk me into this crap."

"It's all I've got."

"It's pathetic."

"I know," I repeated. "In my business, this is what I do when I don't have anything. I just go around turning over rocks, waiting to see what crawls out."

"This isn't a rock; it's a crock."

"She's consistently used Madison and the university as her background story. She even managed to bounce it by a guy who knew a lot about the place. It's the best thing I've got."

"It ain't much," he said again. "Let's go." Flicking away a butt, he suddenly rocketed forward. Most motorized wheelchairs are intended to putt along at a top speed of three or four miles per hour, a demure pace designed to fit nicely into normal foot-traffic flow. Never having been one to go with the flow, Carl Cradduck had commissioned modifications that would have turned many a NASCAR driver green with envy. His chair in high gear was considerably faster than any number of inexpensive foreign cars. A frightening top speed, combined with Carl's utter disregard for his fellow man, invariably turned crowded sidewalks and airport concourses into human bowling alleys. I tried to stay out of the way and pretend we weren't together.

Alumni House was a surprise. From the lush carpets to the Philippine mahogany paneling and hunt club prints, no expense had been spared in an all-out effort to distance this island of good taste from the general squalor of an urban university campus. The result was a kind of no surprise, unevolved English manor-house elegance. Created intact, climate controlled, simultaneously purified and rarefied.

"How may I help you, sir?" The name plate read Pamela Shincke. She had about her an air of competence. Firmly in charge of the reception area. The guardian of the gate. The keeper of the flame. I sensed we were in good hands.

Her appearance provided a much-needed contrast to the rest of the furnishings. She was sporting a smile and one of those modern MTV hairdos with those mysterious radar bangs that I still find it difficult to believe any woman would inflict upon herself intentionally. Maybe after three or four days of unshowered salt and sailing, or after a death-defying ride on the back of a motorcycle, but certainly not purposely.

"We'd like to see copies of the *Badger Annual* from

nineteen-seventy-eight through nineteen-ninety-two," I said.

Since we had no knowledge of the girl's actual age, we'd decided to operate from the premise that, right now, she was somewhere between twenty-five and thirty-five. Allowing for error, we had decided to cover a fourteen-year span—1978 through 1992.

Pamela was eager to help.

"Certainly, sir," she beamed. "Are you gentlemen by any chance Badgers yourselves?"

"Badgers," Carl growled, "we don't need no stinking Badgers."

"Oh," Pamela said. "I get it. The movie with Humphrey Bogart. How cute."

"The annuals?" I said

"Which campus?"

Carl remained calm.

"How many are there?" he asked.

"Two-year or four-year?" she asked.

Carl flicked me a short, murderous glance.

"Four-year," I said quickly.

"Twelve in addition to the main campus here in Madison."

"I see," said Carl through his teeth. "And I take it that each campus issues its own annual?"

"Yes, sir. Altogether, the University of Wisconsin has nearly a hundred fifty thousand students. Just imagine how big just one yearbook for all the campuses would be."

I tried not to.

She picked a brochure from the counter, leaned over, and handed it to Carl. "This might help you, sir. It lists all the campuses, the number of students on each campus, and all that kind of stuff."

"Thank you so much." Carl beamed back. "My colleague and I had better discuss this before we proceed."

"Would you like to use our reading room?"

She gestured toward a large conference room on our immediate left.

"You're too kind," Carl said.

She came out from behind the counter.

"It's my pleasure. Things have been kind of slow around here lately. To tell you the truth, it's nice to have somebody in here. Homecoming's not for another month. That's when we get real busy around here. That and graduation time."

She led us into a large room, decorated in the same dark woods and thick fabrics as the reception area but considerably lightened by a set of leaded windows running along the top of the three exterior walls.

"I was just going to make coffee. Can I get you gentlemen a cup?"

"Please," I said.

"Many thanks," answered Carl.

"If there's anything else you need, just let me know."

"Thanks again," Carl said.

She closed the door behind her. Carl watched her go and then motored up to the edge of the table.

"You suppose she's that nice all the time?" he asked.

"I think it's a distinct possibility."

"Scary."

"Yeah," I agreed.

Carl placed both palms on the table.

"Let's see here, Einstein. Thirteen campuses times twelve years. What's that, about a hundred and a half?"

"Something like that."

"So, you wanna call and get us a flight out of this shit burg or should I do it?"

As a professional investigator, I sensed that Carl was losing his enthusiasm for the task.

"It all points here to Madison," I said quickly. "The address she had given for her missing aunt was in Madison. The stories of her childhood and college days all supposedly took place in Madison. It's gotta be Madison."

"Yeah, but what if, Leo? What if? What if we dragged our moldy asses all the way out here into cheesehead bumfuck and it turns out that the trim went to"—he fingered the list of campuses in his hand—"the Parkside campus or Riverfalls, or maybe even Oshkosh by fucking gosh? What then, huh?"

"No way we can go through that many annuals," I conceded.

"No shit, Sherlock."

"We'll have to try to cover as many bases as possible."

"This is sick."

I persisted. "How many total students did she say they had?"

"Just under a hundred-fifty thousand."

Carl smoothed the list on the table and pulled a pen from his pocket. I leaned over his shoulder.

"If we just do these . . ." He circled Madison, Milwaukee, Eau Claire, and Oshkosh.

"Whitewater too," I added. "It's the only other campus with more than ten thousand students."

"Okay, Madison, Milwaukee, Eau Claire, Osh fucking Kosh, and Whitewater. How many total bodies is that?"

We both mumbled slightly as we totaled the columns.

"Almost two-thirds of them," Carl said.

"Just over ninety-five thousand on those five campuses."

"Even then, that's sixty annuals," he groused.

"We better get started."

Carl folded his arms over his thin chest. No comment. No movement. Just the thousand-yard stare. When I returned ten minutes later with my arms full of annuals, he still hadn't moved.

"I figured we'd do all the Madisons first," I said.

Carl uncrossed his arms, drumming now with his

fingers on the control panel of his chair. "You fuck," he said.

I ignored him. "Should we start at the ends and work toward the middle or start in the middle and work toward the ends?"

No reply. More drumming.

"Okay," I said. "I'll do from seventy-eight through eighty-four. You do eighty-five through ninety-two."

I began to sort the bright red pile.

"Every other year," Carl said.

"Excuse me?"

"Every other fucking year. You do the odds. I'll do the evens. It'll keep us from seeing the same faces too often." He added another "You fuck" as an afterthought.

Scanning pictures looking for a specific face turned out to be harder than I'd imagined. It took me the better part of an hour to find my rhythm. Going too slow slipped me into an inattentive fog where, after about a half hour, I wouldn't have recognized my mother. I had to completely redo the senior section of 1989 when I'd started off too slow. Too fast and I didn't have time to mentally allow for either the ravages of time or the vagaries of fashion. It was trial and error. At my workable speed, it took me about two hours to work my way through my first yearbook. Even then, there was no way to be certain that I hadn't mentally drifted off and missed her somewhere along the way.

By eleven-thirty, Carl hadn't uttered a syllable. He hadn't even gone out for a smoke. Other than to turn pages he hadn't moved. Pamela had appeared at regular intervals to freshen our coffee. I decided not to mention lunch. I was afraid that if he ever got out of the room I'd never get him back in, so I shut up and kept working. Two-thirds of the way through the 1985 edition, I came across a possible.

"Maybe," I said, sliding the book across to Carl.

"Which one?"

"The one with the drink in her hand."

"This one?" He tapped the face.

"Uh huh."

Carl studied the image for no more than five seconds.

"Jesus, Leo. I hope to God you've been doing a shitload better than this over there."

"That's a no, then."

"Look at the hand on this honey."

He pivoted the book back in my direction. "We're looking for a petite woman here, Leo. Look at the paws on this one."

I looked. She had all five fingers. Nothing came immediately to mind.

"Look." He tapped the page harder now. "This one has fingers longer than our trim's whole hand. Large Marge here could palm it and take it into the paint. Jesus. Gimme seventy-nine."

I handed it over.

"Pay attention, for chrissakes," he said over the

top of the book. I did the best I could. By quarter to
three, my stomach was growling as I was finishing
my third annual. The faces were beginning to swim
before my eyes. The steady stream of coffee provided by the ever-affable Pamela failed to stem the
swirling tide of hopeful faces. I was now using my
finger, as if touching each face would somehow make
it more distinct. No help. Everybody was beginning
to look like Mr. Potato Head. Grudgingly, I con-
cluded that we were, as Carl had suggested, wasting
time.

"Maybe we should—" I started.

Carl sat with his arms folded over his thin chest,
staring at me.

"When I was sixteen, my mother married a
drunken pipe-fitter name Hallinan," he said.

I waited.

"A real asshole. One of those low-grade morons
with a cutesy little aphorism for every occasion."

He paused.

"So?"

"Two of his rectal tidbits come to mind here,
Leo."

"Such as?"

"Whenever I did anything right, which was none
too often, he'd always say, 'Even a blind pig will
occasionally root up an acorn.'"

"A nurturing type."

"Yeah. Big time," Carl mused. "And whenever
he'd fuck up, which was a regular Friday-night

occurrence, and the old lady would have to go down to the station house and bail his hairy ass out, he'd always say he'd been saved because 'God protects fools and drunks, and only the good die young.'"

I waited for the tie-in. None was forthcoming.

"I'm all ears," I said.

He uncrossed his arms and held out his right hand.

"Gimme nineteen eighty-one."

No point in asking why. Instead, I rummaged through the pile and slid the volume over to his side of the table.

He consulted the index, thumbed his way about three quarters of the way to the back, and began to slowly go through the pages.

"Maybe we should—" I started again.

Without looking up. "Shut up, will ya."

Pamela made another pass, refilling our cups. Carl took no notice. After twenty minutes, he closed the volume and slid it back over toward me. "I think what galls me the most is the idea that that asshole Hallinan might have been right."

"How so?"

"Obviously some higher power must be in charge of looking out for hummers like you, Leo. There's no other possible explanation."

"Oh."

"Shit yeah. No doubt about it. We shoulda crapped out here, Leo. Big time. If there was any justice at all, we shoulda pissed away a bunch of old

Warheads' dinero and come home with nothin' more than heartburn from this shitty coffee." He sat back in his chair. "I mean, we've got fourteen years times thirteen campuses, not a goddamn thing to go on other than some half-assed idea that this twat might have spent time at a university at some time in her life. We've got half the books being scanned by the Helen Keller of photo identification, who probably wouldn't be able to tell the difference between Joan Rivers and the Lindbergh baby, and what happens?"

"Hauptmann turns out to be innocent?"

"What happens is, right there as big as life in the second book I look at is daddy's little girl just staring me right in the fucking face with that same deer-in-the-headlights look she gets whenever she spots a camera."

"You're kidding."

"Yeah, I'm renowned for being a real barrel of laughs. Ask anybody. They'll tell ya."

He picked up the volume nearest his left arm and worked toward the back. "Talk about steppin' in shit. One crummy picture and Moe and Larry manage to stumble on it. Nineteen eighty only. Nothing in either seventy-nine or eighty-one." He tapped the book. "Just this one."

I walked around behind his chair. The black-and-white image was captioned "Fall Sports Banquet." Standard-issue yearbook photo. The flash had captured the front three and a half tables of what the receding shadows revealed to have been a much larger gathering. Thick-necked young men in rented formal attire. Chiffon off the shoulder for the young women. Grandma's jewelry. Good bones. Good teeth. Corsages and boutonnieres. The scattered place settings and facial expressions confirmed that dessert had long since come and gone. This party was well into the shank of the evening.

I studied the female faces at the center table. The stark light of the flash had washed the edges from their features, leaving only the man-in-the-moon eyes, nose, and mouth floating off-center in amorphous auras of dull white. I leaned closer, nearly resting my nose on the page. No help.

I ventured a quick glance back Carl's way. He met my gaze. I shrugged. Shaking his head, he placed the tip of his index finger slightly above the coiffured head of a gorgeous brunette seated at the rear of the center table. There, at the next table back, her face adrift now above Carl's fingernail, was a younger, thinner, but easily recognizable Allison Stark. A brunette back then. Caught off guard by the flash, her expression showed neither the forced gaiety nor the weary waxiness of those around her but instead revealed an intensity of focus discernibly inappropriate for the occasion.

"Sure enough," was all I could think to say.

"What else do you notice?" he asked.

"Why don't we just save time and have you tell me."

"Go on, look."

I looked. I was about to plead for mercy when it struck me.

"She's sitting between two women."

"Good, Leo. Very good. Notice how at every other table we can see the seating order is like it ought to be—boy girl, boy girl. Except right there where our girl is, suddenly it's three girls in a row."

"No empty seats, either," I said.

"Not a happy camper."

"Look at the dress."

This one was easy.

"She seems lost in it."

"Ycah," hc said. "It's way too big for her. Way out of style too."

As usual, Carl was right. The voluminous dress with what appeared to be fabric roses sewn onto the shoulders reminded me of one of those thirties nightclub movies.

"Maybe she just had bad taste," I suggested.

"More likely she borrowed the dress."

We sat in silence staring at the picture. Finally, Carl sat back in his chair and cast a glance at the door.

"Shall we?" he asked.

"You think you can stand all that affability?"

"I'll grin and bear it," I said.

We called in unison, "Pamela!"

15

STATE ROUTE 78 WEAVES TWO LANES through the smooth green hills of Southern Wisconsin, through Daleyville, past the cutoff to Forward, and south to Blanchardville, where you either turn west toward the shores of Yellowstone Lake or stay on 78 as it continues south down toward Illinois. The blustery morning wind had climbed above the trees. Thin shards of cloud, low in the bright blue sky, kept pace as we drove south. Summer had lingered here. The leaves on the native oaks and maples had only just begun to turn color at the tips. Under different circumstances, it could have been a scenic trip. Not today.

Forty miles of log trucks and motor homes had sapped what minuscule patience Carl had started with. We'd been stuck behind a load of small cedar logs for the past twenty miles. The truncated front end of the van, when combined with Carl's maniacal tailgating, reduced me to stomping imaginary brakes as he simultaneously chain-smoked and manipulated the hand controls like a deranged railroad engineer.

"How much farther?" he groused, inching even closer to the logs. I could count the growth rings. Metal cutouts of naked women undulated on the swaying mudflaps. A hail of loosened bark and kicked-up gravel ticked rhythmically off the van. Again, I involuntarily pumped the brakes like a dog scratching dream fleas.

"Four or five miles and we should be on the outskirts of beautiful Argyle, Wisconsin."

"I'll gird my loins for the excitement."

For the umpteenth time, he slipped a foot of the van out into the northbound lane only to be very nearly vaporized by oncoming traffic.

"Assholes," he muttered as a blue-and-white tour bus whizzed by, nearly taking the mirror.

"Yeah," I agreed. "Bastards got some nerve driving north."

"Stuff it, Leo. You hear me. You got me out here followin' these fuckin' Lincoln Logs up the road from the twelfth century to see a broad whose sole claim to fame is being the Badger alumni chairperson for nineteen-eighty. Yeah, I'm betting the ranch on this one."

"You never know till you try. All we want her to do is put a name on a face for us."

"Yeah, from a fifteen-year-old dinner party."

"We'll show her the composite you made. Maybe that will help."

"Maybe pigs will fly."

"She's not only alumni chairperson, she's also in the picture. What else could we ask for."

"Trust me, Leo, right about now I got a hell of a list of other things I could ask for."

"It's worth a try. People let themselves get appointed alumni chairpersons because they want an excuse to keep their noses in other people's business. They just have to know what's going on. They know who's having a baby, who's getting a divorce. They send just the right little card for each occasion. They like that crap. That's why they do it."

"So you keep telling me."

"Maureen Hennesey is the alumni liaison for my class."

Carl shot me a sideways look.

"The charity dame with the Margaret Thatcher hair?"

"The very same."

Maureen had, as they say, married well. While her husband, Lester, busied himself at the task of massaging the family millions, she divided her time between a series of short-lived affairs with sundry instructors and serving on the boards of nearly every charitable institution in King County. No solvent business-person had been spared Maureen's tireless fundraising efforts. Her grandiose style of coercive insistence was legendary. I had his attention now.

"Really," he said.

"No shit."

"Last time she hit me up for the opera"—he removed both hands from the wheel, pointing his palms at the headliner—"like I give a shit about the opera. I tried to poor-mouth it, you know, like business was off, I was cutting back my charities, that sort of shit. She's real polite and understanding and all. And then proceeds to read me chapter and verse of every gift I've made in the past year and a half. She even knew about some bags of cement I'd donated to the neighborhood Pony League. I mean stuff I bought on my own and had Mark deliver. She even knew about that, for chrissakes."

"Maureen knows everything. See?"

"Hmmm," was as close as he got to agreeing.

We travelled the last three miles in silence.

IT TOOK SOME DOING TO GET CARL INSIDE. The three steps up to the front door were out of the question. Reading my mind, Carl stepped out of character and tried to make things easy.

"Forget it, Leo. You'll rupture yourself and then I'd have to haul your big ass all the way back to Seattle. Go get 'em. I'll wait here."

I threaded my way through a maze of bicycles up onto the front porch and rang the bell. Almost instantly, the door was opened by a slight woman in her thirties. She was dressed for jogging. White Nike

tank top, shiny blue synthetic shorts, new blue ten-
nies. She stuck out her hand. "I'm Anne Siemons.
You must be Mr. Waterman."

I said I was.

Peering over my shoulder, she spotted Carl in the
van.

"Isn't your friend going to join us? Pamela at the
university said there were two of you."

"He's in a wheelchair," I said.

"Oh. I'm sorry." She looked at her front porch
with new eyes. "What a mess. My apologies. The
kids are at the lake. Seems like there just aren't
enough hours in the day since Bud left."

I waited for an explanation of Bud, but didn't get
one.

"The garage is at ground level. He can come in
through there."

She backed the Volvo station wagon out of the
garage so we could roll Carl in through the kitchen.
Even then it was tight. In order to get Carl past the
washer and dryer, I had to lift the front of the chair
while Carl inched incrementally forward. We
repeated the process several times, until we con-
quered the corner and rolled into the kitchen.
Handicapped access had obviously not worked its
way down to suburban home design.

I followed Carl and Siemons down a short hall
into the living room. What had once been expensive
furniture was now frayed and threadbare. Folded
laundry was piled on nearly every flat surface. A

newspaper and magazine collection worthy of the
Library of Congress lay strewn about the floor.
Seated on a stained blue couch was a large blond
woman of about Siemons's age, wearing a red sleeveless dress of indeterminate shape. No shoes. No
jewelry. No smile.

"This is my friend and neighbor, Janet Behnoud,"
said Siemons. "Janet was going to the lake with the
kids, but I made her stay."

We introduced ourselves as we settled in around
a smoked-glass coffee table covered with round
watermarks. On the table, amid flecks of ashes
and what appeared to be blobs of grape jelly, a copy
of the *Badger Annual* of 1980 was propped open like
a tepee.

I pulled a copy of the banquet picture from my
pocket and smoothed it on the table. Janet Behnoud
took a quick look and sat back heavily on the couch.
Anne Siemons watched her friend as if expecting
directions, then turned her attention to the photo.

"That's me," she said, indicating a younger version of herself, bottom center of the photo.

"Yes," Carl confirmed.

"Jimmy Furchert," she pointed again. "He was my
date."

Using the chipped nail of her right index finger,
she began to move clockwise around the picture.
"And Kelly Hill and Dave Dennett, Maranda Mallory
and Cory Flynn, Mike Williams with Julie Miller, Jeff
Swogger and his date." Again, the women locked

eyes. Siemons tried to talk past it. "They're married now. And Janet. And over here—where you can't see"—she pointed to an area on the right that had been cut off by the photographer—"were Milt Hagen and Katie Seaver."

She stopped, looking at us as if for the first time. Somewhere in the house, a washer was in spin cycle.

"Milt owns a—" Again she stopped.

The distant washer began to refill. Again Anne Siemons looked to her friend. More loud silence passed between the two women.

"I feel like I'm in one of those gothic novels," I finally said.

The women stared.

"The kind where the suspects sit around the drawing-room table and cast these meaningful glances at one another as the music rises behind them. These looks you two keep passing have got me waiting for the music. Somebody want to clue me in here, or what?"

When it became apparent that explanations were not forthcoming, Carl leaned forward to the coffee table, stuck his thumb into the propped-open yearbook, and eased it over. Fall sports banquet. Page two hundred fifty-three.

"Lucky guess?" he asked.

"When Pamela called from the university—" Anne Siemons began.

"We were there when she called you," I interrupted. "She just asked if you'd help us identify somebody in the book. No page number or anything."

"We've come a long way," said Carl.

"It's about her, isn't it?"

A sudden chill caused me to shudder.

"Her, who?" Carl asked.

"Her," Siemons said. "The little dark one in the back there." She nodded at the picture in my hand as if unwilling to even point. Siemons blinked twice, sliding her gaze from the book to Carl to me then back to the picture in my hand.

"That's why I asked Janet to stay."

Reaching out now she pointed to the figure nearest the camera on the bottom right. Much thinner, not quite as blond, but the resemblance was easy to see now.

I addressed myself to her. "So Ms.—"

"Ben-nowed," she pronounced for me. "You won't believe how people butcher the pronunciation. Bennowed," she repeated.

"So, Ms. Behnoud, what was it that takes two of you to tell?"

Siemons adjusted the blue plastic band in her hair. "This is so embarrassing," she said.

"She was following him," Behnoud blurted.

"Following whom?"

"Jeff Swogger." She touched the curly head of an uncomfortable-looking young man at the head table. "They didn't have a word for it then, but she was stalking him. That's what they'd call it now."

"He didn't even know her," Anne added quickly. "He was only a freshman, but he started in the defensive backfield somewhere, which was really unusual. That's how come he was in the picture at all. It turned out later that she had followed him from all the way back where he came from."

"Which was where?" Carl asked.

"Someplace in Washington State," Janet said.

"All the way to Wisconsin. This girl followed some perfect stranger from Washington to Wisconsin. That's pretty damn weird," Carl said.

"You don't know the half of it," giggled Siemons.

"Let's back up here," I suggested. "This guy Swogger." I pointed to the curly-haired specimen sitting next to the gorgeous brunette. "This is him, right?" They both agreed it was. "Who was his date for the party?"

"The girl next to him." Anne Siemons touched the brunette. "She was his high school sweetheart. The only girl he'd ever dated. They got married right after he graduated. I don't know exactly when. I'd graduated by then. They're still married. We exchange cards."

Carl and I exchanged a meaningful glance of our own.

"Who brought the girl then?" I asked.

"Nobody."

"How'd she get in?"

A shrug. "She had a ticket."

"How?"

"God only knows. It was strictly by invitation," said Janet.

"So what happened then?"

"A scene."

Anne rolled her eyes. "The scene to end all scenes."

"So, Swogger is there with his future wife, and this girl who got in God knows how is there too, glaring at them from the next table."

"Nobody really noticed her until way after dinner, when she started screaming at them."

"Screaming?"

Behnoud rose from the couch and moved slowly to the center of the room. "After the dinner was over and everything"—she measured the room with her arms—"the band started playing again, and everybody got up and danced. Jeff and his date stayed at the table."

"I don't think his religious beliefs permitted dancing," Anne said.

"And?"

Janet swam her arms again. "And, we're all out there dancing around, and right over the top of the music, and I mean the music was loud, you start to hear this screaming start. Biblical verses. Scripture of some sort. About whores and whoremasters and concubines and eternal damnation for the wicked and about how Jeff was her eternal intended."

I look to Anne Siemons for confirmation.

She held up her right hand. Girl Scout's honor.

"That's the exact words she used, 'eternal intended.'"

"Absolutely at the top of her lungs," she added.

Janet carried on.

"Yeah, and by this time people have stopped dancing and are drifting over to see what's going on. It wasn't like you could ignore it or anything. Hell, even the band stopped playing." She brought her arms suddenly to her sides. "That's when she started yelling about how she'd known from the first moment she'd seen him in his football uniform back home that he was her intended. About how she'd made a pilgrimage here just to be near him. I mean, the place was in dead silence by then."

"What did Swogger do?"

"He tried to help her."

"Help her what?" Carl asked.

"Help her get control of herself, I guess."

Carl's confusion was palpable. Anne Siemons piped up.

"You'd have to know Jeff, Mr. Cradduck. Jeff was everything the rest of those football knuckleheads weren't. He was thoughtful, sincere and kind and sensitive and . . . I know it sounds corny, but Jeff was just a genuinely nice person. He was a philosophy major. Became a minister. You'd have to know him to really understand."

Janet jumped in. "His first reaction was that this screaming maniac was a person who needed help.

That was just how he was. He always put other people first. The rest of us, I mean, we were glued in place. Nobody knew whether to shit or go blind."

"How did he try to help her?"

"He went over to try to calm her. To help her get a grip."

"And then?"

This time, the women looked toward opposite walls. Finally, Anne mumbled.

"And then she took out her breasts."

"She what?"

"You heard right," Janet said. "She reached down into this huge old gown she was wearing and pulled her tits out."

"No!"

"Yes." In unison.

"And?"

"And what? She offered them to him. Held them in her hands and started yelling at him that these were her gifts to him."

"Jesus," Carl whispered.

"I'm afraid to ask what happened then."

"Well, about that time some of the other girls started to realize that their big, strong, football player boyfriends weren't going to be of any help. The guys, they were just standing there taking this all in. I mean these gonzos are there just staring at this poor thing's chest, you know, drooling. At that point, a bunch of the girls took matters into their own hands. They pushed her out a side door into the alley—with her screaming all the way, I might add."

"Did somebody call the police?"

"She ran off up the alley."

"Wow," was all I could think to say.

"Tell them what she said," Janet said to Anne.

"I can't. It's too embarrassing."

"Anne was one of the girls who got her out of there. Go ahead, tell him. I'll get the words wrong. You tell it better."

I suspected that this particular story had been the narrative highlight of innumerable baby showers and Tupperware parties. Anne didn't require further encouragement.

"Okay, so she's standing there in the alley, tucking herself back into her dress. Breathing hard, but really calm all of a sudden. Like the cold air has brought her back to her senses or something. And I was really mad at that point. I mean she'd ruined the whole darn evening that I'd worked so hard for. I almost never swear, but I did this time. I yelled at her. I yelled something like 'What the hell is the matter with you?' Something along those lines anyway, and do you know what she said?"

"What?"

"She said—and these are her exact words—she said, just as calm as could be, 'He shot his seed into her. I know he did. Don't ask me how I know. I just do. He filled her up, and of course, I can't have that.' She said it just like that. Like a schoolteacher or something. 'Of course, I can't have that.' And then she ran off up the alley. Everybody was too stunned to do anything."

"Seed?"

"I swear." Right hand aloft again.

"Jesus," Carl said.

"Jeff was just . . . crushed. He never played football again. Went right to some divinity school after that year. I think he was just so embarrassed by the whole thing that he couldn't face anybody at the university again. I mean, everybody in the place just felt so bad for him. I really can't describe it. It was one of those moments of such incredible embarrassment that it made people almost wish it was happening to them." She hesitated. "You know . . . because watching it happen to somebody like Jeff was somehow even more painful."

"I know what you mean," was the best I could manage.

"It was indescribable," Janet said. "After that, the band tried to get things going again and all, but nobody's heart was in it. They didn't even make it through one song. People just stood around for a few minutes looking at each other and then went looking for their coats. Nobody even knew what to say. Within a half hour the place was empty."

"Hell of a night," I offered lamely.

Anne Siemons agreed. "Even now, I can still remember the day when I got my annual at the end of that year, the first thing I did was check the banquet pictures, before I even looked for my own senior picture or anything else. And this morning, the minute Pamela called to say that a detective wanted to see if I could identify someone in a picture from nineteen eighty, that was the first thing to come to mind. And even after all these years, when I called Janet about five seconds after Pamela called me from the alumni office, it was the first thing she thought of too."

"I just knew," Janet Behnoud said. "I just did."

I went for the sixty-four-thousand-dollar question.

"Who was she? She must have had a name?"

As I figured, they shrugged in unison.

"Nobody knows," said Anne.

"No one I know ever saw her again," Janet added.

"And this Swogger fellow didn't know her from Adam?" Carl asked.

"Never seen her before in his life."

Carl drummed his fingers on the arm of the chair. I checked my fingernails. After a time I said, "You said you had an address for Jeff Swogger."

Anne rose and headed back toward the kitchen. Janet leaned that way, thought about following, but instead stayed put.

"That's how come we were acting so weird before," she explained. "It's almost like we've been waiting all these years for this thing to somehow come home to roost, if you can understand that."

"Sure as hell isn't something you could forget," Carl said.

"It's more than that," she said. "It's more like being married to a drunk for all these years. Believe me, I know all about that. When you're married to a drunk, you spend your life waiting for the call. The one that tells you he's been fired, or he's in jail, or he's dead, or he's killed somebody else's family. Every time the phone rings, your stomach flips over because you know it's inevitable, sooner or later the call is going to come."

Anne returned with a blue three-by-five card. She stood her ground two paces from me. "This isn't going to be any trouble for Jeff, is it? I mean, he's got a really wonderful life going on. He's important to a lot of people. I wouldn't want to do anything that caused Jeff any trouble."

"I don't see how it could. It's just that we just don't have anything else to go on. We need to put a name on that girl. And what you've told us here today is all we've got."

She passed me the card. I had to laugh.

"What's so funny?" Behnoud wanted to know.

I read the card aloud. "The Reverend Jeffrey Swogger, Northwest Christian Center, Fifteen sixty-six Northeast One forty-eighth, Redmond, Washington."

"That's rich," Carl snorted. "All of fifteen miles from home."

"What goes around comes around," said Siemons gravely.

Behnoud saved the day. "Well," she said to her friend, "you gave him the address, now tell him the rest."

I waited. Carl stopped drumming his fingers.

"This gets weirder," Siemons said.

"I'm all ears," said Carl.

"You're not the first people who ever came here asking about her."

16

"CONNLEY RETIRED. TOOK HIS THIRTY YEARS and headed for the weeds."

"When was that?" I asked.

"Eighty-six, eighty-seven. Somewhere in there."

Flush with fitness. Strapping was the word for this guy. His wide wedge-shaped body hummed beneath the hand-tailored blue uniform of the Madison Fire Department. Small features. Dark curly hair, light blue eyes.

"Any idea as to Mr. Connley's current where-abouts?"

"Depends on who wants to know," he said agreeably.

I showed him my PI license. "I wanted to ask him about an old case."

"He'd like that."

"He would?"

"Oh, sure. He'll talk your ear off. He comes in all the time. With those old-timers, firefighting is like in their blood. They can't help it. He stayed away for a couple of years there. Then, when his missus died a few years back, after a while he started coming in again. Volunteering. Consulting. Doing whatever he could. You know. He's on tonight over at Seventh Street." The rest was easy.

The much-fingered business card that Anne Siemons had produced read, "William S. Connley, Criminal Investigation Division, Madison Fire Department." Red logo. Two phone numbers. Home and department, I presumed. I'd tried both. Neither was still active.

He was about sixty. A big man, thick everywhere. A long oval face made longer by a vast freckled dome over which he insistently combed irregular fronds of wispy gray hair. William Connley had also once been strapping. Now, even with the aluminum cane, he shuffled with an odd broken gait as his left leg threatened to disappear behind him with each step. The result was a severe list toward the maimed side, a tilt so gravity-defying that each subsequent step seemed miraculous. He settled his bulk into a chair next to Carl. We shook hands and exchanged names.

"Floor collapsed on me over in Buckeye back in eighty-five," he announced. "Broke my back. They stuck me answering the phone."

He looked speculatively at Carl.

"Car accident in seventy-seven," Carl said.

"Hughes says you guys want to talk about an old case of mine."

I kept it simple and recent. We were trying to put a name on a picture. The picture in the annual. Siemons and Behnoud and the banquet story. He absentmindedly pushed his fingers through the burn holes in the front of his soiled navy cardigan sweater while I ran it down for him. When I finished, he said, "You didn't say why."

"No, I didn't."

He waited.

"I don't mean to be impolite or anything, Mr. Connley—I mean, I'm not purposely trying to be mysterious."

"Bill," he interrupted.

"It's just such a strange deal," I continued. "I don't even know if it's a case at all. I'm not sure what to say about it."

He held up a hand. "Tell you what. I'll tell you what I know. When I get done, then you can decide what you want to tell me, okay?"

Hughes was right. Connley liked to talk. He started at the beginning, ran down his entire career, the triumphs, the tragedies, the accident, losing his wife to colon cancer, the whole thing. It seemed like he hadn't had an audience in a long time. It took him the better part of forty minutes to work his way up to 1980.

"So, back in the middle of nineteen eighty. Early July. Stan Roker and I were the whole damn arson team back then. Managed to get along without Harvard degrees too."

He looked to us for agreement and got it.

Satisfied, he went on. "We ran into anything too wild, we called the Staties. Nowadays—" He stopped himself. "Anyway, what happens is this. First couple of days in July, the old Miles place burns down. By modern standards probably more of a mansion than a house. It's like three stories, twenty-five rooms, woodframe construction, probably ninety years old at the time. Sits way back on its own ten acres inside the city limits. Not visible from the road. By the time we get an alarm and the first unit arrives, the entire structure is fully engaged and already beginning to collapse. Chief Petersen decides there's no possibility of anything being alive inside, so no sense risking anybody's life, tells the units commanders to just keep it from setting the surrounding woods on fire."

"Anything suspicious about the fire?" I asked.

"Lemme finish now," he said. "But no. Place was so far gone when we got there. That old. Wood construction. It burned itself into a heap. Anyhow, the place belonged to Victoria Miles. Everybody in town knew that. About eighty at the time. Family was one of the original settlers of the area. Her husband was Charles G. Miles. Probably don't mean much to either of you, made his fortune in lumber, but he was real prominent around here. Died in the late sixties."

"The name rings a bell," said Carl. "Was he an art collector or something like that?"

"Yeah, good." He slapped a meaty paw down onto Carl's arm. "A collector, but not art. Other stuff. Coins. Stamps. Chinese porcelain. Crap like that."

"He used to loan the stuff out to museums," Carl said.

"Sure did. He was real famous for it."

"I saw his collection of Roman coins once back in New York. That's where I remember the name from. It was supposedly the finest collection of its kind in the world."

"That's him all right."

I stepped back and leaned against the wall.

"So," Connley continued, "when things cool down we dig one body out of the rubble. The old lady. Or that's what the coroner says. Damn near nothing left of it, but he gets a good dental match. Okay, so far so good. These things are unfortunate, but they happen. The place was a firetrap. She was an old woman. She lived alone."

He held up a meaty finger.

"Ah," prompted Carl.

"Right. Hang on now, Carl. Heh. Heh. Well, the smoke no sooner clears when we got her next of kin lightin' a fire under us. All very concerned, you know. None of 'em had seen her in years, of course, but now they're all her favorite relative. You know how it is. Truth is, everybody wanted the case cleared so they can get their piece of the pie. I guess the old lady still had the first dime her old man ever left her, which was a hell of a lot of dimes. So, at this point, her family is breathing down our necks when we get contacted by her insurance company. They're shittin' a brick. They're still carrying a two-million-dollar policy on the old man's collections."

This got the reaction he'd been looking for.

"And get this," he continued, "that wasn't the value of the collections—no sir, the collections were worth more like six or seven. Two was just all they were willing to insure them for as long as Miles insisted on keeping the stuff at home."

"At home. Like in the house?" Carl asked.

"You got it. And the only way they'd insure it at all was if he built himself a fireproof vault in the basement."

"Which, I take it, he did."

"Big as life. Fifteen by thirty, to be exact. Steel and firebrick. Took three construction cranes working in tandem six hours to get it up out of the basement."

He paused for effect. Looking at each of us in turn.

"Nothing. Bare as a baby's ass. The old lady's personal papers. Nothing else. Not an airmail stamp or a copper penny. Nothing."

"Burned up?" I asked.

"Hold your horses," Connley admonished.

Chastened, I returned to my wall.

"Some of it, the porcelain, it turned out was still out on loan to museums. About two million worth. Never for the life of me been able to imagine two mil worth of dishes, but you know, to each his own. Even with that, there should have been about three mil in coins and stamps in there. Nothing." He sliced the air with his arm. "Not one damn thing."

"So her relatives are raising hell," Carl suggested.

Connley wagged his big head.

"They could give a shit. The stuff was insured. They just wanted their money. The fire just saved them the trouble of selling the stuff. Hell, as I remember, the property itself sold for three mil or so even without the house. It was the insurance company that was losing its mind. They were looking for any excuse not to pay. Negligence. Arson. Any damn thing."

He waited to see if I would interrupt again. When I didn't, he went on.

"So, about this time, Stan—my partner Stan Roker—gets off his big ass and gets around to checking with local tradesmen. You know, the old lady didn't go out, so Stan figured she must have had stuff sent in and that maybe those folks knew something. He was mostly just trying to cover our asses. Make damn sure we did everything we could—and guess what?"

He gave me a grin. "You can ask what now," he said.

"What?"

"Stan turns up this kid, David Lund, who works for Hansen's Market. It's not there anymore, but at the time, it was a family market about four blocks from the old lady's house. Seems the kid had been delivering groceries and whatever else the old lady wanted for the past couple of years. The kid claims that when he first started, he used to deliver them to the old woman herself, but that since about September of seventy-nine the old lady had a live-in companion. A young girl. Dark, under twenty. Said her name was Michelle. No last name, just Michelle."

"Anybody else know about this girl?" asked Carl.

"Nary a soul. We checked them all. Meter readers, social workers, everybody. Nothing. All we got is the kid. And the kid's been in a couple of scrapes with the law, minor drug things, nothin' serious, but just enough so we're not real sure what to do with his girl story. So—to give credit where it's due, Stan, it was his idea, wants to know how the old lady went about hiring this mystery girl. I mean, as far as we know, she hasn't been in public for a couple of years. We check with the local agencies. Far as they know the old lady drove off the last housekeeper a couple of years before. None of them would have worked with her if she'd asked, which she didn't."

Connley gave an exaggerated shrug.

"The paper," Carl suggested.

"Exactamundo. First week in September seventy-nine. There it was, an ad for a live-in companion, the old lady's phone number and all."

"Oooh," I said.

"*Oooh* is right," Connley agreed. "So Stan and I roust the Lund kid again. He's still on probation, so we can push him pretty hard. He sticks with his story. We drag the kid down to Madison PD and run him through the mug books for a couple of days. Nothing. By this time, the family is really pressuring the department to sign off on this thing so the estate can be settled. There's a lot of heat being passed around, and most of it is coming right at Stan and me. Chief Petersen don't like this Lund kid or his story one bit. He's on our asses to tie the thing up. Anyway, as a last resort, we sit the Lund kid down with a police artist and come up with a likeness."

I overcame the urge to pull Carl's likeness from my coat pocket.

"Identikit?" asked Carl.

"Yeah. Pretty primitive compared to what they got today, but in those days, poor ignorant bastards like us thought it was the cat's ass. Sooo—we just started passing the likeness around when the word comes down from above that the case is closed. Chief Petersen decides that we can't hold up the wheels of progress on the word of some stoner kid. Yeah, he's a bit intrigued by the newspaper ad we found, but like he says, that was then, this is now. Most likely the girl took off a long time ago. The old lady was notoriously hard on help. The Lund kid's story that the girl was there as late as two weeks before the fire don't hold water for the chief. He figures the kid is just looking to get his name in the paper. Tells us to wrap it up and submit a final report."

Connley now was visibly excited. The story had gained a momentum of its own. He wouldn't require further prompting.

"So, Stan and I are back in the office the next day huntin'-and-peckin' up a report when the phone rings. It's the trainee of the month from over at the Seventh Street station. Been on the job all of a month or so. Fresh out of the university. Back there in the early eighties was when you started to have to have a college degree to even apply. Nowadays, they all got degrees in Fire Science, whatever the hell that is, or forensics or some such crap. Anyway, the kid, I can't remember his name, he says he just saw the likeness on the station board and says he thinks he's seen the girl before. Well, you know, I figure the kid is just trying to make a name for himself. Draw a little limelight. That kind of thing can make quite a difference at promotion time, if the brass remember your name. So I'm on my guard, right. Well, the kid then proceeds to tell me this completely off-the-wall story about this girl losing her mind and exposing herself at this dinner he was at. This stands my ears straight up. I mean, the story was way too wacko to be made up."

"The sports banquet," I said.

"Right. He says there's a picture of her in the nineteen eighty annual. Gives me the page number and everything. So I hustle over to the university and, sure enough, it's right where he said it was. It's a pretty damn good match for the Identikit too."

Carl gave me a small nod of the head. I reached into my jacket pocket and unfolded the photographic likeness of Allison Stark. I dropped it into Connley's lap.

"Look anything like this?" I asked.

Connley fished in his shirt pocket and came out with a pair of black half glasses which he rested on the end of his nose.

"Eyes are just fine. Just need 'em for reading," he said, peering at the picture. He studied the likeness for a full minute before he spoke. "As best as I can remember—it was what, fifteen years ago—but as best as I can remember, that was pretty much her. It's hard to tell. This is a photograph, that was more like a cartoon, but it sure as hell could be the same person."

He handed me back the papers.

"So you went to see Anne Siemons."

"Right. She told me essentially the same story that the trainee told me about the party and the girl exposing herself and all."

He folded the glasses and returned them to his shirt pocket.

"So Stan and I are all excited. I mean none of this actually advanced the investigation, but we figured it was just too weird to ignore."

He patted the glasses as if to confirm their presence.

"Well, to make a long story short, the chief didn't agree."

"Not with the missing stuff, the newspaper ad, the Lund kid, the whole sports banquet scene. Not even with all of that?" Carl asked.

"You gotta understand. Petersen was under a lot of pressure. The family had big-time clout, and we had absolutely no hard evidence. Nothin'. We didn't even know for sure that anything was missing. For all we knew it burned up in the fire. And now we were mucking around in an incident that could have been embarrassing to the university. And listen fellas, if there's anybody in this town you don't want to get on the bad side of, it's the university. They own this town. They're the only reason this town is here. Making them look bad was not a good idea."

"But you had corroboration of the Lund kid's story," I said.

Connley shook his head sadly.

"Not as far as the chief was concerned. Petersen was from the old school. He didn't make distinctions about drugs. As far as he was concerned, the Lund kid was a drug addict. Which again, as far as he was concerned, left us with a partially corroborated story of a junkie as our only lead. I can't say as I blame him. He just wasn't willing to take any more heat on what we had. He said that was the end; we shut it down."

"And that was the end of it?" I asked.

"That was it," he confirmed. "After the insurance paid off, I sent a list of the coins and stamps out on the national wire, just to see if any of it would show up, but it never did."

"That's not surprising," I said. "Most serious collectors aren't like your Mr. Miles. They don't collect the stuff to share with others. They hoard it strictly for themselves. Stuff that rare would just disappear into a private collection and never be seen again."

"Probably the wackiest case I ever worked on," he said. "Well, Leo, you want to share the rest of this with me or what? You got me curious now."

I started at the beginning and laid it out for him. He sat with his big hands folded in his lap, listening intently. When I'd finished, he retrieved his cane and struggled to his feet. He checked his watch.

"I'm helpin' out. Relieving the dispatcher tonight. They figure I can still handle that. I gotta go."

We both thanked him for his time. He started to go, then stopped.

"So you think it's the same girl?" he asked.

"It's the same girl," Carl said flatly.

Connley looked to me. "Believe him," I said. "If Carl says it's the same girl, it's the same girl."

He took half a minute to digest the information.

"And you know for sure that she's the one bilked this guy out of a bunch of money in this real estate deal a while back."

"Yes."

"When was that?"

"Last summer."

And it's the same girl who married this friend's son?"

"It's her," Carl said again.

"That happened this year."

Now Bill Connley turned to face me.

"And your friend, he didn't think she went down with the ship?"

"No, he didn't."

"Any particular reason?"

"Nothing worth talking about," I said. "Same kind of vague maybes you guys had about the fire."

"Quite a gap in there. Between nineteen eighty and ninety-five. Fifteen years is a long time. Even supposing she did burn up the old lady and got off with the stuff, the best she could have hoped for was maybe ten cents on the dollar for identifiable stuff like that. A kid probably didn't get that much. Maybe two hundred thousand if she was lucky. That's not enough to last fifteen years."

"Not, it's not," I agreed.

"What do you suppose she's been doing all these years?"

"I don't want to think about it," I said.

"Probably not working at McDonald's," mused Carl.

We watched as Connley crabbed down the polished hall and disappeared into the elevator. Carl started to speak, changed his mind, and instead pushed the forward button on his chair. His sudden reticence lasted through the hotel, through leaving the van at the airport, all the way until we had heeded the first call to board. We sat in the back of the plane, watching the first-class passengers stowing their gear.

"She's like lions," he said, as a stout woman in blue jeans wrestled a plaid overnighter into a distant overhead compartment. "She hunts the weak. She spots 'em, cuts 'em off from the herd, runs 'em down, devours 'em, and then returns to the shade with a full belly to sleep it off."

"I've been trying not to think that."

"Think it," he said.

"'Kinda makes you wonder if she went down with the ship."

"Doesn't make me wonder. Lions don't go down with the ship. Wildebeest go down with the ship."

17

IN TWO SHORT DAYS, MY ANSWERING MACHINE had gone into meltdown. The more messages it collects, the shorter it gets with the callers. As it approaches the end of its tiny tape, you have about five seconds to leave a message before it cuts you off. The last three messages were all from my attorney, Jed James.

"Leo. Give me a call when you get a chance. Things have—" Click-hummmm.

"Why don't you fix that damn—" Click-hummmm. "Call me, Leo, you—"

From his offices in Pioneer Square, Jed terrorized the local law enforcement community. His years as the ACLU's chief litigator back East had given him both a firm grounding in litigation and a combative politically incorrect manner seldom seen west of Chicago. Jed was the champion of rights. No particular kind. No agenda. Just rights. No cow was too sacred. No infringement too slight.

Facing the prospect of reversal, judges made it a point to have pressing matters that prevented them from presiding over Jed's cases. Knowing Jed's penchant for media attention, the King County prosecutor's office made it a point to plea-bargain with unusual vigor. Having been pummeled in the past, most experienced private attorneys took substantially less and settled out of court.

"James, Junkin, Rose and Smith."

"Hi, Suzanne. It's Leo."

"Hisself has been most upset by your absence."

"Hisself is usually upset."

"We wouldn't have it any other way. Hang on. I'll see what his majesty is doing."

He started right in.

"You ever thought that just maybe you got your money's worth out of that answering machine, Leo. Come on, 'fess up, how long you had that thing?"

"Better part of fifteen years."

"And the idea of maybe replacing it with something just a bit more technologically proficient doesn't come immediately to mind?"

"It still works," I protested.

"Christmas," he said, partially covering the mouthpiece. "Suzanne—!" I could hear him shouting. "Mark it down. For Christmas this year, Leo gets a new answering machine."

"Oh, now you've spoiled the surprise," I pouted.

"The Boys are going to lose the house."

"Just like that?"

"Just like that."

"Defeatism is unlike you, Jed."

"It's realism. O. J.'s defense team couldn't save 'em now. They never actually owned it anyway."

"How's that?"

"The old lady hadn't paid the taxes for the past twelve years. Property with unpaid taxes can't officially change hands until the taxes are paid."

"So, if they paid the taxes—"

"Thirty-four thousand in taxes. Another seventeen in assessments? And that's just the tax end of it. The house has got a clogged sewer line spewing effluent into their neighbors' yards. The city won't fix it because of the unpaid assessments. Their neighbors are in the last stages of a public nuisance complaint that I'm also out of appeals on. They're going to win. It's a done deal. The old lady's estate is going to get the house back. The city is going to sell it at a fire-sale price, pay itself off the top, and let the Boys and the rest of her relations fight it out for the rest."

"How long?"

"There'll be a seal on that place in under two weeks."

"Have you told them?"

"For all the good it's done. I stopped over night before last. You can't call anymore, you know. GTE cut the phone off."

"Really?"

"Yup. And the city is shutting down their services one at a time. So I stopped by to give them the bad news."

I could hear him chuckling on the other end.

"I'm afraid to ask."

"They were just hammered, Leo, I mean twisted, knee-walking drunk, playing cards back there in the kitchen. I used that same line I just used with you— that the place was going to have a seal on it within two weeks. They started doing seal impressions, you know barking and slapping their arms together, tossing slices of pizza at each other like fish. By the way, did they tell you about the pizza?"

"Yeah, they did."

"They were still barking when I left."

"Sorry," I said.

"Not to worry, Leo. I've gotten to be as fond of them as you are, but we're at the end of the line here. Make sure they understand, okay?"

"I'll take care of it," I assured him.

"New subject," he said. "Can you handle a skip trace for me?"

"Nope. Sorry."

"It's easy money."

"I've got something important going on now. I'm going down to Portland this afternoon."

"What could be more important than easy money?"

"Lions."

"I'm not going to ask. Bye, Leo."

"Bye, Jed."

Rebecca was in a meeting. Marge was not taking phone calls. No way I was returning Cousin Paul's calls. He wanted me to confirm a Monday luncheon at his club. There were four messages from H. R. McColl, first two from a secretary, followed by two from the great man himself. Fishing for an address for my severance check, I guessed. Unfortunately for Mr. McColl, Mr. Waterman was, quite regrettably, going to be away from his desk.

The Reverend Swogger, according to the church secretary, would be just delighted to meet with me at four-thirty this afternoon, no matter what I wanted, sandwiching me, she said, between his meeting with the board of governors and his weekly taping, whatever that was.

Somehow it had gotten to be nearly three in the afternoon. Mark had been waiting when Carl and I, after a four-hour layover in Salt Lake City, had rolled down the Sea-Tac gangway a little after two in the morning. For some reason I'd arrived home wired and unable to sleep. I hadn't rolled out until nearly noon. My internal clock was way off. A four-thirty appointment, twenty miles away had seemed easy. Now I felt rushed.

18

WHATEVER THE REVEREND SWOGGER WAS DOING, it was working. I don't know whether he'd been saving any souls, but he sure as hell had been saving his pennies. On the north side of the road, inside a large fenced enclosure, an enormous old Quonset hut crouched beneath the old-growth firs like an ancient armadillo, its ribbed metal shell mottled by rust and awash with tree debris. A red banner emblazoned with news of a revival meeting the following Friday adorned the side. My guess was that this had been the original church building. No more.

Diagonally, across the street to the east, sat what the secretary had modestly called the new church. Without the blue glass spire pushing heavenward like a prow of some celestial ship, the building could just as well have been a shopping mall. Steel and rock and glass, the five connected buildings occupied a full suburban block.

The block immediately to the south was occupied by the Evergreen Christian School, four freestanding buildings surrounded by playgrounds, basketball courts, and a full-size baseball field. The two com- pounds were connected by a massive parking lot—a rough estimate suggested about five hundred or so spaces. Figure two-point-something true believers per car, and the church probably held somewhere in the vicinity of twelve hundred souls. The wages of sin obviously were not frozen.

I pulled to a stop in the main parking lot. A large green sign offered a map and a campus directory. Youth hall, gymnasium, and swimming pool to the left of the church in the big square building. Youth office and Krupp Hall on the second floor. The matching building on the far right held the activity room, the choir room, the sanctuary, the chapel, and the church offices. Behind the complex, a small rectangle was labeled PRIVATE. Some wit had added an S.

Predictably, I'd parked on the wrong side of the building and had to cover three full sides before I came to a black metal door marked "Church Office." It was open. Behind me now, one block over, a residence made of the same materials as the church sat on the corner. A long way from the traditional rectory, it looked like it belonged on a golf course. The sign on the gate also read PRIVATE. No S this time.

Turning away from the house, I stepped inside the office and shook the mist from my hair. Neutral, off-white walls, thick cream-colored carpet. The beige oak desk was unoccupied. The anteroom was empty. I checked the place out.

There were three pictures of Jesus and five of the Reverend Swogger. The bookcase on the near wall held several piles of brochures. Another picture of the Reverend Jeffrey Swogger adorned each. Schedule of church services. Six every Sunday in the new church and six more across the street in the old. At six-thirty, a sunrise service with country-style music. A traditional service at nine with a sixty-voice choir. At ten-thirty the modern service, which included a ten-piece band, sixteen vocalists, and three interpretive dancers. A broadcast schedule for the TV program. Food bank applications. A large, yellow four-fold with all of the church's summer programs for youth. I pocketed one of each.

"Hello," I said as loud as I could without screaming.

"Come in," resonated from the depths of the building.

I followed the carpet down a short hall toward, appropriately enough, the light. He met me at the door, hand out.

The Reverend Swogger was going to his grave with the same wide-eyed, adolescent face he'd been born with. The intervening fifteen years had only served to solemnize his boyish features; a slight thickening here, a thin web of lines there, but otherwise he could still have been twenty.

He was bigger than I expected, six-two and a solid

two-ten or so, more of a linebacker now than a defensive back. The clump of curly brown hair had long since been tamed by fifty-dollar haircuts. Thousand-dollar blue suit, rounded collar, custom-made shirt, plain burgundy tie, gold cross tie tack.

"You must be Mr. Waterman," he said, indicating a red leather chair to the left of the desk. "Please, sit down."

I confirmed that I was and took a seat. Only the black lacquer desk in the near right-hand corner of the room suggested an office. The decor was more like an amiable front parlor—lace curtains and flowered chintz, deep sofas and landscapes, comfort for the body, succor for the soul.

He settled comfortably into his black high-backed chair.

"Mary said you wanted to see me on a personal matter."

"Yes," I said.

He smiled warmly and spread his hands. "How can I be of service?"

"This is quite a church you've got here," I said for an opener.

"Between eleven and fifteen thousand people attend our services every week," he said with obvious pride. "That's in person. It's hard to get an accurate TV count."

"Going to church has come a long way."

"The message hasn't changed," he assured me. "It's only the packaging that's different. Willow

Creek Community up in North Everett had an Easter program where they dramatized the Passion of Christ. The whole thing took twelve minutes, and you didn't even have to get out of your car. Drew nine thousand."

When I looked dumbfounded, he gave me the canned speech.

"We minister to the secular suburbs, to the unchurched, to those who quit organized religion years ago. The papers like to call us megachurches. We see ourselves more as missionaries. Quitting church does not eliminate the need for the spiritual. The need for religion is something we all carry inside. Modern churches merely seek to service the need in its present form. It's all about servicing needs."

I was polite. I said, "Interesting," instead of "bullshit."

"Now what personal matter can I help you with?"

"Actually," I said, "it's not personal about me, it's personal about you."

"Me?" He smiled and folded his hands on the desktop. "Have we met before?"

"Not to my knowledge."

"You're not one of my parishioners." It was a statement.

"You know all of them?"

"At least by sight. I don't get around to the shut-ins as much as I should. These days, we use the TV program for that, but I'm sure I'd remember you if you were."

"You attended the University of Wisconsin?"

He leaned slightly forward. "Briefly."

"Played football?"

He was genuinely amused. Not in the least threatened, just curious.

"Also briefly. You seem to know quite a bit about me, Mr. Waterman. May I ask what you do for a living?"

"I'm a private investigator."

"From Seattle?"

"Yes."

I pulled my license from my pocket and slid it across the desk, where he gave it a cursory glance before sliding it back.

"May I ask what it is that you are investigating?"

"I'm not quite sure, Reverend. It could be—"

Over my left shoulder, next to the wall of windows, the door at the far end of the room swung open. His eyes moved to the door.

"Excuse me, but I'm—" the Reverend said.

A tea cart tinkled as it pushed through the opening, followed by a woman in a white blouse and a denim jumper. She was tall, her long dark hair streaked with gray.

"Oh," she said when she looked up and saw me. "I'm sorry. I'll come back. I was—"

She was the dark-haired beauty in the banquet picture.

"Oh, it's you. No. No. Come in," he said.

He turned to me.

"This is my wife, Katherine."

We exchanged long-distance greetings as she pulled the cart the rest of the way into the room to her husband's side with an elegant economy of motion usually only seen in models.

"Mr. Waterman here is from Seattle. He's a private investigator."

Like many suburbanites, Swogger spoke of the city like it was a distant planet, rather than twenty minutes from his front door.

She perched on the edge of his desk. "Really. I thought those were just in the movies," she said.

"He's here to investigate us on a personal matter."

She smiled as best she could and gently picked lint from her husband's shoulder. "Are they on to us at last?" she said in mock despair.

"I'm afraid so," he said. He turned his attention back to me. "You were saying—"

"I was saying—" I started. "I . . . oh hell. Excuse me, I—"

He waved me off. "Not to worry. I am familiar with the word."

She left her hand on his shoulder as they waited. I rummaged about for an opener, failed, and started babbling.

"Nineteen eighty, the University of Wisconsin fall sports banquet. The girl who—" I blurted.

"Oh dear," she said. "That crazy girl."

"Has something happened to her?" he asked.

"I don't know," I answered.

For the first time, the Reverend Swogger seemed mildly annoyed.

"I don't mean to be rude, Mr. Waterman, but could you perhaps start at the beginning? I'm afraid you've got me completely confused."

I did. I gave them an abridged edition, starting with Allison Stark and moving backward, through Lake Chelan, all the way to Madison. Leaving out the possible murder and mayhem, making it sound like a routine skip trace. She absently rubbed his shoulder as I laid it out.

When I'd finished, the Reverend Swogger unlaced his fingers and asked, "And your friend didn't believe that she was killed in the boating accident with his son?"

"No, he didn't."

"And you?"

"I'm keeping an open mind."

"You said the police are treating it as an accident."

"Yes, they are."

"And after investigating, you think otherwise?"

"I think it's possible."

"You think all of these people, over all that time, with all of these different identities, are the same person."

"Also a possibility."

"Now that sounds like the movies," Katherine Swogger said.

"I can't disagree with you there," I said. "But it's

all I've got. I'm hoping that maybe if I can find out who she started out to be, I can fill in some of the blanks and maybe put this thing to rest once and for all."

"What can we do to help?" he asked after a moment.

She began picking lint again.

"I've gotten as far as nineteen eighty and that night at the sports banquet. That's as far back as I've gotten."

He placed his hand over hers on his shoulder and nodded.

"I'm afraid we're not going to be of much help. I've thought about that night many times since then. I do quite a few high school functions, convocations, banquets, you know, that kind of thing. Every time I do one, I wonder what I might have done differently that night and whatever became of that poor girl. I mean"—he spread his hands—"the road not taken and all of that."

"It's not the kind of thing a person forgets," I offered.

"Most assuredly not."

"Had either of you ever seen her before?"

"Never," they answered together.

"And since?"

"Never," he said again.

"And you have no recollection of seeing her or running into her or anything back when you were playing high school football?"

"I played B-8 football, Mr. Waterman. For Hamilton, in the North Cascade League. That's a long way from the bright lights."

I had to agree. My parents had, for most of my childhood, maintained a summer getaway another twenty miles up the Cascade Highway at Ross Lake. Every August, the old man would tool the Buick up from Seattle for a glorious week of watching my mother clean the cabin. Just about the time she got the place what she considered to be fit for human habitation and had finally stopped mumbling, it was time to go back to the city. The joys of youth.

A hint of nostalgia surfaced now in him.

"This was places like Lyman and Hamilton, Birdsview, Concrete, Rockport, and Marblemount. A six-team league. Ten games. We played everybody twice. Believe me, mostly it was just our families in the stands."

"You must have been pretty good to have gotten a major college scholarship from a B-8 school."

"I had my fifteen minutes of fame," he admitted.

"Oh, don't be so modest, Jeffrey. You made All-State," she scoffed. "Everybody knew who you were. You were a star."

"In Skagit County maybe, but that was about it." He turned to his wife. "What was the most people you ever saw at one of our games?" he asked quickly.

Katherine Swogger thought it over.

"He does have a point, Mr.—"

"Waterman."

"If she'd been at his games, I'd surely have seen her," Katherine Swogger said. "I never missed a game. On a good night, there were maybe three hundred, if both towns showed up in force. Sometimes when the weather was terrible, it would be more like fifty people total. I don't see how she could have developed such an obsession about Jeffrey without me seeing her."

Swogger nodded agreement. "Believe me, my high school football career was no big deal."

"She seemed to think so."

"All the more frightening," he said.

"Is that why you stopped playing?"

He considered this at length.

"I suppose—with the aid of hindsight—that's probably part of it," he hedged. "I didn't realize it then, but I suppose that's true. At the time, it seemed like it was more of a matter of having another set of priorities."

He smiled up to his wife, who returned his gaze.

"But there's no denying it, Mr. Waterman. Even with other factors at work, that night at the sports banquet had a major effect on my decision to give up football. It certainly wasn't my fault or anything, but . . . somehow, just the fact that it worked out that way—that scene happened at all—left a taste in my mouth that I just couldn't get rid of."

"You were the victim," I insisted.

He wagged his curly head.

"I don't believe in victims, Mr. Waterman. I

believe that people are responsible for their lives. Not just for what they intended to happen but for what happens. Somehow, wittingly or not, I was part of that moment. I had engendered something that I had not intended and which I could not control. All I could think of was not to put myself in that position again. I'm at a loss for words."

"Interesting," I said again.

"Oh, the tea," said Katherine Swogger. "I forgot the tea."

She turned to me. "Could I offer—"

"No. No thanks," I said. "I've got to be going."

Katherine Swogger wheeled the rattling cart across the room and began fussing with the service, laying out cream and sugar cubes in cut crystal, setting a steaming amber cup before her husband, pouring a cup for herself, and then hovering with the pot. I put my hand over the third cup.

"Thanks anyway," I smiled.

I pecked away at them for another couple of minutes. Prying, looking for any dimly remembered fact. Like the others, however, that night had not skulked off into the gloom but was still bright in their minds. No help there.

"I'm sorry you've come for so little, Mr. Waterman. I wish there were more I could do for you," he said when I ran out of gas.

"One does what one can, Reverend."

"Are you sure—" She reached for the pot again.

I pulled myself from the seat.

"I'd better be going."

She leaned in close to me. I could smell Ivory soap.

"You *will* keep in touch with us, won't you? We'd very much like to know if you find out anything about that poor girl."

I lied and said I would.

19

I KEPT MOVING AROUND THE KITCHEN, trying to stay warm. As Jed had predicted, the city was shutting them out. Yesterday the phones, today the gas. Words became steam in the cold morning air. I kept my hands in my pockets as I paced.

"Who found the place?" I asked.

"The Speaker," said George. George sat, arms akimbo, impervious to the cold, bolt upright in his customary chair, wearing only a yellowed sleeveless undershirt, a wadded pair of plaid boxer shorts, and black Reeboks.

"How in hell does a guy who doesn't talk find anything?"

"He talks," said Harold, who had the oven on fullblast, door open, leaning close, wrapped head to toe in a green army blanket.

"When?" I asked. "I've known the guy for ten years and never heard him say a word."

"He used to talk to Buddy," said Ralph, whose

ribbed neck protruded from the folds of a thick, red-velvet bathrobe.

"Now he only talks to George," said Harold.

"I inherited him," George sneered.

"Like the house," added Ralph.

"Only him we get to keep," Harold said.

Unaccustomed to participating in this part of the day, they were slack-faced and sullen. I'd spent the last half hour rousting them out of bed, handing out cash, and making it clear to them that the jig was about up on the house. Sometimes I admired their ability to ignore nearly anything, to put anything they didn't want to think about completely out of mind. Not this morning. This morning, I'd gotten fingerpointing nasty with them. This time they listened. They didn't like it, but they listened. They were pissed at me and not volunteering anything.

"So, what's the story?" I prodded.

"No story," said George.

"Don't make me drag this out of you. I'm not in the mood."

"Nothin' much to tell, that's all," said George. "She had a little room on First Avenue, down the hill from the market, upstairs over that pawn shop by the museum. You know where I mean?"

I said I did.

"A buck and a half a month. A single. Dirty. Real piece of shit. Like something the city puts you in. That's the story."

"Small," said Ralph.

"Real small," affirmed Harold.

"You could raise veal in it," added George.

"How'd she pay?"

"Cash. The day she moved in."

"How long had she been there?"

"Not even a whole month."

"Any line on where she came from?"

"Nothin'," said George. "All we found out for sure is that she knew she was leaving."

"How do you figure?"

"She gave the super all her stuff."

"Really? Just gave it to him?"

"Yep. Told him she and her family was going to the land of milk and honey and wouldn't be needing it any more. She told him she was going to get new and better stuff."

"Milk and honey?"

"That's what he said," said Harold. "Milk and honey."

"He also said she was a retard," said George.

"Challenged," corrected Ralph.

"Who the fuck appointed you to the political correctness patrol, huh, birdbrain? Who?" George snapped.

This time of the morning, they could get nasty in a hurry.

"I've got an out-of-town assignment for you guys."

"Like out of town where?" George asked.

"Like out in the country. Up north."

"Country? You mean like with trees and stuff?" asked Harold.

"Like that, yeah," I said.

"We don't do country, Leo," said George. "I don't smell bus fumes, I get real nervous. I break out. Besides that, Ralph starts doin' his flop act on log trucks he's gonna get killed. Naw. Thanks but no thanks. No country."

"I always end up in a cell with some guy named Bubba," groused Harold.

"Da—da—da, da, da, da, da, da—daaaaa—" George doing *Deliverance* theme.

"They never like me in the country," said Ralph.

"Don't worry, they'll like you just fine in that dress," snapped George.

"It's not a dress; it's a robe," Ralph protested weakly.

"They'll bug your eyes out like a frog."

"Stop it," I said.

"Fucker thinks he's Tallulah Bankhead."

"It's warm," Ralph insisted.

"Don't worry, shitforbrains. They'll have somethin' even warmer for ya."

I tried money again.

"Four guys. Seventy dollars a day. Two days at least. Plus I'm good for all motel rooms and food."

No answer.

"You guys are about to hit the streets again. I'm sure you can use a little extra money."

"We got some money. We'll get more from the house," said George.

"Yeah, in about two years when the lawyers get through picking the bones, you'll be able to split a bottle of Mad Dog."

Still no answer. I tried again, this time with enthusiasm.

"A couple of nights in motel rooms. Good meals. You'll have a stake in your pockets. Huh? Waddaya say?"

"And treats after we get done working," said Ralph.

Treats meant booze. Vast quantities of cheap booze.

"Only," I said, waving a finger in a wide arc, "*after* you get done working. Otherwise no booze. I hold all the booze until we're done for the day. Swear to God, you get drunk on this job, I'll leave your ass out there with the hicks. I swear. You can find your own way back. I'm serious. This thing we're gonna do is the last chance I've got. If we don't turn something here, I'm going to have to bag it."

The prospect of seven or eight consecutive hours of mandatory sobriety produced a pathetic wave of foot shuffling and head wagging.

Harold tried to hedge. "Maybe just a bracer in the—"

Left to their own devices, with money in their pockets, the Boys' day followed a strict pattern. They liked to have a little eye-opener before attempting anything more serious than getting out of bed. Something light. A couple or three beers maybe. By ten or so, were they going to be required to actually venture outdoors, they would concur on the advisability of a stiff mid-morning bracer. Thus suitably fueled, they would immediately begin the search for just the right place for lunch and a few modest cocktails. Après lunch, predictably feeling somewhat sluggish, they would further medicate themselves with an afternoon pick-me-up or four, which, remarkably enough, segued neatly into happy hour, where, as the name implics, all restraints were temporarily rescinded. No day, of course, could end without a final nip to help them sleep. Any unanticipated drinking need could be dismissed as merely a phlegm cutter. You had to admire guys who had their bases covered.

"That's how it's gotta be, fellas. No ifs. No buts. That's it. You hear me?" Nothing. "Is it understood? Somebody tell me they understood."

I laid the big lumber on them. "If you guys can't manage that, I'll find some guys who can."

Each man looked at me hard. This mention of mythical other guys was pure heresy. They were my guys, and everyone knew it. It was their single remaining claim to fame. It was their entitlement to preferred bar stools and sunny park benches. They worked as detectives. They'd been in the papers. One of them could always produce a caked, yellowed copy of some old *Times* article. Now that they knew I was serious, a long silence ensued.

"You promise no more than two days?" asked Harold.

"I promise."

He looked to George. George sat with his thin arms folded over his chest, again refusing to make eye contact with me.

"We bring the Speaker," he said finally.

"No way," I howled. "I'm not paying a mute to canvass for me."

"The Speaker," he repeated.

"We'll take Norman," I countered.

"Norman needs to watch the house."

"The Speaker found the girl's place," said Harold.

"We'll assume that was his moment of lucidity for the nineties. I'll take Norman, or maybe Waldo or Big Frank, but I won't take the Speaker. That's final."

"Waldo could come over and watch the place," said Ralph.

Harold and Ralph looked to George for a sign.

"Okay, okay, Norman," he huffed. "How we gonna get there? That little tub you drive sure ain't gonna get all of us anyplace, not to mention our stuff. You got a plan for all that crap, Leo?"

"Sure do, George. I know just where I can borrow us some transportation."

I SAW HIM BEFORE HE SAW ME. He was glad-handing a tall young redhead in an ankle-length black leather coat when I walked in the showroom door. He was working his way from little tweaks on her elbow to an exploratory pat on her ass when he caught sight of me, and froze in his tracks. Without missing a beat, he guided the woman to the nearest salesman and headed my way.

Tony Moldonado stood in close. He was wearing a blue suit with a wide pinstripe, red carnation in his buttonhole, paisley tie, freshly shined shoes. He smelled of Old Spice.

"I knew it," he said.

"Knew what?"

"I knew you'd be coming around to shake me down, and I'm tellin' you right now you ain't getting nickel one—"

"I'm not here for money," I said quickly.

"You're not?" His eyes narrowed. "What then?"

"I need a favor."

"How much?"

"It's not a how much; it's a what."

"Okay then, what?"

"I need a van."

"Wadda you, crazy? You think I'm gonna give you a van? You think vans grow on trees?"

"This is a community-property state, Tony. Keep that in mind."

In disgust, he paced a full circle around me, ending back where he'd started. I decided to make it easy for him.

"I just want to borrow a van for a couple of days. Nothing fancy. Used would be fine."

Kindness was a mistake. "Our insurance doesn't permit—" he started.

"I've still got the camera."

"What camera?"

"The one with the pictures of you holding your cock in that cheap motel room. You remember? The room with Bo Peep with her drawers down around her ankles, and the big bad wolves? That room."

He gave me a dumb look.

I playfully bopped him on the shoulder. "You remember. The room down there by the airport where you'd been poking anything and everything that walked or crawled in. You remember that room, don't you, Tony?"

He shrugged. "Maybe we got a parts van."

"Just for a couple of days."

"The seats aren't in it."

"Have you still got the seats?"

"Sure."

"Howzabout you put them back in," I suggested.

"We could do that."

"And clean it up."

He shrugged again. As long as I had him on the ropes, I threw a couple more jabs. "Oh yeah, I forgot. Have your guys fill it up and check the fluids, will you? Thanks."

His shoulders sank even further. He looked like the Bridge Troll.

"What time is it?" I asked.

Tony checked his watch. "Ten-twenty."

"Can you have it ready by one?"

"I suppose," he grumbled.

"See you at one."

SOMETHING ABOUT THE RINGING OF A TELEPHONE drives reason from my mind. Anything to stop the ringing. I sprinted across the apartment.

"Hello."

"Ah, Leo." Cousin Paul's strangled tenor.

"I was just going to call you," I lied.

"Oh, I'm sure you were. Most assuredly."

"I was," I insisted.

"Hmmm. Be that as it may, cousin. There remains the matter of the liberation of your trust fund and our luncheon date."

"There does indeed," I agreed. "Did you have a date in mind?"

"I had this afternoon in mind."

"No can do. I'm leaving town."

"When then?"

"What's today?" I asked.

"Wednesday."

"Let's see. I'm going to be gone for a couple of days. What about next Wednesday?"

"One o'clock."

"One o'clock."

"The Seattle Club."

"Yup."

"Tie and jacket. At least tie and jacket. Suits are preferred, but you know, if you don't have—"

"I don't."

"One o'clock, Wednesday."

"I'm looking forward to it."

"I'm sure."

On my way home from Eastlake Chevrolet, I'd double-parked in front of the Boys' house, poked my head in, and told them to be packed and ready at one. It was just short of eleven. Plenty of time for me to pack a few things and make a trip to the liquor store.

I left a message on Rebecca's home phone telling her I was going to be out of town for a couple of days.

The phone again.

"Yo," I answered.

"Not very businesslike." It was Marge.

"Sorry," I said. "How you doin'?"

She took a deep breath. "I'm doin'. That's about all I can say." A pause. "Heck's family all went back home this morning. This is the first chance I've had to sit down."

"Try to take it easy," I advised lamely.

"Has Howard McColl contacted you?"

"He's tried. I was away from my desk."

"So, he hasn't fired you then."

"Nope."

"Good."

"Good?"

"I've been out of it for a few days."

Another pause.

"Quite understandable," I threw into the void.

"What's not understandable to me is that the estimable Mr. McColl should take it upon himself to reorganize my affairs."

"Oh, I assumed he was lending a hand."

"What? I'm just some poor dearie who can't manage without the strong, guiding hand of a man. Is that it?"

She was rolling now. I didn't want to interrupt with an answer.

"I don't want to disillusion all you strong silent types but Sea Sundstrom was—is—my creation. Whatever wonderful other virtues Heck may have possessed, and God knows—" She paused to collect herself. When she started again, it was with measured control. "And God knows I miss him. But corporate life was just not his cup of tea. Way too many i's to dot and t's to cross for him. Too many people saying one thing and meaning another.

Heck, God love him, couldn't even be hard enough on the guys in the warehouse. He just didn't have it in him. This is mine. I did this." She stopped.

A beep. One of us had another call coming in.

"I never doubted it," I said with conviction.

"I want you to keep at the investigation," she said.

"Okay," I said. "This is it, anyway."

"What is?" she asked.

"If this little trip I'm gonna take doesn't pan out, we'll have to discuss what to do next. It may be time to try the cops or maybe just hang it up."

Another beep.

"Is that yours or mine?" she said.

"No idea."

"Hang on."

I hung.

"It's Howard. Do you want to listen in while I fire him?"

"I'll pass," I said.

"I've got to be sure about all of this."

"I understand," I said. "You want a full report?"

"Stay at it, Leo."

Hmmmmm.

20

WE'D COVERED NEARLY THIRTY MILES before Harold cracked the silence. As we crested the small rise before the Marysville exit, he leaned forward and read my mind.

"This is Marysville, huh? Isn't this where all that stuff was being dumped, you know—back when Buddy got killed?"

"Yeah," I said. "This is it. About eight miles west of here. Out on the Tulalip reservation."

I thought that was going to be it, but I was wrong.

"You shoulda known, Leo," Ralph said suddenly.

I knew what he meant. I'd had this same conversation with myself more often than I liked. "Yeah, I know," I said.

"We talk about it a lot," said Harold. "You done all the right things, Leo. I mean you told him all the right stuff, no denying that. But you still shoulda known how he was."

"Ain't like he was gonna do what you told him," George said from my right.

"He never did what nobody told him," Ralph added.

"You shoulda known," Harold repeated.

"I know," I said again.

This time, they let it ride. George and I briefly locked eyes as we searched the air between us for silent signs of Buddy.

They'd been waiting at the curb like refugees when I'd pulled up in the borrowed van. Norman, a huge khaki sack thrown over his shoulder, towered above the others in a gray tweed overcoat. Ralph had covered several turtlenecks with an aged madras sport coat. He looked like the Michelin Man gone plaid. In spite of the bright blue sky, George and Harold wore matching yellow rain slickers like the Bobbsey twins. The Speaker stood lone sentry on the porch, his lank hair hanging straight down, wearing his sandwich board—still "Ozone Schmo-zone"—as mute and impassive as the post he was leaning on.

"All aboard," I shouted.

The sheer volume of luggage should have alerted me, but I was hassled and hurried and not paying much attention. They would have pulled it off if Ralph hadn't missed the seat with his Hefty bag, which slipped to the floor with a crack of broken glass. The sickly sweet smell of peach schnapps spread like airborne honey through the interior air.

"Hold it. Hold it," I hollered. "Everybody out.

Get the bags out too. Obviously we need a reality check here."

"What's the problem?" demanded George.

"What," I demanded. "You don't smell it?"

"Smell what?" asked Harold.

"I don't smell nothin'," said Ralph. "Harold, you smell anything?"

"I think maybe you busted your aftershave," tried Harold.

"Ralph doesn't shave," I said.

"I meant mouthwash," said Harold weakly as they dragged themselves and their luggage out onto the narrow grass strip.

"Open all the bags."

"Who the hell are you, U.S. Customs?" George snapped.

"That's right, and the custom is that I'm holding all the booze."

"Cram it, Leo. Nobody appointed you God or nothin'."

I ignored him. "Open up. Come on, open up."

No movement. I undid the safety pin securing the nearest bag.

They stood forlornly in the street as I went through the assortment of sacks, baskets and Hefty bags they used for luggage, picking carefully through the sodden clothes and broken glass of Ralph's green Hefty cinch sack. In the end, the tally was: four fifths of assorted whiskey, the shattered half-gallon of peach schnapps, two pints of hundred-proof vodka, and one large can of Sterno.

"Sterno?" I couldn't believe it. "Sterno?"

"We might need to impress the natives with fire," said Norman.

I confiscated all of it.

"Maybe you better go inside and get some dry stuff," I suggested to Ralph. "This stuff is pretty wet."

He shrugged. The minimalist approach. Simplify. Simplify.

"Well, leave the bag open. It'll dry."

George sat up front with me. Ralph and Harold commandeered the second seat. Nearly Normal Norman sat in back, facing the rear, clutching the seatback on either side, his huge maned head thoroughly obscuring the rear window. Within a couple of miles, the rancid mist rising from Ralph's bag had so permeated the interior air as to make it possible, by simply closing the eyes and conjuring the sounds of wheeling desert birds, to visualize oneself immediately downwind of the Cairo dump. The rest, as they say, was silence.

I dropped off the interstate at Burlington and took the Cascade Highway east, winding through Sedro Woolley in silence, past the sign for the Northern State Multi Service Center—what, until some time back in the early seventies, used to be Northern State Hospital. For nearly seventy years the state of Washington had used Northern State

Hospital as its repository for the seriously addled. Among Seattle's informal community of screaming drunks, brain-fried druggies, and muttering droolers, Northern State's medieval methods were the stuff of street legend. Each of us knew somebody who'd taken the one-way trip to Northern State. The walls seemed to be reaching out to us.

I broke the spell.

"Okay. We're almost there. Here's the deal. You guys listening?"

I checked the mirror. No eye contact. A couple of grunts.

"All we want to know is, does anybody recognize the girl in the picture? Nothing more than that. If you get anybody to hit on the picture, come get me. I'll take it from there."

I paused to let it sink in.

"What did I just say?" I pushed. Nothing. I tried again.

"Hey, I'm not kiddin' here. Somebody tell me what I just said."

"You said we was too goddamn stupid to do anything except to show some picture to the hicks, and if anything needin' a brain came up we was to call you right away," George said from my right.

"I just—" I started. Shit. He had a point. That had indeed been more or less the message. "Okay, George is right." I sighed. "I'm sorry. If you're going to work, you might as well do the job. If anybody even seems to recognize the picture, find out everything you can and then find me and report. We'll all figure out what to do from there."

The Timber Country Saw Shop came right before the turn to Lyman. As I turned right, I spotted a sign a quarter-mile down the highway: EAT. We wound down into the town. Main Street was five blocks long. The first short block contained the only two public buildings. On the left was the post office. On the right was the Lyman Tavern. Both were painted a uniform white. The post office was entered at ground level. A dark-haired young woman, big-time pregnant, wheeled a baby in a stroller out the door. Her striated belly had rolled the top of her blue stretch pants and now bobbed at large beneath an orange-and-white maternity blouse. On the right, the Lyman Tavern was three steps up to a narrow front porch supported by elaborately turned posts. Half a dozen pickups nosed into the north side of the building.

I drove another three blocks and pulled over to the side of the road. "Everybody out," I announced as I opened my door and got out. I walked around to the double doors on the passenger side and yanked them open. Another round of mumbling, bumbling, and stumbling and I had them standing in the fine gravel that separated Main Street from the lawn of the modest blue house behind me.

They blinked disbelievingly at their surroundings as I passed out pictures. I wanted to get them going before the bitching started.

"Okay. We need to ask as many people as we can in the time we've got. The longer they've lived here the better. You're gonna find that most of these people have been here a long time. Be polite. Ask them for help. Say something like, 'Excuse me. I was wondering if you could help me.' For the most part, people will help if you approach them in that manner."

George waggled his hand like a schoolboy who needed to take a piss. I knew better, but acknowledged him anyway.

"What?"

"Excuse me, sir, but I was wondering if maybe you couldn't help us get the fuck out of here." The other three almost smiled.

"As a matter of fact, my good man, you've come to the right fellow. You do just what I tell you and I'll have you out of this lovely little hamlet inside of an hour."

He wanted to respond, but I kept talking.

"Harold. You go down there to the end of town." I pointed south. "This is Third, so you do all up and down First and Second." I stepped out from behind the front of the van and peered up and down the street. It looked to go no more than three blocks on either side of Main. "George, you and Norman do Third and Fourth. Ralph can do Fifth by himself."

"Ralph can always manage a fifth by himself," said Harold.

They yukked it up. I went on.

"If there's a No Trespassing or No Peddlers sign, skip the place. Sometimes out in the country like this, people *really*, I repeat *really* don't want to be bothered. Sometimes out here in the sticks you're gonna find types that have been waiting thirty years for something that looks like you guys to show up on the front porch so they can blow them away. Don't take any chances. Be safe. You guys hear me?"

They all let me know they understood.

"Don't mess with any dogs. Thank everybody when you're done. If they want to know how come you want to know, tell them the missing heir story like we did when we found the Abrams girl."

Again they agreed. I handed each man a folder of photos and a roll of half-inch masking tape.

"Okay, let's go then," I began. "We'll all meet back here in this spot in an hour, and"—I waved a finger—"stay out of the tavern."

"What are you gonna do?" asked Ralph.

"I'm gonna drive back out to the highway and talk to the people in the saw shop and the people in the restaurant. Then, depending on what I find out from them, I'm gonna come back here and see how you guys are doing and then maybe take a lap around town. I want to see if there isn't some place in town where folks hang business cards or maybe put up announcements about stuff they want to sell. I'll put one of the small pictures with a phone number up. If any of you guys comes upon a place where you can hang one without pissing anybody off, then put one up. That's what the tape is for. Each of you has a bunch of pictures that have my number on the bottom."

They pawed through their respective folders.

"Save those for hanging up. Show the big ones without the number. Somebody wants to keep a picture, let 'em. I've got plenty. An hour." I checked my watch. "It's two-twenty. So three-twenty, right here. Got it?"

They must have. Each man trudged off in his appointed direction clutching a folder.

Nothing doing at either the Timberland Saw Shop or the Riggin' Room Café. Friendly? Yes. Concerned? Maybe. Helpful? No. Both places let me tack up a picture. I continued past the café, just in case there was another business of some sort just up the road. Not a thing. I retraced my steps back into Lyman, this time taking an immediate left off Main, riding the perimeter. Lyman was a typical Northwest mill town, twenty years after the mill closed down. Anybody with any place to go had long since gone. What was left was just marking time.

Postwar single-family houses originally financed by the company, never better than adequate, now moss-encrusted, sagged in varying degrees toward equilibrium with the natural contours of their untended yards. Like the clear-cut scars on the sides of the surrounding mountains, they stood in testament to simpler times. I turned right. The closer I got to the river, the better the upkeep of the homes.

The copper-colored Skagit River blew by First Avenue, garnished with fresh leaves and limbs, torn loose by some upriver storm. Freshly mowed grass, well-tended shrubs along the river. Recent retirees, I guessed, moved out to the country to fish away their golden years.

I took a full lap and then cruised the streets looking for any trace of the Lyman school, passing Allison Stark's picture taped to a pole on Fourth and catching a glimpse of Harold as he backed out the front door of a small yellow house on Second and Main. Apparently, the school had vanished from the earth.

I left the van at the pickup spot and showed the picture around the post office. Nada. Norman was slouching on the front of the van as I crossed the street to the Tavern. He'd shed his tweed overcoat and attracted a crowd. A white-haired boy on a blue bike rode wobbly semicircles at Norman's feet while his little sister stood agape, looking straight up at the strange, massive apparition.

Same thing at the Tavern. The place was so dark, the bartender had to click on the light over the register to look at the picture. He held it there for the patrons. No go.

"Was the old Lyman school in that big empty area between Second and Third?" I asked the bartender.

"Used to be," he said.

A little fellow on the nearest stool, green John Deere cap worn at an angle on the very top of his head, piped in. "Till eighty-two. Said we had to consolidate. Then they made all the kids go to Sedro Woolley."

"Took what damn little heart the town had left," said somebody down the bar.

John Deere agreed. "Even when we didn't have nothin'. We could always beat Hamilton."

"Concrete too sometimes," somebody added from the gloom. "We turned out some damn good athletes. Got some major college scholarships. Don't usually get them for B-8 neither."

"Then they closed us down."

The bartender dried a glass. "Had a couple of kids get hurt in the old building. The thing got to be an eyesore. We bulldozed it down back in—"

"Eighty-six," said another voice.

"Eighty-five," came from the far end of the room.

"Eighty-six."

"You're both wrong, as usual," said a rough female voice.

I slipped out the door while they worked it out. The Boys had gathered around the van. The kids were gone. Their expressions told me all I needed to know.

"Nothin'," said George as I approached.

"Anybody else get anything useful?"

"I got some blueberry pie," said Ralph with a grin. "A real nice widow name of Williamson down the end of Fifth Street."

"Lyman was founded in eighteen seventy-two by

a guy named Williamson," said Norman. "Grew hops. Had big plans for—"

I cut the travelogue off. "Everybody in," I hollered.

We duplicated the process at Hamilton, where the gutted remains of the old school building stood like a peeling Greek temple a scant block off Pettit, the main drag. No hits. We followed the Skagit east to Birdsview and Grassmere, both barely wide spots in the road, talking to anyone who would talk, taping up pictures, ending up, just before full dark, at the North Cascades Motel on the outskirts of Concrete.

I bought us three rooms. A couple of doubles for them to share and a single for me. Coming out of the motel office, I didn't bother to check for them in the van. The pink neon sign said COCKTAILS. They were bellied up to the short bar, slurping 'em down like antelope at a water hole. I wedged myself in between George and Norman.

"Good day's work, fellas," I said.

They gargled agreement.

"I've got an idea," I said.

They were wary.

"Why don't we get some food, a bag of ice, and some cups from the store and take it down by the river and have us a little party? It's a nice night out. That way, you guys won't be blowing all your money in here, and we can party to our heart's content without disturbing anybody. We've got enough booze to float a driftboat. What say?"

They checked with each other. Why-not faces.

George was still parched and pissy.

"You wouldn't be worried about our deportment now, would you, Leo? You're afraid we can't have a few in polite company without pukin' on our shoes. Is that it?"

Everyone stopped swallowing and strained to hear.

"If you guys want to stay in here and pay a couple, three bucks a shot, that's your business. I just think we'd have a better time for a whole lot less money, that's all."

"We?" said George. "You mean, like his majesty is going to have a few with the peasants?"

For the first time all day, I had everyone's attention.

"Damn right," I said quickly.

"We better get to the store before it closes," said Harold.

Ralph inhaled both ends of a fresh boilermaker and followed Norman out the door.

21

I SAT ON THE FLOOR IN THE OPEN DOOR OF THE VAN, gently massaging my right knee. Norman wandered nearby, flossing his teeth with a matchbook cover. George, Harold, and Ralph were lounging in a bed of pink-and-white petunias, heads thrown back, catching a little sun. For them, this was just another Thursday. I, on the other hand, felt like I'd been threshed and baled. Squinting painfully in the clear midmorning light, I laid out the plans for the day.

"Okay, listen up," I started. "Don't make me repeat myself."

"He don't look so good, do he, fellas?" joked Harold.

"A little green around the gills, if you ask me," said George.

"Didn't eat his breakfast neither," said Norman, who, not coincidentally, had kindly eaten it for me.

"I don't know how you guys do it," I confessed.

"Practice. Practice. Practice," said Ralph.

The only thing they liked better than drinking

was talking about drinking, about who had gotten how shitfaced, on what, with whom and when, which in turn generally led to a nostalgic romp through the vomiting hall of fame. I wasn't in the mood for color commentary. God knows we'd consumed enough booze before I'd stumbled back to my room and gone comatose. Either giant moths had gnawed out the knee of my jeans, or somewhere along the way, I must have taken a fall. The crusted bruise that I'd discovered in the shower this morning pretty much ruled out the moth hypothesis.

"George."

"Yo."

"You and Harold and Norman are going to divide Concrete up among you. George, you do the far end of town. The cops are right up at the end of the street. Talk to them first. Talk to everybody. Put up as many pictures with phone numbers as you can. It's a lot bigger than the places we've been doing, so it's going to take a few hours."

"Seventeen hundred people, give or take. Used to be called Cement City. Produced forty percent of the cement used for Grand Coulee Dam."

Mercifully, Norman stopped on his own. I rolled my eyes at George.

"Don't look at me," he said. "You got him started on this geography shit. I was perfectly happy with the zoo parade."

"What am *I* going to do?" asked Ralph.

"You're coming with me. We're going to head up

to Rockport and Marblemount. That's as far as this trip is going. The two of us ought to be able to cover those two in about the time these guys do Concrete."

"And then?" asked Harold.

"Then, I'm going to buy you guys the best lunch in town and drive you back to Seattle, where I'm going to hand each of you a bunch of money. How's that sound?"

At last, we had consensus.

THE SAUK RIVER LEAKS OUT FROM THE NORTH CASCADES like blue-white breast milk. The same limestone deposits that attracted the Portland Cement Company leach their sedimentary waters into the river, creating an odd moving carpet of pearlescent opacity. The river was, unfortunately, the highlight of the trip.

"We struck out, huh, Leo?" said Ralph as we recrossed the Sauk on our way back to Concrete.

"Unless one of the guys got a hit in Concrete."

"Whatcha gonna do if we come up dry?"

"I'm not sure," I said. "I'm probably going to go to my client and tell her it's over. Then maybe, depending on what she wants to do, maybe take what I've got to the cops."

"What'll the cops do?"

"That's hard to tell. Probably nothing. What I've got so far is pretty borderline. The heat won't usually get involved unless their noses get rubbed in it."

The digital sign on the State Bank of Concrete

blinked 1:38, 62 degrees as we pulled back into town. As I eased the van into an empty parking space, Norman filled the driver's-side window.

"You guys done?" I asked.

He nodded.

"Where's the crew?"

His eyes moved to the Hub Tavern and back. He pushed the button, yanked open my door, and pressed his massive forehead hard against mine. He smelled of mothballs and mildew.

"The lady in the post office," he said.

SHE WAS A STOCKY WOMAN OF SIXTY OR SO, prematurely purple hair cut short, combed like a boy. She wore a striped workshirt under a brown leather vest, blue jeans, and work boots. A deeply undershot lower jaw gave her the aggressive profile of a largemouth bass. She was taking her time, perusing each envelope carefully before sliding it into the back of the appropriate mailbox.

"Didn't say I knew for sure who she was."

"Oh," I said. "Norman thought—"

"Big fella needs to take his head out," she said with finality.

I waited, stretching out over the counter, trying vainly to establish eye contact as she sorted mail.

"Just said I thought I knew those eyes. She used to come in once in a while with her momma. If it's who I'm thinking of, then she musta had her nose fixed. When I seen her she had one of them wavy noses, like it had been broke a bunch of times, but I remember the eyes."

"Whose eyes did you think they were?"

She stopped sorting mail and looked at me for the first time.

"Thought it might have been the older Hasu girl."

I waited for more. It wasn't forthcoming.

"What can you tell me about her?" I tried.

"Stubbornest little thing I ever seen."

"How's that?"

"Her momma used to bring all them kids from the Christian school to town on Saturday afternoons, and give each of 'em a quarter. Her momma was the teacher. Never did like that woman. Always felt like she was lookin' down her nose at me. All them other kids would hustle right over to Howard's for candy, but not that one. No, sir. We used to have this gumball machine in here. The kind where sometimes you got gum and once in a while you'd get some little plastic prize. You remember those?"

I admitted I did.

"Well, that little one—she couldn't have been more than eight or nine at the time—she decided she wanted this funny-looking plastic engagement ring that was in there, and I'm tellin' you, she come in here every Saturday for the better part of two months, cashed her quarter into pennies, and fed 'em into that machine until she got that durn thing. Never seen nothing like it. Most kids lose interest after a while. Not that one though. She was gonna have it, or else."

"You remember her when she got older?"

Wrong question. With a sigh, she set the cardboard box of mail on a scarred oak table and walked over to face me.

"Mister. You listen to me now. I appreciate that you got a job to do, but there's certain kinds of things a lady don't talk to strangers about. You hear what I'm sayin'? Hell. I was married to my last husband for nineteen years, and we never mustered up the gumption to talk about those Hasus and all those goin'-ons, so I sure as hell ain't gonna stand here in front of God and everybody and run off at the mouth to a perfect stranger about it."

"I can appreciate that," I said.

"Good. 'Cause that Hasu family isn't somethin' I'm willin' to talk about. 'Specially not that Terra Hasu. It's not something the community wants dredged up again, neither. I shoulda kept my mouth shut to the big fella. It's just when I saw . . . anyways . . ." She waved me off. "Never mind."

"Sorry," I said for no particular reason.

She went back to her mail, but this time it was just for show, shuffling rather than sorting.

I waited again. She continued to fiddle with the mail in the box, not looking my way. When it became apparent that I wasn't going to fade into the woodwork, she walked back over to the window.

"You want to know about the Hasus, you go talk to Mr. High-and-Mighty Gardner over at the police station. Our non-duly elected sheriff, he knows what I'm talkin' about. You go ask him."

"Gardner," I repeated. "At the police station."

"Bruce Gardner. Chief of Police. You ask him."

"Thanks."

I started for the door. She brought me up short.

"And don't let Mr. Pious fool you. He's got personal knowledge."

24

THE BOYS WERE SHADOWBOXING AND TRADING INSULTS around the vans as I crossed the street. A rogue's gallery of wanted posters' faces adorned the front of the barn-red building. The eyes seemed to follow me in.

Chief Gardner wasn't on duty. Officer Milliken was a leathery little guy with squinty eyes and a thick piece of dried egg yolk decorating his blue tie.

"The chief won't be in till five," he announced.

Allison Stark's visage glared up from the chief's inbasket.

"Could you maybe give him a call? I really need to have a word with him."

"You one of them with the pictures?"

"Yeah, I am." I took out my PI license and showed it to him. He handed it back. I passed him another picture of Allison. He smoothed it on the desk in front of him. He shook his head.

"Never seen her before. But then I've only been around for six years." He smiled. "In these parts, that makes me practically a transient. Chief Gardner, he's born and raised here."

"Could you call him?"

"You say it's important?"

"Yes, it is."

He thought it over.

"Stay here, I'll be right back."

He crossed the room and opened the frosted glass door behind the chief's desk, revealing a small dispatcher's closet. He ignored the radio, instead dialing the old black rotary phone. I couldn't make out what he was saying, so I sauntered over. He covered the mouthpiece.

"Chief says you'll have to wait till five. He's taking his boy fishing this afternoon."

"Tell him I need to talk to him about the Hasu girl."

"Hasu?"

"That's right." I pronounced it again.

He told him, and then he listened. And listened. I couldn't hear the words coming over the line, but the staccato cadence and the movement of Milliken's eyes told me what I needed to know. Gingerly, Milliken set the phone in the cradle.

"Whew boy." He exhaled. "You sure got his attention, mister. I haven't heard him that excited since they tried to recall him for enforcing the parking regulations. Be about fifteen minutes."

I headed across the street to the crew.

It was more like twenty. He slid the blue patrol

car to a stop in front of the station, shouldered open the door, leaving it bouncing on its hinges as he quickstepped into the station, waving a sheaf of papers with the motion of his left hand.

Before I got a chance to move, Gardner was back out the door, trailed by Officer Milliken, who trotted along behind, holding his gun to his hip as he loped along.

He made a beeline for the Boys and me. Gardner was a tall man, stoop-shouldered from years of trying to appear shorter. A redhead with a walrus mustache and an untamed mop of carrot hair combed straight forward on his head. He must have owned Eddie Bauer stock. Crisp red-flannel shirt, green suspenders under a new khaki fishing vest. Several iridescent steelhead flies stuck in the little sheepskin patch on his left shoulder. He pushed a torn handful of Allison Stark posters under my chin.

"Are you responsible for these?" he demanded.

Strips of broken masking tape fluttered like pennants.

"Sure am," I said pleasantly.

His face was nearly as red as his hair. "Who gave you permission?"

"Permission to what?"

"To deface public property."

"What public property?"

He waved the flyers in my face again.

"These damn things are all over town."

"I certainly hope so. It's costing me a fortune."

"Don't get smart with me."

"That'd be a waste of time now, wouldn't it?"

"This is littering," he persisted. "Littering carries a fine of up to five hundred dollars and or thirty days in jail."

From behind me, a voice called out, "I seen 'em jaywalking too, Chief. Why doncha run 'em in for that while you're at it?"

I turned to check out the voice. The crew had formed a menacing semicircle right behind me. The sidewalk between Hub Tavern and the *Concrete Herald* building had filled with locals, several still holding beer glasses.

"Move along now, folks. Go about your business," Gardner shouted over my shoulder. "This is a police matter."

Nobody moved. An undertone of voices rolled over the street. A shrill voice rose from the back of the sidewalk.

"Why don't you and Barney Fife lock 'em all up?"

"Give 'em the death penalty," shouted another.

A derisive chuckle now rippled through the crowd. Officer Milliken's eyes darted around like a spotlight at a prison break.

Chief Gardner opened his mouth to reply, thought better of it, and snapped it shut. Instead he turned his attention back to me.

"I want you and these . . ." He seemed to be lost for a noun. "Gentlemen," he said finally, "on your way. Right now. Don't even stop for gas. Consider yourselves damn lucky I'm not running you in."

With that, he turned on his heel and stalked back toward the station. Somebody in the crowd gave him a wolf whistle.

"What about the girl in the picture?" I said to his back.

He stopped, turned, and wagged a finger at me.

"Don't press your luck."

I walked up close. His breath smelled of old coffee. I spoke softly.

"Look," I whispered. "You're the law here. I respect that." I threw a look back at the crowd. "You seem to have enough trouble of your own. I'm not here to make any of that worse, but you need to understand that I'm not going away. I've put a lot of time and miles on this case and until now I haven't come up with squat."

"You still don't have anything," he said.

"No, Chief Gardner," I said. "Actually, I do. It's not much, but it's more than I had before."

"And what's that?"

"A rumor," I said. "A rumor regarding you and this Hasu girl. We can have this out here in public. You can arrest me, but two hours later, when I'm back on the street, I'll just start knocking on doors again. You need to understand that I'm prepared to knock on every door in this town if that's what it takes."

I gestured to the swelling throng on the sidewalk.

"Excuse me, Chief, but I can't help noticing that folks around these parts don't seem real supportive of your efforts. I've got a feeling that if I work at it hard enough, I can find out what I want to know from one of them."

Before he could respond, I added, "What I'd prefer, though, is that you and I have a nice private discussion. You know, one-on-one. Nice and discreet. It's up to you."

He scanned the crowd as he thought it over.

"Let's take a walk," he said.

25

I WAITED UNTIL WE'D ROUNDED THE CORNER at the east end of main, away from the gaze of the crowd. We walked in the shade, along the red, weathered side of a defunct Albers Feed Store.

"Excuse me for asking, but isn't Chief of Police an elected office around here?"

Gardner gave a derisive snort and stopped in his tracks. "So they keep reminding me."

"So, why all the animosity?"

"Because I insist on acting like a policeman. I had the nerve to enforce the parking regulations, and I don't want drunks driving all over the valley on Saturday nights," he said bitterly.

"Sounds reasonable to me," I said.

"That makes two of us, then. The guy I replaced, Marvin Hansen, he'd been sheriff for forty-one years. He dropped dead three months ago over at the café."

"And you inherited the job."

"In all Marvin's time, nobody ever got a parking

ticket. Nobody ever put money in the meters. Everybody ignored the burning ban. If you got drunk and broke up one of the bars, Marvin just drove you home. If you crashed your truck driving dead drunk, Marvin drove you home and called a wrecker for you."

"Probably explains his job security."

This trenchant observation got me another snort.

"Who said I knew this girl anyway?" he asked as we continued our stroll south out toward the highway.

"I don't see how that's going to improve anybody's situation."

He stopped, drew himself up to his full height, and pinned me with his gaze. "Yeah," he sighed, continuing his walk. "I suppose you're right."

He stopped again and turned back toward me. Stepping in close.

"Why should I tell you anything? Maybe I just run you and those tramps out of town. If I start making some calls, I can run you all the way out of the county."

"I don't doubt it. But that's not gonna be a help. I meant what I said back there. I'm not going away. If that's what it takes, I'll be back tomorrow with more of those guys and my attorney."

He rummaged through the sheaf of torn photos he was still clutching in his left hand and came up with a relatively whole copy. He studied it carefully. "I suppose it does look kind of like her."

"Her name is Terra Hasu," I prompted.

"Yeah. When I was a kid, her family lived way the hell out in the woods up behind Diablo."

"Where did she go to school?" I asked.

"They had their own Christian school down in Hamilton."

I waited. He picked up the thread.

"They were real isolated. They didn't have much to do with anybody outside the church. There were all these wild rumors."

"What rumors?"

"Oh, God. Cannibalism. Demon worship. Kiddie porn. You name it, they were supposed to be involved in it. You listen to these folks, you believe half the valley was linked up in a half-mile daisy-chain cluster fuck." He pointed an upturned palm back the way we'd come. "You saw those people back there. That's how they are. They don't have enough to do. They spend their time making up things about people."

"Okay. So?"

"So about my junior year in high school, Terra started showing up once in a while at school things. Everybody noticed her right away. You know, it's a small town. All those weird rumors. Besides that, her clothes and everything were so weird."

"Weird how?"

"Like old and out of date. Hand-me-downs. The kind of things kids notice right away."

"And are none too kind about."

"You know it."

"What year was that?"

"Seventy-eight, seventy-nine. Right in there some-place."

"So she started showing up at school functions."

"Yeah, and . . . you know . . . word started to get around."

"About the girl?"

"Yeah." He walked around scratching and stretching like a hitter about to enter the batter's box.

"What word?"

"You know."

"What?" I pressed. "She was easy? What?"

"Not exactly."

"What then?"

"That she was one of *them*. That she was wild. I guess that's the word."

"Wild how?"

He looked at me hard. I gave him my best man-of-the-world look.

"Listen, Mr.—"

"Waterman," I said, sticking out a hand. "Leo Waterman."

He reluctantly shook it. Surveying the street again, he released my hand and pushed his deep into his pockets.

"You know, it doesn't look like my prospects in the next election are going to be any too damn good. I can live with that. What I do have going for me, though, is my family. I've got a hell of a wife and three nice kids. If I do talk to you, this is the end of it. When you walk away from here, as far as I'm concerned, this conversation never happened. No depositions. No nothing. You understand me?"

"I understand," I assured him.

"Easy wasn't the right word," he said. "Easy says you could like . . . you know . . . come on to her and she'd . . . come across."

I waited him out. Nearly a minute passed before he spoke again.

"It wasn't anything like that. She did the choosing. She just sort of decided who it was she wanted, and that was it."

"Uh huh."

"I'm not the only one here in town either. There were others. It's just not something . . . you know . . . anybody's gonna talk about."

Out on the highway, an eighteen-wheeler splattered the air with his jake brake. We listened as the roar rolled up over the hills.

"She wasn't like the other girls," he said.

"How so?"

Another long pause.

"Terra knew what you *really* wanted. It was like she could read way down in your mind, down into those things that you feel bad for even thinking about. With her it was more like"—he searched for a word—"theater. And she knew exactly what part you really wanted to play."

There didn't seem to be anything to say, so I didn't.

"Then the shit hit the fan." He took a deep breath.

"You've got to understand that from here on it's just small-town rumor. Nobody knows anything for sure."

"Okay."

"One of the first things I did when Marvin hired me was to try to poke my nose into the case, but it was all sealed up by order of the Skagit District Court. They do that when there's juveniles involved."

"It's a good policy."

He collected his thoughts.

"She killed him."

"She who killed him who?"

"Her mother, Claire. That part is on record. She killed her husband, Wayne. Some say she mutilated him too, but that's just rumor again. What's for sure is that the wife killed him. The poor woman had a long history of mental problems. She's been in and out of Northern State all of her life. I guess she just snapped."

"Did she go to jail?"

"Oh, no," he said. "She went all the way over the edge. Sat right there in court and told the judge her old man needed killing. Calm as could be. Not the slightest hint of remorse. They sent her down to Western State. Social Services took the little kids."

"Terra?"

"That's the part everybody remembers."

"What's that?"

"The competency hearing over in Sedro Woolley."

"What about it?"

"Terra went bonkers. The bailiffs had to carry her out both days. Took three of them."

"You were there?"

"Yeah. I was there. Hell, half of the valley was there. It was during Christmas break. She just went nuts. Screaming about how they hadn't done anything wrong. About how she'd get her momma out no matter how long it took. Big old picture of her being carried out of court was on the front page both days. It was big-time news for around here."

"What happened to her after that?"

He shrugged. "I don't know. I thought maybe they'd thrown her in the can for contempt or something, but she was just gone." He folded his arms over his vest. "What with Wayne Hasu dead and the mom off to the bin, the whole thing just sort of blew over. There was a lot of talk. A bunch of folks moved out of the area. It wasn't the kind of thing folks wanted to hear about anyway. Once they had somebody to blame, they just swept it under the rug."

He kept his gaze high on the scarred slopes to the south. I had a feeling. "And you never saw her again?"

He plucked a small purple flower from the ground and twirled it in his big fingers.

"I didn't see her again until nineteen eighty-nine," he said. "The year I came back here with Judy. She walked right into the station during my shift, big as life. Fine clothes, jewelry. New car. Had her nose fixed and everything."

I cocked an eyebrow. He shrugged.

"Just like that, huh?" I said.

"Just like that."

"Did she say anything about where she'd been all that time?"

"Nope."

I sensed that I'd somehow touched a nerve.

"You still see her?"

He scraped a handful of pebbles from the street, shaking them in his hand as he walked backward. He began throwing the stones, one at a time, at the side of the building.

"When was the last time you saw her?"

He gave a walleyed look, like a dog caught messing the carpet.

"She was here a couple of weeks ago. Looking real fine. Blond this time," he said, suddenly refusing to meet my eyes. "I told Judy I had to take a prisoner to Seattle. We—" He stopped. "I'm not proud of this. Maybe I'm just weak, but once she sets the hook in you, she doesn't let go. She's showed up every year or so, ever since eighty-nine. Every time, I tell myself it's the last time." He shrugged again. "It's a strong drive."

"I understand," I said. "It's been a major player

in most of the real shitty decisions I've made in my life."

We moseyed back up the slope, turning onto Main Street, which, except for an old man sliding along behind a walker, was now deserted. For the first time, he noticed the still-open door of the cruiser.

"My boy's waiting," he said. "We were gonna—"

"Thanks for the help."

He cast me a sideways glance. "You know, even after all this, if she was to walk through the door tomorrow night, or next month, I'll probably do it again," he said quietly.

"I know."

26

"YOU LOOK TERRIBLE."

"Thanks, I needed that."

"You know better than to drink with those guys," Duvall said.

"I guess I needed a refresher course."

The bell on the microwave startled me as it announced my coffee. Rebecca retrieved the cup and slid it over the breakfast bar at me.

"I've been thinking about what you told me. About that girl and her background and all."

"And?"

"I was struck by how the whole story is the perfect recipe for creating a sociopath. It's like her whole history was cast in stone from the very beginning. You take a regular kid, you isolate her from normal human beings, you subject her to years of mental and sexual abuse, and what you get is somebody who's prepared to do whatever it takes to survive."

"You think she's just a poor waif trying to survive?"

"A poor waif, no. Just trying to survive, yes."

"Come on. She's killed at least two people. She's been directly responsible for the death of at least one other. She's ripped off in excess of a couple of million dollars that I know of, and you say the poor thing is just trying to survive."

"Some people need more than others. Look at her life, for gosh sakes, Leo. This is a very needy person."

"Thank you, Dr. Brothers. The bad news is that none of this gets me any closer to finding her."

Rebecca checked her face in the small mirror, loaded her briefcase with paperwork, and picked up her keys.

"I thought this was your day off," I said.

"So many meetings, so little time. Lock up for me, will you?"

"No problema," I said.

She pulled her black raincoat from the hook behind the door.

"What's on your plate this afternoon?"

"I've got a five o'clock with my client."

"You better take a nap before you go."

"That's the plan."

"See you later."

The door closed behind her and then suddenly opened again. She stuck her head back in.

"Where's the mother?"

"If she's still alive, she's probably still in Western State. They tend to get retentive about folks who cut other folks into pieces."

"If her mother's still alive, that's where to look."

"How do you figure?"

"Trust me, Leo. She won't be far from her mother. People who suffer together have strong connections."

FIVE MINUTES INTO MY REPORT, Marge walked out onto her private terrace, seeking cover amid the jungle of potted plants. The breeze off Elliot Bay fanned my note cards onto my shoes. I kept talking as I picked them up. She stood on the concrete, just outside the sliding door, her arms now folded tight over an ivory silk blouse.

"You're sure?" she said when I finished.

"I'm sure."

"What if this person was lying?"

"He wasn't. He had no reason to lie. He saw her a little over two weeks ago. At least three weeks after she was supposed to be dead."

"We should call the police."

"There's a bunch of problems with that."

"Such as?"

"First off, Nicky's death is officially an accident, and the cops are never real anxious to be wrong." Marge started to object. I raised my voice. "Also, she's probably not wanted for anything."

Marge Sundstrom came charging back into the room, waving her arms.

"How can that—that pig not be wanted for anything? She murdered my son."

"I know," I said. "Listen to me, Marge—" She stopped pacing. "This woman is good at this. Early on, she got lucky. The old lady was an easy mark. She was a quick study, though. She learned from the experience. You've gotta give her that. What better place to find the vulnerable than at support groups? There's a kind of twisted brilliance there. There's no telling how many times she's run that little number, either. I'm bettin' a bunch. Over the past fifteen years, she's turned herself into a sophisticated woman of the world who doesn't have any trouble fooling other professionals. She's gotten this far by being smart, by being ruthless, and by being careful."

"But we have a witness."

"That's the other problem," I said. "First of all, it's my word against his. He'd have to be out of his mind to spill his guts to the police. He's got a wife and family. If I were in his position, I'd stonewall the hell out of it. You've got to understand, Marge, the people she leaves behind have been"—I struggled for a word—"compromised, I guess is the word. They've done things they'd never have done if it hadn't been for her."

"What bush is it that you're working so hard at beating around here, Leo? What are you trying so hard not to tell me?"

I took a deep breath. "You remember when we started this, you cracked once that 'a woman's best friend is a man's imagination'?"

"I remember."

"She's an artist with that imagination. I think she's learned how to push all the buttons. She knows how to get people to cross the line, over into a place all their instincts told them to stay out of. Once she gets them over there, they're not about to be telling folks about it."

She thought it over.

"Not Nicky," she said.

I retied my lace on my left sneaker.

"I want her," she said. "I want to wipe that smug look off her little face. I want to see her behind bars."

"Me too."

"What do we do?"

"We follow the mother."

"WHAT YOU'RE ASKING IS DEFINITELY ILLEGAL, probably unethical, and perhaps immoral. Why should I do that for you, Leo? Give me a reason."

I did my best. I told her everything, from Heck's suspicion that Allison hadn't been on board, all the way up to Chief Gardner. Saasha Kennedy was a good listener. You get that way after a few years as a crisis intervention specialist for the state of Washington. We'd met last year in a downtown hotel, where she'd been trying to talk a jumper in off a fourteenth-floor ledge. Later I'd enlisted her help with a particularly precocious young woman I was supposed to be guarding. While she still harbored serious doubts about me, she and Rebecca had become fast friends. We'd doubled to a couple of dinners and movies with Kennedy and Robert Dolan, her significant other.

"You're telling me the truth?" she said when I'd finished. "This isn't one of your more creative ruses?"

"Swear."

"Are you at home?" she asked.

"Yeah."

"I'll call you back. I'm working out of my apartment today. I'll have to annex the files by modem. I don't have a dedicated line, so I'll have to hang up and call you back."

"I'll be here."

I tried Rebecca. Still in a meeting. I went into the bedroom and changed into a pair of gray stonewashed Levis, a burgundy short-sleeved shirt, and my black high-top Nikes.

The phone rang. Kennedy.

"I could only get parts of this. Most of the file is permanently sealed by court order."

"I know."

"Claire Ellen Hasu was involuntarily committed to Western State Hospital in Steilacoom in July of nineteen eighty. Uncontested."

"What's uncontested mean in this context?"

"It means that although there were serious criminal considerations, all parties agreed that she wasn't fit to stand trial."

"Okay."

"Diagnosed as schizophrenic. Partially disassociated. Sometimes unresponsive. Intermittently violent. Security required full-time for staff safety."

"What's all that mean?" I asked.

"It means that sometimes she could appear to be just as normal as pie, but basically she was crazy as a shithouse rat."

"Okay."

"Transferred to Evergreen Psychiatric, in Olympia, in eighty-two. Evergreen is private. Prognosis is unchanged."

"Whoa, wait a minute. How does somebody who disassembles her spouse get transferred to a private facility?"

"It's common—if the family has means and the facility meets state requirements for security, the state is more than happy to get out from under the financial burden. Eager, even. Transferred again in eighty-five to Northbay Convalescent in Bellingham. Ditto to Seattle in eighty-nine."

"This woman needs a travel agent, not a doctor."

"Some experimentation is typical of patients with plenty of money and a poor prognosis. The family wants to feel it's tried everything. They're looking for the miracle cure. They're willing to try anything."

More pages turned. "This history, though, is excessive even for the well-heeled. If you read her treatment history, she's followed every new treatment trend around the state for the past fifteen years. Truly amazing tenacity."

"This woman gives up on nothing," I said.

"Transferred to Hampton Psychiatric in Longview in December nineteen ninety-two. Hampton is quite well respected. They've been around for fifty years."

"What does that kind of care cost?"

"It's a substantial commitment."

"How substantial?"

"Well—let's just take nursing. We'll forget about overhead, administration, security, medication, all those little details. Just round-the-clock nursing."

"Round-the-clock?"

"The patient is on heavy meds and is a high security risk. Twenty-four hours a day, seven days a week, fifty-two weeks a year."

"How much an hour?"

"At least twenty-five bucks an hour. Minimum."

I could hear her pushing buttons. "So, twenty-five bucks, times twenty-four hours, times three hundred sixty-five days is—six hundred bucks a day—times three hundred sixty-five is two hundred nineteen thousand dollars. Now add twenty percent for benefits, and we get—"

"I get the idea," I interrupted.

"A little over two hundred sixty-three thousand. Just for the nursing. As I said, it's quite unusual for the family to be that flush."

"I'll bet."

"Now, Hampton was a semiprivate facility, so you can divide the total cost by about four, but when you factor in the other expenses, it's going to push the figure up. Especially the kind of psychoactive meds she's on now. The meds alone are probably fifty thousand a year."

"Explain," I said.

"You have to understand how far the treatment of schizophrenia has come in the past twenty-five years. It wasn't that long ago; in the sixties, they kept zapping you with electricity until you became docile. Heck, as late as the mid-seventies treatment still consisted of a straitjacket and a padded room. If you gave them a hard time, they wrapped you in wet rubber sheets until the shaking calmed you down."

"What do they do now?"

"Psychoactive meds. That's what she went to Hampton for. They're the cutting edge of private psychoactive research."

"And?" I could hear pages being turned.

"And they worked. She got her first significant change in prognosis in what—thirteen years? Thorazine alleviated nearly all of her symptoms."

"Nearly all?"

"The most recent notation says she suffers occasional psychotic episodes under extreme stress."

"So she found her miracle."

"That remains to be seen. This is all too new. Nobody knows what the long-term effects are going to be. There isn't a sufficient sample to tell about long-term side effects or whether, over time, the body builds up a resistance to the drugs, things like that."

"So, she's in Longview."

"Not quite. Let me finish. September eighth of this year, she was transferred again to something called Mountainview Recovery in Issaquah."

"A little over two months ago."

"Right."

"What do you know about Mountainview?"

"Nothing." I could hear pages turning again. "I've got the state directory here. Chartered in November of seventy-four. Private, which means we're talking about really big bucks now. Used to be privately owned and operated. Changed hands earlier this year. Closed for reorganization until August of ninety-five."

"At least this clears up one of my loose ends."

"What's that?" she asked.

"Well," I said. "I've been trying to figure out how she goes through as much money as she does."

"She's just trying to get her mama cured."

"It would sound pretty noble if I didn't know where she was getting the money."

"Find her, Leo. Before she hurts someone else."

"I will," I promised.

27

I CAME BLINKING OUT OF THE MOUNT BAKER TUNNEL and cruised down the western high-rise onto the new floating bridge just as the sun put in a belated guest appearance. I had to flip the switch on the mirror to keep from being blinded by the slim orange sliver burning low over the Olympics. A stiff southern breeze had punched the water on the right side of the bridge into a series of small, disorganized white-caps. On the left side, the water was dark and flat.

I traversed Mercer Island, ran by Factoria, and followed I–90 out past Issaquah. I drove past the private road twice before I realized it was a driveway. No number. No sign. No mailbox. I thought it was just a turnout across from the white rambler with a big picture window. The overhanging trees absorbed the last remaining light. I nosed the Fiat into the darkness, turned on the headlights, and followed the road up and to the left. Another seventy yards, and then a sharp right. Up and right, then same thing back to the left. The road was a series of switchbacks that zigzagged all the way up the south side of the hill. The little car began to labor up the ever-steeper slopes. I downshifted to first and continued up.

At about the better part of a mile from the main road, I stopped in front of an ornate metal gate. Two small turnouts, one on each side of the gate, ran parallel to the high metal fence, just enough room for a car to back in and then head down the hill. A small white porcelain sign at the left of the gate read MOUNTAINVIEW RECOVERY. To the right of the gate, a white call box was bolted to the other brick column.

I could hear the slow clicking cadence of a distant sprinkler as it arched back and forth. The dim lights of a large two-story house shone dusky yellow through the trees. I backed the Fiat into the right-hand turnaround, walked back to the gate, and pushed the button on the box.

A loud set of chimes rang somewhere in the building.

"Yes?" An accent of some sort.

Two anodized lanterns on top of the gateposts suddenly buzzed on, throwing a thin circle of white light over the gate area.

"My name is Waterman. I'd like to see whoever is in charge."

"You have an appointment?"

He sounded a bit like Hector. Probably Hispanic.

"No. But I—"

"Sorry. Only by appointment."

With a snap of static, he was gone. I heard the whirring then as a small camera mounted on top of the gate header scanned the area and settled on me. Smiling for the camera, I leaned on the button long enough to make the chimes sound like the circus was in town. Nothing. I respected the process this time with a bigger smile. Still nothing.

I was debating the wisdom of climbing the fence when they appeared on the other side. Two Hispanic youths, not much more than twenty. Five-eight or so, a hundred fifty pounds max, dressed in white from head to foot.

"You must go," said the one on the left with the pencil-thin mustache. "Or we call the police."

I took a business card from my pocket, walked forward, and offered it through the fence. They looked at one another like I was trying to hand them a roadkill rat. When I kept waving it, Lefty stepped forward and plucked it from my fingers. His lips moved as he tried to decipher the card. Visibly frustrated now, he turned to his mate. "*Yo lo llevo a la jefa. Quedate aqui y cuidalo.*"

Still decoding, Lefty trotted my card off into the gloom. The other guy took a step back away from the gate and began stiffly pacing back and forth like a Beefeater at the Tower of London.

The click of a single sprinkler was joined in chorus by another. Closer I could hear the thick drops striking the ground. In the localized artificial light, Beefeater was now stalked by his shadow when he marched left and pushed it before him like a wheel-barrow when moving right.

It was another ten minutes before Lefty returned. He'd found a friend. Either they had a mold some-where on the grounds where they made these guys, or they were reproducing through cell division. Lefty turned the handle on the back of the gate, pulled it open about three feet, and beckoned me in. "You follow," he said.

I followed. Down a wide flagstone walk bordered by bricks set on edge, cutting through a well-mani-cured lawn surrounded by world-class shrubbery. Lefty led the way; the other two brought up the rear.

It must at one time have been a private home, a neocolonial manse. Maybe thirty rooms when it was new. This was the kind of place where secrets got buried. Where, if you had the cash, you stashed that alcoholic ex-wife, that idiot brother Waldo who liked to wave his pee-pee in public, or old Uncle Frank who just couldn't keep his hands off little boys. As long as you kept paying the freight, Mountainview Recovery would keep them out of your hair and out of the papers.

We climbed the two steps up to the twelve-panel doors on the front of the building. Using a key attached to his belt, Lefty opened the door in the middle. It swung open silently on oiled hinges. On the way by, I grabbed the edge of the door and tested it with a fingernail. Steel, not wood.

With the same key, he opened the first door on the right. The room seemed to be part library, part office. The spaces between the windows on the left wall were covered with framed medical degrees and official-looking plaques honoring civic contributions. The right wall held books on built-in floor-to-ceiling shelves. An old-fashioned sliding ladder provided access to the upper reaches.

Lefty led me to the far end of the room, where an elegant teak desk, a bit too big for Ping-Pong, was flanked by four red leather chairs with brass studs hammered in along the seams.

"Here," he said, indicating nothing in particular.

"Yes, we are," I agreed.

After he backed out of the room and closed the door behind him, I walked over to the windows. I scratched at the windowpane in front of me. Plastic of some sort, about a half inch thick. What I had thought was standard window leadings was instead more stainless steel. It would take a lumberjack a half hour with a splitting maul to hack his way through one of these babies.

I checked out the books. Mostly ancient decorator stuff, chosen for the color of their bindings rather than for the quality of their content.

The large oil painting occupying the central position behind the desk was of a woman in her thirties. Medium-length curly brown hair, held back over the ears by a pair of gold clasps. A pointed chin that seemed to poke out at the viewer. Pale blue eyes, showing white all around, as if in a constant state of surprise. The brass plaque on the table beneath the picture read "Medical Administrator— Dr. Lila Dawson."

I was still admiring the artwork when a voice came from behind.

"I hope you have a good reason for disturbing our patients, Mr.—" She checked my card. "Waterman." She said it slowly. She made it sound like a silly name. Some vagrant designation, ignominiously bestowed on the substantially less fortunate.

The painter had removed her rough edges. In the flesh, she was older, thinner, and much more intense. Her heavily veined hands held my card as she scanned it through her black half-glasses.

"My apologies," I offered. Without being asked, I sat in the red chair to the right of the desk. She walked around me and sat behind the desk, placing my card in the exact center of the blotter, meticulously squaring it up to the edges.

"Anyone can have cards printed," she said when she was satisfied.

"Anyone can have their portrait painted."

Lila Dawson donned her glasses, sat back in her chair, and looked me over like a lunch menu.

"I don't think I like you," she said.

"That's not very sensitive. You keep that up, you're gonna hurt my feelings. Then *I'll* need rehabilitation."

She removed her glasses now, allowing them to dangle from the gold chain around her neck.

"Because I am responsible for the well-being of so many, you'll excuse me if I have little talent for levity, Mr. Waterman."

"You're doing just fine," I assured her.

The eyes opened even further.

"You find disturbing the solitude of seriously ill patients to be a laughing matter?"

"Certainly not," I assured her. "I rang the bell. That's the way it's done in polite society, isn't it?"

"You should have called ahead for an appointment."

"Would I have gotten one?"

A thin smile.

"I just have a few simple questions about one of your patients."

She treated me to a stare that was supposed to melt me into a slobbering mass of protoplasm. "All information concerning my patients is strictly confidential."

"Claire Hasu is one of your patients. Is that correct?"

She opened the center drawer on her desk and poked around inside.

"I am not at liberty to share that with you. Now if that will be all—" She let it hang.

"Not even close," I said. "I have no desire to breach any kind of confidentiality. I just—"

The door hissed behind me. Huey, Dewey, and Louie stepped into the room, standing with their backs to the door. I turned back to Dr. Dawson.

"I only want to know—"

She stood up. "These unfortunate souls have enough problems without the likes of you. Can you imagine the agony that their families go through? Can you imagine a life without control of your senses or even your most elemental bodily functions? Can you?" Her voice rose. "Can you imagine yourself completely in the hands of others? When even your most basic need is at the whim of someone else? Can you? Would you like that, Mr. Water . . . man? Would that give you pleasure?"

When I didn't answer she spoke over my shoulder. "Mr. Waterman will be leaving."

I rose from the chair. "Mr. Waterman will be back," I said. "With a state inspector and a couple of policemen. Thanks for your time."

She stood to face me, her face suddenly quivering as if she were getting an electric shock.

Again she spoke over my shoulder. "*Tienes lista las medicina?*"

I didn't hear an answer, but I could feel them moving behind me. I stood up and stepped to the desk. I lifted a decorative crystal sphere from its wooden base on the desk and palmed it like a softball. Lefty was coming down the center rug, his right hand cupped at his side. Dewey and Louie were carrying out a flanking movement along the walls.

"I'm leaving, Doctor," I said to her. "No need for—"

"*Agarallo!*" she cried.

I was a step slow. The sphere caught Lefty square in the forehead, but not before he pierced my left shoulder with whatever he'd been hiding. He fell at my feet. I reached down and jerked at the chain that held his key, tearing a belt loop free, coming away with it. He groaned and rolled over onto his face. Dewey and Louie feinted at me but kept their distance.

Brandishing the sphere, I began to back toward the door. I checked over my shoulder for reinforcements. A syringe, plunger down, was imbedded in my shoulder. I pawed at it with my free hand, knocking it to the floor.

The doctor stayed put; her face was lopsided now, without symmetry. "No. No, no," she ordered. "*El no llega legos. La medicina lo calma.*"

They shadowed me up the room but made no move to stop me as I fumbled the key into the lock and backed out the door. As I kicked the door shut, my right arm was suddenly pinned to my side by a face I couldn't keep still. I reached around the face, grabbed the back of the neck, and drove my forehead hard into the center of the swirl. I heard the crack and scrape of bone. The grasp loosened. I brought the sphere up from my shoetops. It caught him under the chin to the crushed-rock sound of teeth crushing teeth. The apparition disappeared. I swung in a circle, looking for new challengers. Bad move.

My eyes failed to keep up with my head. The disparity upset my equilibrium; I went to one knee. Whatever Lefty had injected into my shoulder was beginning to take effect. I weaved out the front door, missed the first step, and sprawled out onto the flagstones. Even through the injection, I could feel the searing pain in my left elbow.

I started forward but inadvertently veered left around the main building as if driven by the wind. My legs felt heavy and useless like I was running uphill in deep sand. I kept leaning left and running until I came to the fence on the south side of the building. Like the windows, the fence was at once decorative and formidable. Eight feet tall, wrought-iron spikes with fancy spearpoints on top. It would take an agile and determined patient to climb out into the woods.

The world was animated and quivering with life. Each leaf, each blade of grass, was alive and moving independently of its brethren as if undulating to some underlying cosmic rhythm. It was all I could do not to stand and gawk in wonder. I hadn't felt this good since seventy-nine. I moved forward along the fence, working toward my car, using my hands to maintain my balance, searching in braille for an opening in the fence.

I could hear voices to my right. Moving closer. My path along the fence line was blocked by a massive rhododendron. Beams of light bobbed and criss-crossed over the lawn area. I squatted next to the bush, lost my balance, and sat heavily. The lights moved closer.

I crawled in between the rhodie and the fence, separated from the yard by the massive twisted trunk of the bush. The legs of two white-clad orderlies danced by the small opening in the roots. I wiggled my body down into the soft loam. Years of beauty bark had lined the dower bed with a soft, spongelike carpet. My hand felt the bottom of one of the fence spikes. Instinctively, I began to dig, moving the bark up and forward, piling the soft material around the roots of the shrub, creating an earthwork to further shield me from the yard.

The lights and the legs came by again, this time lingering on my hiding place. I peeked through the roots. Dewey and Louie. With Lefty and the other guy out of commission, they seemed to be all that was left.

"*Que es eso ayi?*"

"*Donde?*"

The lights swept back and forth, centering on my hidey-hole. I ducked my head and waited to be found. Inexplicably, the whole scene suddenly seemed wildly amusing. I had to push my face into the ground to avoid laughing out loud.

A sudden clamor arose from the other end of the

grounds. I could hear high-pitched yelling, but couldn't make out the words. The legs thundered off a run, their four-legged vibrations fast fading.

Sputtering, I rose to my knees, clearing my eyes and spitting bark, digging now like a dog for a bone, using both hands to send a rooster tail of dirt out behind me. Within two minutes, I had hollowed out a space large enough for me to wiggle out under the fence.

Once out, I giggled my way around the perimeter, bouncing off trees, falling twice, until I was at the back of the Fiat. The main gate was still closed. Back inside the fence, several shadows were moving my way on foot. I ran, slow motion, to the Fiat, threw open the door, and climbed in. I felt around the ignition. No keys. The wheel was locked. Thank God I'd used The Club. I began to laugh hysterically. Tears ran down my cheeks as I wrenched the wheel back and forth in a frenzy. On the fifth try, the pin that locked the steering wheel snapped. The shadows were getting shorter. There were three of them. I counted again. Three.

I fell out the door, climbed to my feet, and began to push the little car forward. As it reached the slope, it gained momentum, rolling smoothly, nearly leaving me behind as it moved down the hill. At the last moment, I crawled inside and aimed the little car at the road in the middle.

Through the glare, the gate was sliding to the right. There were four now. The doctor, Dewey, and

Louie. And another who stood beside the gate, arm pointed accusingly in my direction. I was studying the face when I missed the first switchback. I took the scenic route across the dogleg, plowing over a couple of scrub oaks, pulverizing a rotted stump, and then popping out the other side onto the pavement again.

I wrenched the wheel hard to the left and tried to focus my fading vision by using only one eye. I found the brake in time to baby it around the next corner, and the next. I gave up the brakes. The little car fishtailed wildly. I was still fighting the wheel when I broke from the woods onto the final straight stretch of the driveway, nearly blind now. Rolling fast toward the distant yellow light. I floored the brakes four times before I realized I was pumping the clutch. The Fiat was moving fast, running smooth like a sled. It was momentarily airborne as it left the driveway and bounced over the berm of the county road. The yellow light down the hill drew closer. A smaller blue light moved in the center of the field of yellow. I tried for the brakes again, missed again, and began to laugh. I aimed for the blue.

28

"THOSE ARE THE OATFIELDS."

"What are they doing here?"

"They just got through with your insurance agent."

"Why? Do I know them?"

"You ran over their television set."

"I did?"

"Yes, you did."

"Don't tell me."

"It was in their living room," Rebecca volunteered.

I winced. "My car?"

"Toast," she said, tossing me a white plastic bag. "That's what's left from the car. The tow truck driver gave it to me."

"And all the suits?"

"You know very well what the suits are."

"They can't all be cops."

"Wanna bet?"

"Wadda they want?"

"In a word, Leo—you. They want you. Jed's kept them at bay for thirty-six hours, but the jig is up."

"Tell them I'm still delirious."

"They assigned that Dr. Loftus to you before I got here. Officially, you're his patient. He's declared you fit as a fiddle. There's nothing I can do. Are you ready?"

"No."

"Good. I'll send them in."

They filed in, ten strong. Two Staties in uniform. Two plainclothes from King County. Two more uniforms from Issaquah. Two Portland detectives, a lonesome-looking Idaho State Police sergeant, and a guy in a blue suit who didn't bother to introduce himself.

Jed immediately took the offensive.

"Gentlemen," he began, after hand-shaking and card-swapping was over. "It must be understood at the outset that my client Mr. Waterman, like any public-spirited citizen, is anxious to cooperate in any way possible with any and all duly empowered law enforcement officials." Before they could comment, he held up a single finger and continued, "It must also be noted, however, that his cooperation must in no way compromise his constitutional guarantees regarding self-incrimination.

"In other words, if we don't guarantee not to charge him with anything, he's not going to tell us a thing.

"That is, I suppose, a somewhat crude but none-theless accurate translation of the spirit of the statement."

"That's a yes," I offered.

The younger of the two Issaquah cops, neatly shaved head glinting in the harsh overhead lights, took immediate issue. "Wait a minute, here. We've got your client dead to rights for reckless endanger-ment, reckless driving, DWI, destruction of private property, vehicular assault, and failure to provide proof of insurance. This maniac destroyed a house, for gosh sake. You think we're gonna roll over on all of that?"

"Life is a system of tradeoffs," Jed assured him.

The Statie with all the stripes jumped in. "I have been authorized to waive all charges in return for complete cooperation."

"Not by the city of Issaquah, you haven't."

Jed sauntered over to the door and pulled it open.

"Tell you what, fellas, you guys work out your jurisdictional problems and then get back to us. Okay?"

The Oatfields still sat stone-silent in the hall as the cops filed out.

"Why all the different cops?"

"Good question," Jed said. "That's why we're standing mute until we get a guarantee. I have no idea what they all want. What's for sure is that if the state is willing to deal, they must figure they've got bigger fish to fry. Besides that, the guy in the blue suit smells of Club Fed to me."

"What's the Issaquah cop so worked up about?"

"He's still pissed off about what a good time you were having when they arrived. He claims you kept hugging him and insisting he do a commercial for The Club."

"I was delirious."

"What else is new?"

When they came back in, Blue Suit did all the talking.

"Agreed," he said as he came through the door. This time, however, instead of slouching in the corner, he came over to the left side of the bed. He handed me several pieces of paper, folded once down the center. "Have you seen this before?" he asked.

He was about fifty, with thick brown hair without a tinge of gray, combed in the Ronald Reagan Bob's Big Boy style, so thin and fit it looked like he was sucking in his cheeks. His hands showed the work of a professional manicurist.

I flipped the pages open. "It's a copy of a report I gave to my client."

"Mrs. Henry Sundstrom."

"Yes."

"To the best of your knowledge, is the information accurate?"

"What's this, the Ollie North hour?"

He shot Jed an exasperated look. Jed passed it over to me.

"Okay. To the best of my knowledge, yes it is."

Jed came over to the right side of my bed. "Quid pro quo, gentlemen. Before we go any further, why don't you give us some idea about why so many jurisdictions are interested in this matter?"

"We believe that we may have a pattern of crime here that crosses state boundaries. We sent a copy of this report out over the regional wire yesterday morning. We got some very unexpected results. Several local jurisdictions"—he nodded at the other cops—"have open files, some as old as ten years, in which the crimes are similar and the suspect meets this Terra Hasu's general description."

"Which explains your presence," Jed said pointedly.

Blue Suit ignored him. "King County had already been called to the scene. As a matter of fact, they arrived before Issaquah."

"Called by whom?" Jed asked.

Blue Suit cast a glance at the two King County detectives. The shorter of the two pulled a notepad from his pocket and flipped through the pages. "We got a call at seven forty-two from a Saasha Kennedy."

"Why would Kennedy call the King County Police?" I asked.

"Ms. Kennedy, whom I believe you had spoken

with earlier in the day—" He waited for confirmation. I let him wait. "Ms. Kennedy, in the course of collecting information about Mountainview Recovery, happened to ask the computer system for a list of other patients."

"And," I prompted.

"There were no other patients."

"None?"

"Nary a one."

Blue Suit took the lead again. "Quite rightly, this raised some serious red flags for a mental health professional like Ms. Kennedy. She acted appropriately and called it in."

"I don't understand," I said.

The other King County dick stepped forward and held a picture in front of my face. A bit heavier, a bit younger, but that lopsided look was not something I was soon going to forget.

"Have you ever seen this woman?" Blue Suit asked. "Dr. Lila Dawson," I said without hesitation.

The cops exchanged "I told you so" looks.

"Actually," Blue Suit said, "Claire Ellen Hasu."

"Who?"

"The woman in the picture."

"You're shitting me. She's—" I stammered.

"Gone," said Blue Suit. "All that's left up there now are four illegal Panamanians, one with a fractured skull, one needing some serious dental work. None of them has one word to say." He hesitated for

effect. "We also found a woman under heavy seda-
tion in the security section. We ran her prints. You
want to guess?"

"Dr. Lila Dawson."

"Touchdown," he said, slightly raising his hands.
"We'll know more if and when the doctors can bring
her around. Right now, they're not promising anything. They think she's been kept under for the
better part of a month. Could be permanent brain
damage."

"Jesus," Jed muttered.

Before I could digest this information, Blue Suit
took over.

"It looks like somebody bought the damn hospital, hired a director, the staff, jumped through all
the state hoops, just so they could transfer the Hasu
woman into it."

"How could that happen?" I asked.

He got defensive. "It was a real treatment center,
that's how. Mountainview has been there for twenty
years. It's not like this was some fly-by-night operation. Whoever did this had their shit together. They
bought the place. The administrator was creden-
tialed. The hospital was accredited. Claire Hasu was
their first patient since they reopened. Think about
it. Every hospital has to have a first patient. She
was it. In this case, however, she was also their last
patient."

"They were on their way up the road too," said the
first King County cop. "We think the only holdup

was coming up with some identity paperwork for the older Hasu woman. Our forensics guys found a partially burned envelope in the fireplace from the Pacific County Bureau of Vital Statistics. We think she got her hands on a birth certificate. Whose, we don't know. With a birth certificate and a few weeks, you can become just about anybody you want to be. We're checking with Social Security and DMV now."

"Then you came knocking on the door," said Statie with stripes, "and seriously gummed up the works."

I sat up in the bed, stuffing pillows behind me for support.

"This is classic government work," I said. "The inmates end up running the asylum, and nobody's at fault."

"The people in Longview sent her up in their own ambulance. There was no breach of security on their end. We've interviewed the crew. According to them, Ms. Hasu was responding well to her medication. Talking to the crew. Excited about a change in scenery. Quite pleasant, according to them. They were met by Dr. Dawson, two Hispanic orderlies, and the family. Dr. Dawson herself signed her in."

"The family?"

"A daughter. In her thirties. We've got an artist down at Longview with the EMT who did the driving. We'll come up with—"

"Don't bother," I said. I pulled the manila folder out of the plastic bag on the bed and handed him a composite of Allison Stark. "Show that to them. See what they say."

"And you figure the switch happened right then?" asked Jed.

"That's what we're postulating. We figure no sooner was the Hampton ambulance out of sight then the real Dr. Dawson found herself under lock and key in the security wing."

"What do you figure they had in mind for the doctor?" I asked.

"Maybe they just leave her there with the Panamanians," said the Statie with all the stripes.

"Or—if you take the whole thing one step further—" said Blue Suit, "what could happen next is that poor Claire Hasu dies suddenly; the state gets notified; the remains get properly buried, and the two of them are home free. Nobody is even looking for them."

"Jesus," Jed repeated. "So, either way, as soon as she had her paperwork together, mother and daughter were going to just disappear."

"That's how it looks," said Blue Suit.

"Any leads?" I asked.

"We've got public transportation covered. Nothing there yet. We'll get them. It just may take a while. But fortunately, Mr. Waterman, that's not going to be your problem any more."

Blue Suit sat on the edge of the bed. "We want you to know that we appreciate the job you've done.

Without you this might never have come to light. You did a heck of a job."

He patted my arm twice, nodded at Jed, and then led the procession from the room.

Rebecca caught the door just before it swung shut and stepped inside.

"Loverboy here just skated on enough charges to keep him inside for thirty years," Jed announced.

"Thanks to you," she said.

"Gotta go," said Jed. "See if you can stay out of trouble, will ya?"

I told him I'd try.

"Dr. Loftus has released you as of five o'clock," Duvall said when he'd gone.

"Where's my stuff?" I asked.

"Your clothes are in the closet."

I threw my feet over the side of the bed. Even before touching down, I could tell that I was sore all over. I hobbled over to the closet and retrieved my clothes.

Rebecca caught me up, while I struggled to dress. "You made the papers again. Section two. Page one."

"Cheap advertising."

"Carl called."

"What, pray tell, did Carl have to say?"

"He said he never wants to hear any shit about his driving again."

Pushing my second arm through the sleeve pulled

a deep groan from me. I rested before starting on the buttons.

"Your cousin Paul called."

"Let me guess; he still expects me for lunch on Wednesday."

"On the money, honey. Also, the usual assortment of other Watermans called the hospital, checking on your condition."

"And you gave them the usual round of thanks."

"Yes, I did. And"—she crossed the room and pulled a piece of paper from her raincoat pocket—"Saasha Kennedy called me at home this morning. She was concerned that you were going to be upset with her for calling the police."

"Tell her not to worry. If anything, she may have saved my ass. God knows what might have happened if the County Mounties hadn't showed up right after I hit the house."

"Good. I'll call her this afternoon. She'll be relieved." Duvall unfolded the paper. "She wanted me to pass something on to you. It was complicated, so I took some notes." She began to read. "At the time of Claire Hasu's commitment, there were three minor children. Terra, who was seventeen. We know about her. There also was a son named Anthony, who was fifteen at the time. Anthony, as nearly as Saasha could find out, is alive and well, working as a roofer somewhere in Southern California."

I was working on tying my shoes when I suddenly grew numb.

"The youngest was six. Moderately handicapped. A little girl named Norma."

"Whoa," I said. "Norma?"

"That's what she said."

"There's a Norma Hasu?"

"No. Different last name. All the kids had different last names. Anthony was a Runyon. Norma's last name was"—she spelled it—"W-u-r-t-h-o-v-e-r. Wurthover."

"Whatever," I mumbled.

"Isn't that the name of the girl your friend Heck thought was on board with his son?"

"Sure is."

"Surely she wouldn't—"

Duvall went back to reading.

"Norma Wurthover graduated from a job-training program in Bothell three months ago. Right after that, she moved out of her group home in Kenmore. DSHS hasn't heard from her since." Rebecca checked the back of the paper. "That's it."

"Damn," I said.

"Not a sister," Rebecca said. "It must be a coincidence. Nobody would do that to a sister."

"Messes hell out of your family-values theory, doesn't it?"

"Why would she do that? Give me one good reason."

"I'll tell you what I think happened," I said. "After she graduated from that job program, I think Norma became a serious fly in the old ointment. I think she asked the Social Services people where her mother was, and I think they told her. Unless I'm mistaken, she made her way out to Mountainview and paid old mom a visit."

"You're making this up."

"Norma told a woman at the marina that she'd seen her momma and that her momma was all better now and had a real important job."

"You're kidding."

"I wish I was."

"Why kill the poor thing?"

"I'm betting that somebody who plans out every little detail like Allison Stark is not going to want a loose cannon like Norma wandering around running off at the mouth. Besides that, having parts of two bodies recovered only made things easier."

Duvall looked sick.

I fought off a wave of dizziness as I tied my other shoe.

"You don't look so good. Maybe you should lie down," she said.

"Let's get out of here."

"You are going to butt out of this, aren't you?"

"I don't have any choice. If I knew where they were, I'd sure as hell go after them. But I don't, so that's that. Things are at the APB manhunt stage of things. They could be anywhere. That's what the cops do best. Let's get out of here."

29

"TAKE THE LAKEVIEW BOULEVARD EXIT," I SAID.

Rebecca jerked the Miata hard to the right, swerving out of the mouth of the Mercer exit, forcing her way across all five lanes just in time to dive off at Lakeview.

"You should go home."

"I want to check on the Boys."

"You're on foot, remember."

"I left that van I borrowed in the Boys' driveway. I'll drive it."

"The house or the Zoo?"

"I paid them yesterday."

Four full-dress Harleys were backed in on the downhill side of Lynn when Rebecca let me out next to the Zoo.

"Thanks for the ride," I said. "I'll call you later."

She handed me the white plastic bag. "Don't forget your car."

"How thoughtful of you."

"Don't mention it."

I pulled open the battered door and stepped into the darkness. The aged bar that ran down the right side was full. Four ancient bikers occupied the stools closest to the door. The Boys were playing snooker on the huge six-by-twelve-foot table in the back. I made it all the way to the table before they noticed me.

"It's Evel Knievel," bellowed Harold.

The noise startled George, who got so far under the cue ball he lofted it completely over the rail and onto the floor, where it began bumping over the uneven planks toward the back room. Harold gave chase.

"Jesus Christ. What in hell?" Then he saw me. "Leo," he said. "It's Lazarus come back from the dead."

"Did ya really waste a whole house?" asked Ralph.

"As I understand it, it was just the family room."

He seemed disappointed. Norman, the Speaker, Earlene, Mary, and a short Asian guy who seemed to think he knew me appeared out of the darkness to hear the story and offer congratulations on a job well done.

"I get another shot," said George.

"No way," howled Ralph, waving the ball. "You scratched."

"Bullshit," George shot back. "How in hell am I supposta—"

Tuning them out, I lugged myself up onto one of the tall stools surrounding the table and flopped the bag up onto the counter. I dumped it out and began to paw through the dusty contents. The folder full of Carl's composites. The last four registrations. One eight-track tape—Moby Grape. Two old Les Schwab tire guarantees. Three partially melted cough drops. Heck's green bag of receipts. Three petrified french fries. A pair of sunglasses with one lens. A dollar forty-seven in change and a road map of Montana.

The little Asian guy appeared at my elbow holding a pool cue. He was wearing a soiled blue-and-white baseball cap with a peeling silhouette of the Space Needle on the front. One of those cheap foam jobs, the crown several inches too tall. It made him look like a TV bass fisherman. Billy-Bob Fung. Grinning maniacally, he clapped me on the back. His eyes were clouded and unfocused. He kept on grinning until I looked up, at which point he scrambled back across the room to Earlene and Mary.

I went back to poking around in the remnants of my beloved Fiat when wild laughter erupted from the rear. Earlene, Mary, and Billy-Bob all hid their heads when I turned around.

"Something funny?" I asked.

If it wasn't before, it was now. The three of them burst into beer-spewing torrents of laughter. Billy-Bob lurched over to me again, jabbed a stubby finger at Heck's bag, and then rushed over to whisper into the Speaker's ear. It must have been a doozy. Even the Speaker cracked a smile.

"What? What?" I shouted. "Somebody want to clue me in here or what."

No go. All this produced was more mirth. George missed again.

"Hey, hey," he groused. "How in hell are we supposed to concentrate here?"

The Speaker leaned over and whispered in his ear. George looked my way, leaned his cue against the wall, and walked over.

"They think you're a pervert."

"Why's that?"

"The bag."

I held up the white plastic bag.

"No, the other one. The green one."

I put my finger on it. "This one?"

From across the way, Billy-Bob howled, "Spikee butt plug." The three of them dissolved into a drunken rugby serum.

"It's from that pervo shop on First Avenue, you know, the one with all the rubber gear on display." He tapped the bag. "See the chains?"

"I thought they were like interlocking rings, you know, like the Olympic symbol."

"Leo been a baaaaad boy," cooed Earlene. Predictably, this produced another round of hysterics.

"Naw. They're chains. They got their windows lined with the same paper. It's like their logo. We all walked past it twenty times a day when we was lookin' for that girl."

"I have to make a call," I said, digging in my pocket for change. "Get the fellas and meet me at the house."

30

ONE OF THE TWINS ANSWERED THE PHONE. "Flood residence."

"Mr. Ortega, please."

"Your name?"

"Leo Waterman."

"Hold on."

Frankie took his sweetass time. "Yeah."

"Frankie, it's Leo."

"Tell me something I don't know."

"I need a favor."

"What makes you think you got one coming?"

"That's for Tim to decide, I guess."

I heard him sigh. "Hold on," he said.

Tim Flood and my old man had started out together working as labor organizers for Dave Beck and the Teamsters. My father had parlayed his local notoriety into eleven terms on the Seattle city council. Tim had gone in another direction. He'd used his Teamster connections to become the Northwest's biggest and most successful fence. Like any good conglomerate, Tim had branched out. If Seattle had anything that could be termed organized crime, Tim was it. These days he was mostly legitimate. Mostly. Old habits die hard.

Last year, I'd bailed Tim's granddaughter, Caroline Nobel, out of a mess. I was hoping he still felt grateful. Frankie Ortega had worked for Tim Flood for as long as I could remember. Tim liked to call Frankie his arranger. If you got behind in your payments to Tim, Frankie arranged for your furniture to disappear. If you still didn't get your vig paid on time, Frankie arranged some sort of colorful maiming. A broken arm, something like that. Nothing too serious. Nothing fatal. The dead can't pay.

He was back. "So what do you need?"

I told him.

"That shithole belongs to Pinky Taylor. He's got this nephew of his, Marty something, running it. Marty's an asshole of the first order. You're right. They ain't gonna tell you shit. Most likely they'd hit you up for some change, feed you a bunch of crap, then try to sell your ass to whoever it is you're looking for some more. That's how they operate."

"That's what I figured. You think you can convince him?"

"I said he was dumb fuck, Leo. I didn't say nothing about him being suicidal."

Point made, he changed the subject.

"You know, the kid's doing good. She enrolled at the Evergreen State College this year."

"Great."

"Still got that ecology bug up her chimney, though. Tim's got us recycling, for chrissakes."

"Responsible citizenship," I said.

This got what passed for a laugh from Frankie Ortega.

"Yeah, that's right. Okay, Leo. Tim figures we owe you one. You be there at seven-thirty. You're gonna want to get right in there after we leave, while Marty's still got the fear of God in him. He's a dumb fuck. You give him some time to sit around and think about it, he's gonna get stupid again."

"I'll be there."

AT SEVEN-THIRTY SHARP, Frankie and the twins came marching up Pike Street, under the red, blinking LOANS sign, parting the regular citizens like a plow through a spring field. Whoever had invented the business suit had never intended it to cover anything as large as the twins. If you'd never seem them in action, their blocky bulk, combined with their remarkably splayfooted stride, could have been comic. If you'd seen them work, suppressing a smile was easy.

All hundred and sixty pounds of Frankie Ortega was resplendent in a light yellow suit, white tie, brown-and-white two-tone shoes. He left one of the twins outside while he and the other went in. As he stepped through the entrance, Frankie flipped the sign on the door to CLOSED.

The place was called the Pleasure Palace. It had occupied this corner of Second and Pike since sometime back in the sixties, a leftover from the sexual revolution. Upstairs they offered peep shows and movie booths. Downstairs it was books, magazines, and equipment. Two mannequins in full rubber gear cavorted in the front window. They were having a handcuff sale. This week only.

George, Ralph, Harold, and I were waiting across the street in front of the Drug Emporium.

"So, what are you guys gonna do when the city takes the house?" I asked casually.

"Big Frank says they got some rooms on his floor down at the Franklin Hotel," offered Harold. "We was thinkin' of movin' in there."

"That way, we could stay together," Ralph said.

"Who else would put up with you two?" George asked.

The door of the Pleasure Palace burst open. A customer, horn-rimmed glasses, was suddenly propelled sideways out the door. He stood blinking on the sidewalk. A green sport coat sailed out the door onto the sidewalk. He picked it up. For a moment, the guy thought about rushing back inside. Then he looked to his right. The sight of the outdoor twin glowering at him was all the motivation he needed to get moving up the street.

The other four customers came out in a knot. All middle-aged white men, they came stumbling out into the street looking dazed. I was watching a little bald guy trying to dislodge his shirttail from his zipper when Harold piped up. "Hey, Leo," he said. "Ain't you related to the guy in the blue suit?"

I shifted my attention to the guy in question. Cousin Paul stood on Second Avenue adjusting his tie. I started across the street. As I approached from the rear, he turned to leave and ran smack into me.

"Howdy cuz," I said. "The businessman's lunch? What's your office—three, maybe four blocks from here? You do this often?"

He was dumbfounded. "Oh . . . Leo . . . I—you— I—it's not what it seems. I—"

I patted his shoulder. "It never is, cuz. It never is."

George's voice came from behind me. "Should we check him, Leo? See if his shorts are on backward?" The crew yukked it up.

Horrified, Paul took me by the shoulder and pulled me aside.

"Now, Leo, you wouldn't, you know how Nancy is—"

"My lips are sealed," I promised with a big grin.

"Come on now, Leo. This isn't funny."

"I'll cut you a deal, Paul. You forget about lunch on Wednesday and all that trust fund shit, and I'll forget about this. How's that?"

His relief was palpable. "You mean it?"

Before I could answer, Frankie and the indoor twin were coming out the door of the Pleasure Palace.

"Duty calls," I said to Paul.

Frankie twitched his perfect little mustache at me and followed the twins back up Pike. I grabbed the sticky door handle and went inside.

Tony Moldonado would have loved the place. The right-hand wall was dedicated to books and magazines. As nearly as I could tell, no fetish was left unaccounted for. Standup racks ran down the center of the store. Videos of all types adorned the racks. *Dickman and Throbbin'. When the West Was Wet. Rumped and Dumped. California Reamin'. Romancing the Bone. Call Me Fido. Jesus.*

An orange beaded curtain at the back of the store partially obscured the way upstairs. A long, high counter ran along the left side of the store. Behind the counter, under the wide, watchful eyes of Juanita the Inflatable Senorita, was the equipment collection. Full executioner garb, restraints, gags, hoods, ropes, sprockets, gears, pulleys, studded bustiers, a museum-quality assortment of faux appendages in a variety of textures, styles, shapes, and colors, many of truly epic proportions, some conveniently built for two, others, as the yellowed sign suggested, "for those hard-to-reach areas." Had I but known what I was missing.

Marty sat behind the counter, his head cradled in his hands. His forehead was beginning to puff and turn purple. The back of his greasy hair stood straight out as if someone had grabbed him by the back of the head and slammed his forehead onto the counter several times. I pushed both pictures under his pitted face.

"You know them?" I asked.

"What the fuck's the matter with you?" he whined. "You didn't have to send those animals in here. All you had to do was ask."

"Yeah. I'm sure you would have been anxious to help."

"Hey, man, I told the other guy. Ain't my fault the dumb fuck walks out and gets his big dumb ass run over."

I hustled down the counter; the lock on the gate was already shattered. I burst through it, ran up the three steps, and started toward Marty, who had evacuated his seat and was cowering against a wall covered with studded dog collars. "Hey. Hey." He held his hands in front of him. "Hey. Hey, man."

"That dumb fuck was a friend of mine," I said quietly.

"Sorry. Okay? Sorry."

"How much did you beat him for?"

"Hey man, I didn't—"

I stepped on his right foot, which instinctively brought his hands down, then punched him in the forehead. He slid down the wall, dragging several leashes and collars down into his lap. The impact shook Juanita loose from her moorings. She fluttered down from the ceiling, her rubicund apertures coming to rest astride Marty's shoulders.

"How much?" I repeated.

"Five hundred bucks," he whispered up from the floor.

"The pictures."

"Yeah. Yeah. I seen 'em both. Him just once. Her a bunch of times. They was mostly mail order, though."

I stepped back to give him room.

"The address."

Keeping his eyes on me at all times, he clawed himself to his feet and pulled a small black metal box out from under the counter. He picked through the cards, finally pulling one half-way out. I reached over and pulled it free. "Thanks," I said. Flat on her back now, Juanita seemed to be whistling.

I read the address. I should have known.

31

THE INTERIOR OF THE HOUSE WAS DARK, illuminated only by the glowing light switches that flickered from within the darkness like the narrow eyes of forest creatures. I pushed the doorbell. Nothing. I tried again, this time longer. A momentary change in the scant light suggested movement in the back of the house. I knocked.

After a moment, I could feel her presence behind the door. "Mrs. Swogger, it's Leo Waterman," I said. Nothing. "From Seattle. I spoke to you and your husband a while back."

"I remember."

"I know it's kind of late, but I'd like to have a word with you."

"My husband isn't home."

"That's okay. It's you I wanted to talk to."

I thought I heard her breathe. "Please," she said. "You'll have to come back when my husband is at home."

"If I could just have a few words with you—"

"Please," was all she said.

"He's never home when she's around, is he?"

Her next breath I heard for sure. "I don't . . . please don't."

"Help me stop her," I said.

I had my left hand on the front of the house, so I could feel her lean heavily against the wall. "You don't have to live with this," I said. "Nobody should have to put up with this."

Any response was obliterated by the deep booming of bass notes as a black Mazda pickup truck, windows tinted solid black, its frame nearly dragging the ground, rounded the corner immediately to the north and cruised slowly down the street, away from where I stood. I shifted my weight from foot to foot as I watched the purple taillights recede. The lights disappeared around the corner. I listened as the booming bass notes spread their sonic ripples in ever more distant circles, finally giving way to the rushing sound of the wind high in the fir trees.

I was about to speak again when a rattling chain from inside stopped me. The door opened a foot. Her eyes were wide. Her long hair was unbraided, hanging loose about her like a prayer shawl. She clutched a white terrycloth bathrobe hard at the neck.

"Please go," she said through the crack.

"I can't."

"He's my husband."

"Not when she's around."

She nodded at the floor.

"Where are they?" I asked.

She shook her head slowly. "You mustn't judge him by this, Mr. Waterman. He has needs . . . he . . . he's done so much good."

"I'm sure he has."

"He just can't break free. She . . . she won't—"

"She never lets anything go. With her, nobody gets out alive."

Katherine Swogger's eyes were full now. She released the door and stepped back into the room. I followed her in, closing the door behind me. I reached over and switched on the floor lamp to the right of the door. Her face was all lines and shadows and sorrow. These weren't her first tears of the evening. She turned her back on me. We stood that way for a long time. The furnace kicked on, sending warm air up my right pant leg. I moved off the heat register, across the room, intending to put a comforting hand on her shoulder.

"Don't," she said, before I got there.

"How long?" I said. "How long are you going to let this thing tear your life apart? It's time for it to stop. Help me, and I'll stop it."

"God, how I've wanted to. They wouldn't let me stop," she said in a very small voice. "They made me . . . do . . . things. Things I—"

"Her father got what he deserved. It's time the rest of them paid."

She gave me a dismissive wave of her hand.

"Wayne Hasu had nothing to do with it. He was just a fool. It was always Claire. Claire's a monster. He was going to the police. She—" She stopped, shaking her head in some silent conversation. "Never mind."

"Tell me where they are."

"I can't."

"You know Claire's loose, don't you?"

Her eyes opened wide. "No. You're lying. How can that be?"

"It's a long story. Trust me. Terra managed it. Wherever Terra and your husband are, she's there too."

She turned away again, flexing her toes in the carpet, tugging at her twisted lower lip. "Oh God," she said. "I can't stand the thought that she's there watching, giving directions."

"Don't you ever get tired of being a victim? How can you sit here while your husband is out doing God knows what with her?"

She turned back toward me now, squaring her shoulders, pulling the hair out of her face. I thought for a moment she was going to strike out at me. "Better with her than with me," she said.

"It needs to stop," I said again. "It has to stop for him too."

"I can't."

"Right now, as far as the law is concerned, the worst your husband is looking at is harboring a fugitive, and that's only if they can prove he knew she was on the run."

"She called him last night."

"You listen in, don't you?"

"If you want to survive, it's a habit you learn."

"I wondered how come you were surprised I was there with your husband, but at the same time seemed to have the tea set up for three."

"You're not lying to me. Claire is out."

"I swear," I said. "Just about every police department in the Northwest is looking for them right now. It's just a matter of time. This is the only chance you're going to get. Do the right thing here, and you can buy a lot of goodwill for your husband."

She thought it over.

"I have to be there," she said after a minute.

"Are you sure?" I asked.

"I think so. I need to see this end."

"Where are they?" I said again.

She told me.

"I need to use the phone."

"In the kitchen."

"It'll be all right," I said lamely.

"No, it won't," she said.

32

THE HIGH BREEZE HAD WORKED ITS WAY DOWN to ground level, pulling with it a thin, insistent rain that swirled unpredictably up sleeves and down shirtfronts. Katherine Swogger, Marge Sundstrom, and I had been standing in the meager shelter of a barren oak tree across the street from the duplex for the better part of an hour when the Statie with the stripes crossed the street to us.

His plastic hat cover had collected a pint of water, which rolled off the wide brim as he walked. "The warrants are in order," he announced.

I felt Katherine shudder on my left. The cop addressed himself to her.

The duplex was a shabby prefab affair, mirror images, left and right. Looked like two bedrooms and maybe a loft. Brown plywood siding, three concrete steps leading up to bright yellow doors. Wrought-iron railings. Both units were dark behind heavy curtains.

"The church owns both units?"

"Yes," she said. "They're used sometimes as safe houses for battered women. Sometimes as temporary shelter for homeless families."

Behind him, two black-clad entry teams moved into position in front, while two more quick-stepped around back. Each team carried a heavy fabricated battering ram up the short flight of steps that separated the front doors from the street. "I'm way out of line letting the three of you be here," he said. "Anything breaks down, Waterman, you get these ladies the hell out of the way in a New York minute, you got it?"

I said I did.

He turned to leave. Katherine Swogger reached out and put a hand on his arm. "Please, officer," she said. "Don't hurt him."

"My men are trained to exercise due restraint."

He tried to leave, but she stopped him again. The cop was patient.

"Don't let them bring him out like . . . Tell them to fix him up, please," she said finally.

His eyes narrowed, but he stayed professional. "I'll take care of it."

With the crook of a finger, he summoned the two radio officers down from the porch. They leaned in close, throwing glances our way as he spoke, returning to their positions when he'd finished.

Without any visible signal being passed, both front doors were suddenly assaulted. On the right, the yellow door shattered, and bounced inward on its single remaining hinge, and then swung fully open, leaning awkwardly against the porch rail. The inside of the door was adorned with a colorful poster: LOVE SHOULDN'T HURT. The team disappeared inside.

On the left, the lock held, leaving the ram buried in the cheap hollow-core door. While the officer struggled to pull the heavy ram free, one of the others reared back and planted his booted foot just above the lock. The door burst open, dragging the ram, still imbedded, with it. The armed officers went in back to back.

The undercurrent of weather was drowned amid the shouts coming from the duplex. One by one the lights in both units came on. The shouting died down. The three cops still outside shooed the neighbors back to their homes. Katherine Swogger leaned heavily on my left side. Marge had slipped her arm through mine. She was shaking so hard her teeth were chattering. "Take it easy," I said. "It'll be over soon."

The team on the left appeared on the front porch.

"Empty," the sergeant shouted.

One by one the officers walked back into the street and waited. A shadow appeared in the door of the right unit. Both women tensed. The sergeant walked briskly over to the Statie with the stripes. I disengaged myself from the women. "Stay here," I said. As I closed the distance, I began to pick up parts of the conversation.

"Well then, give him a frigging shower," said Statie. He saw me coming out of the corner of his eye and motioned me over. He was angry.

"Did you know what was going on in there?"

"No, and don't tell me," I said.

"I been at this twenty-four years, but this is the capper," he huffed. "Jumping Jesus." He spoke to the sergeant. "Bring the women out. Make sure they're decent. We'll transport them separately."

As the sergeant hurried back inside, I walked back over to Marge and Katherine. "They're bringing the women out," I said. The two women stood huddled together, fused by some unspeakable kinship.

Claire Hasu came out first, her eyes rolling in her head like a spooked horse, handcuffed behind, an officer on each elbow, her head sticking out from the top of an orange police-issue poncho. Her feet and legs were bare and otherworldly, seemingly translucent, in the purple glare of the mercury vapor lights.

A red-and-white Shephard ambulance pulled up in front of the house, partially muffling her voice, blocking our view. The doors were opened from the inside. Two white-shirted EMTs stepped out into the rain.

Terra came out next. Same arrangement. Another orange poncho, this one cinched in place by a bungee cord around the waist. In the odd artificial light, her black-clad legs all but disappeared, leaving her torso to float on air. From behind the ambulance, Claire's voice rose again.

"Tell them they've made a mistake. Tell them," she said as Terra was led by.

"Be quiet," Terra said without looking at her mother.

Claire offered pointless resistance as they pulled her, skidding on her bare heels, around to the back of the ambulance, lifted her onto a collapsible gurney, and pulled the straps tight.

Whatever else she had to say was cut off as they lifted her into the ambulance. Two members of the assault team, bulky flack vests still in place, climbed in after her, pulling the doors shut behind them. Without turning on its lights, the ambulance purred off down the street.

Terra didn't watch it go. Her eyes were locked on Marge Sundstrom, who had crept out from beneath the tree and stood now in the rain-slick road no more than twenty feet from the woman she had known as Allison Stark. Marge opened her mouth to speak, then closed it.

A white state police cruiser came to a stop between the two women. The driver hustled around and opened the door. Only Allison's head was visible above the car. Her lips curled as she spoke.

"You cow," she said in an even tone. "I only wish I had a chance to work on you. I'd make you bark like a dog." The cop tried to push her into the car.

She kicked a leg out backward and locked her chin onto the roof. "You want to hear about your precious Nicky? How he liked it with the Vaseline. How he liked me to—"

The Statie with the stripes shouldered his way through the other cops, grabbed her by the hair, bent her head to her waist, and, using his knee as a catapult, launched her into the backseat.

"Get her the hell out of here!" he shouted at the driver.

As the police car pulled away, Marge stood transfixed in the middle of the street, her feet wide apart, hands thrust deep in the patch pockets of her plaid wool coat. She stood for a long moment after the car had gone, then turned quickly and walked toward me.

"I'll be in the van," she said, brushing my shoulder on the way by.

By the time they brought Jeffrey Swogger out, fifteen minutes later, Katherine had gravitated across the street. She stood tall among the knot of police officers along the sidewalk, her wet black raincoat shimmering with reflected light.

His curly hair was soaked and plastered to his skull. He wore the same blue suit he'd worn when I met him, except without the tie and the belt this time. They'd done the best they could. Although his face was ruddy from a recent scrubbing, the lips were still a bit too bright, the eyelids still a shade too defined. Katherine called his name. He tried to speak. The lips moved, but nothing seemed to come out.

"Oh, they're gonna love him down at King County," said one of the cops behind me. A second cruiser pulled to the curb.

I turned and walked around the corner to the van. My legs were stiff. I felt like the Tin Man. Marge sat low in the passenger seat, staring out the side window into the darkness.

"You okay?" I asked, as I buckled up.

She took a deep breath. "That wasn't nearly as much fun as I thought it was going to be."

"Funny, but I think that's what the Reverend just said."

The little smile told me she was going to be all right.

THE BUM'S RUSH

George lifted a stiff hand to my elbow as we closed the distance. Twenty years on the streets had filed his instincts smooth. He knew. This was trouble . . .

Nobody loves you when you're down and out – except maybe Leo Waterman. As a man who has transformed a crew of residentially challenged devotees of cheap alcohol into a crack surveillance team, Leo has a soft spot for society's downtrodden.

When a homeless woman says she's the mother of a deceased rock idol, Leo takes it upon himself to investigate the lady's claim, thereby embroiling 'the Boys' and his own already bruised body in a high-speed, life-threatening pursuit of the truth.

'Waterman is a big, bullheaded, wisecracking galoot with a mischievous sense of humour that makes him one of the most likeable characters in the genre'
Booklist

The Bum's Rush, the third Leo Waterman novel, will be published by Pan Books in May 2007

The opening scenes follow here.

1

IN THE LOW DARKNESS OF THE ALLEY, the sole delineation of blood from blackness was a certain vibration of line where the animal movement ended and the uneven bricks began. Ahead in the gloom, a succession of shoulders moved as a single beast, ears hot and full of blood, lips mumbling encouragement to some bizarre ballet being danced down on the rough gray stones.

George lifted a stiff hand to my elbow as we closed the distance. Twenty years on the streets had filed his instincts smooth. He knew. This was trouble. Without willing it so, I found myself stopped. George's hand fell to his side. Harold wedged himself tight between my right shoulder and the wall. Inside the circle of men, white smoke from a trash fire rose up the west wall, adding further insult to the overhead ocean of airborne waste that had been hanging low over the city for the better part of two weeks. An inversion, they called it.

"That's it, git 'er." A slurred voice rolled along the alley, oddly amplifying the silence left in its wake. I could hear it now. Under the shoe noise and the grunting. First the sporadic ticking of the fire, then, down at the bottom, a continuous, rhythmic keening, at times almost a whistle, rising insistently from the ground. I willed my legs forward, but apparently they had other plans. Before I could get a grip, Norman shouldered me aside and strode out ahead.

Arriving at the circle of men, he reached in and separated the nearest pair with enough force to create a staggering chain reaction around the entire circle. On his left, the force ricocheted the heads of two loose-necked drunks. A bottle shattered on the pavement. An emaciated guy of about thirty, his blue watchcap dislodged and rolling at his feet, stumbled to one knee, clutching his ear. On the right, the old guy in the tweed overcoat was squeezed, seed-like, out into the center of the circle where he stood blinking and chewing his gums, waiting for his numbed nerves to give him some sort of hint as to what in hell had just happened. I followed Norman through the breach.

Two figures rolled and kicked amid the damp refuse. Up close, the sound I'd heard back in the mouth of the alley was less a whine of terror and more a groan of strained resistance. Sitting astride a struggling figure, blue bandana worn pirate style, was a ragged specimen—forty going on seventy-five—his leathery face a maze of booze-etched crevices, landscaped here and there by a thin beard and mustache. He tore at the clothes of the other figure, who was scrunched into a defensive posture, one hand with a death lock on the belt line of a sagging pair of trousers, the other clawing at the dangling sleeve of a green satin jacket, torn to strings at the shoulder, revealing an oblong breast, big brown nipple slightly off center, peeking from beneath a bunched flannel shirt.

With a single lengthened stride, Norman punted the pirate back to Penzance. The ungodly force of the huge boot completely separated him from his victim, propelling him airborne express to the far side of the circle of men, where he came to rest, rocking silently on his spine, face smoothed with purple blood, bug-eyed paralyzed at the feet of a pair of Indians who seemed unable to comprehend this sudden change in tonight's entertainment schedule.

The remaining figure immediately regained her feet and tottered toward the east wall, the free hand hauling her drawers back up over her hips, one eye, visible through her hair, never leaving Norman. Instinctively, I reached to help. She backed against the wall, pulled her right fist back into her sleeve, and waited for my next move.

George stepped between us. "Leave her be, Leo," he said. "Don't be such a goddamn social worker."

"She needs—" I started.

He stepped in closer. "Yeah. She needs a lotta shit, Leo, and ain't none of it gonna come from you neither. 'Less of course you wanna take her away from all this. You gonna marry her or something?"

Over George's left shoulder, I could see that she was halfway back the way we'd come, eyes welded to us, using the wall for support.

The pirate had rolled onto his side and retched up a small pool of thick liquid that struggled to spread itself upon the dirt. The eight or nine spectators began to stagger off into the darkness.

"Ally ally infree." Norman roared from behind me. He held down the center like a ragged obelisk. Bigger even than usual. Wearing everything he owned. The better part of six-seven, his massive arms spread as if in embrace, his gnarled hands beckoning. On the street they called him Nearly Normal Norman, or sometimes just Normal. It was a joke. You only had to once look into Norman's eyes to be absolutely certain that this person was not watching the same channel as the rest of us. A couple of years back, the last time he'd earned himself a state-mandated tune-up, I'd watched six cops and a couple of paramedics fail to get him into an ambulance. The third wave of reinforcements finally tracked him down over in Hing Hay Park, where he was contentedly feeding corned-beef hash to the park's feral pigeons.

As the gathering crowd jeered, they'd cornered him in the pagoda and Tasared him six times. He'd seemed to devour the voltage like some walking storage battery, his eyes glowing ever brighter after each shot of juice. It wasn't until they'd busted the third syringe off in him that he even began to slow down. I don't care what anybody says, I still contend that if he hadn't been naked, they'd never have taken him.

The pirate, resting now on his knees and forehead, groaned piteously and again began to heave, this time dry.

Normal slid a massive arm around the nearest Indian. "They call you Little Bird, don't they?"

"Some do," the guy agreed, looking straight up at Normal.

Normal inclined his head toward the other fellow. "What's your buddy's name?" he asked.

"Na-Ke-Dan-Sto-Li," the guy answered slowly, carefully wrapping his moist mouth around each syllable.

"What's that mean?" I asked.

"Dances with vodka," the guy said.

Normal embraced the pair as they yukked it up.

George approached the old guy in the overcoat.

"Hey, Monty," he said. "Your name's Monty, ain't it?"

The old guy's eyes, thick and milky with cataracts, rolled in his head like a spooked horse. A constant marination in fortified wines had begun to tenderize the old boy. Begun to separate skin from bone, leaving the impression that the slender sinews holding the face could, at any moment, give way and allow the whole mess to slide south, circle the drain of his toothless mouth, and disappear altogether down the cosmic gullet.

"I ain't done nothin'," he said, looking around, searching for the voice. "I was just watchin'."

Harold stepped around me, pulled a wad of singles out of his pocket, and hustled over to the two younger guys, who stood stock-still, eyes frozen on Norman. George approached the old guy.

"It's me, George Paris. Remember me?"

The dazed look on his face suggested that the old guy didn't remember anything more distant than his last forty-ouncer.

"Used to live in that room across the hall from you down in the Pine Tree, back in eighty-five. You remember?"

The old guy squinted, the act nearly throwing him off balance. For the first time, a glimmer of recognition crossed his face.

"Oh," he stammered. "George, yeah, you and that other guy."

George pulled a pint of peach schnapps from his coat pocket, unscrewed the top, and handed it to the old codger.

"Right, Ralph. Ralph Batista. You remember old

Ralph? That's who we're lookin' for. We're lookin' for Ralph. You—"

The old man's face closed like a leg trap. He licked his lips and handed the pint back without taking a drink.

"Don't know nothin' about none of that," he said.

He turned to leave. A low growl from Norman stopped him cold. He turned back to George. His eyes were full of water. "Come on, man. I ain't done nothin'. I don't know nothin'. Come on."

They stood, lockjawed, staring at each other for a long moment.

"Go on, get outta here," George said finally. The guy didn't need to be told twice. He started down the alley toward the woman.

"Go the other way," I said. He did.

I stood and watched as the boys alternately bribed and threatened the rest of them. Even from a distance, it was apparent that they were getting nowhere. It had been that way all night. I checked my watch. Twelve-fifteen. A sudden wind cut through the alley, carrying the smells of fryer grease and salt water, swirling the white smoke to the walls, leaving a foul-smelling landscape of muted shadows and fog.

We'd started at noon, down under the viaduct, kicking cardboard houses, rousting sleeping drunks, passing out sandwiches, singles, and booze. We'd braced every derelict in a ten-block area. We'd been by the Gospel Mission twice. We'd worked our way through the flocks of juicers and junkies congregated in Occidental Park. We'd pulled 'em out of their warm hideyholes in parking garages and vestibules. Nada. Nobody had seen Ralph. Guys he'd known for twenty years were suddenly having trouble remembering his name. My mouth was dry and smooth like ceramic. My stomach felt like it was full of scrap metal.

The pirate had pulled himself to his feet. I could hear the breath wheeze from his wet lips as he lurched off.

George appeared at my side. "Nobody knows shit," he said.

Back in the early seventies, George's banking career had fallen victim to both merger mania and an unquenchable taste for single-malt Scotch. His grim demeanor, well-defined features, and slicked-back white hair made him look like a defrocked boxing announcer. Anyone who didn't look into his eyes or down at his mismatched shoes could quite easily mistake him for a functioning member of society.

Harold and Norman pushed their way through the oily smoke to my side. Harold shook his head sadly. Harold had, for better than twenty years, managed a shoe department for the Bon, but like many of the denizens of the district, had surfed himself into the streets on a wave of cheap booze and failed marriages. He used to be taller. Every year seemed to carve more meat from his already skeletal frame. I'd always figured his huge Adam's apple and cab-door ears would surely be the last to go, found on some Pioneer Square sidewalk, mistaken by some wino for an escaped cue ball and a couple of dried apricots.

"We've been about everywhere I can think of," I said. "Any of you guys got an idea?" This led to a prolonged round of head shaking and foot shuffling.

"Maybe he left town," said George, finally.

"Oh, bullshit," shot Harold. "Other than that time Leo took us all out in the sticks, Ralph ain't been out of Seattle in thirty-five years. You just feel guilty, that's all, so shut the fuck up."

Harold's attitude was tantamount to a peasant's rebellion. Shovels, rakes, flaming torches, the whole thing. Since Buddy Knox's death, George had always served unchallenged as leader and spokesman for this little group. To my knowledge, other than some occasional bickering when they were out of booze for a protracted period of time—say, fifteen minutes—George had never been challenged.

"Guilty," he spat. "What in hell have I got to be guilty about? I wanted to hear that kinda shit, I'd call one of my exes."

"If you hadn't thrown him out—"

"He's a fucking wet-brain. He spends his whole goddamn check and then sponges off—"

"Hey, hey," I interrupted. "This isn't getting us anywhere. Are you guys sure you never seen this guy who came by for his check?"

"I told you," George said impatiently. "Some little mulatto in a fur hat said Ralph had sent him for his pension check. I told him to piss off. Ralph wanted his check, he could hustle his ass up and get it."

Norman was stomping out the remains of the fire, using both feet, turning, dancing to his own music. "Global warming," he said when he noticed I was watching. "Average world temperature is fifty-eight degrees now. Up two degrees in twenty years."

I knew better than to disagree with him.

"I need a drink," George mumbled.

Couldn't say I disagreed with that either.

Visit **www.panmacmillan.com** to read more about all our books and to buy them. You will also find features, author interviews and news of any author events, and you can sign up for e-newsletters so that you're always first to hear about our new releases.

www.panmacmillan.com

GIFT SELECTOR
YOUR ACCOUNT
WISH LIST
WAITING LIST

HOME | ABOUT US | IMPRINTS | TRADE/MEDIA | CONTACT US | ADVANCED SEARCH | SEARCH | GO

BOOK CATEGORIES | WHAT'S NEW | AUTHORS/ILLUSTRATORS | BESTSELLERS | READING GROUPS

Coming Soon...

Reading Groups

Competitions
Feeling Lucky?

Extracts
Sneak Previews

Interviews

Events
Meet Our Stars

Reviews
What The Critics Say

News & Awards

Editor's Choice
What We're Reading